CU00338886

THE LIARS BENEATH

HEATHER VAN FLEET

WISE WOLF
BOOKS

WISE WOLF BOOKS
An Imprint of Wolfpack Publishing
wisewolfbooks.com

THE LIARS BENEATH. Text copyright © 2022 Heather Van Fleet. All
rights reserved.

This is a work of fiction. All of the characters, organizations,
publications, and events portrayed in this novel are either products of
the author's imagination or are used fictitiously.

Cover design by Wise Wolf Books

ISBN 978-1-953944-58-0 (paperback)
ISBN 978-1-953944-64-1 (ebook)
LCCN 2021948862

To Emma. My fifteen year old queen, my Podcast partner in crime. Someday I'll write the fantasy book of your dreams. For now, this will have to do.

THE LIARS BENEATH

THE WARS BENEATH

1

July
Present Day

SPLINTERS TEAR at the undersides of my nails when I squeeze the church pew ahead of me. The raw skin burns, but I welcome the pain, needing it to distract me from the ache in my chest.

In front of me sits an old man who's scratching at his comb-over toupee. The side falls down past his right ear, leading way to the baldness beneath. I huff, irritated because I can't see the front of the church around his oversized head...not that I want to. Not when I know what's there.

Her coffin.

Her face.

The results of my biggest mistake.

"And now a reading from the book of Ecclesiastes, chapter three, verses one through eight." The minister

1

clears his throat, talking nonsense Rose would've laughed at.

Instead of listening, I relax under Dad's arm, while Mom clings to my right hand. Settled and sheltered, I shut my eyes, welcoming the darkness. It promises peace, an almost believable sense that this isn't happening.

In a world away from grief, I'm with my best friend again—the echo of her voice whispering promises of forever in my ear. We climb trees, fish with my father early in the mornings on his boat, then spend our afternoons swimming in the river alcove off Colton Road.

Our space, our world, she tells me.

Yes. Always, I smile and say.

"...and a time to heal; a time to break down, and a time to build up..."

I clutch Mom's hand even tighter, bottom lip trembling. The minister tries to pull me back in, but I won't let him. Not now.

Slipping back into my memories, I inhale the smoke from summer bonfires, taste the s'more goop dripping from between my lips, listen to Rose's laughter while she watches me shove four marshmallows into my mouth at the same time.

Away from the church, in the dark, non-lonely recess of my mind, mud squishes beneath my boots with every step we take along the dam near my house. Rose teases me for being scared of falling into the water, her blue eyes filled with mirth.

With the setting sun at her back and a hand over my forehead blocking the glaring light, I watch her long-limbed body teeter close to the edge, balanced on one foot like a ballerina. As always, she's completely fearless.

But then the rush of water drifts closer, her lips part in a silent scream, and I gasp...

More tears fill my eyes when they pop back open, and my recollections become nightmares with the snap of a twig beneath my feet, though I wasn't there the night she died.

The sole source of Rose's end was the exact same thing I feared falling into for so long. Irony is cruel.

Two weeks ago, I was finishing up the first of my college applications, readying for senior year. Now I'm preparing for a future knowing Rose would be by my side every step of the way.

We were best friends. Like sisters even. Joined at the hip since the age of ten, living the dream of two girls eager to become women. Rose was the other half to my whole. Together, we could have accomplished anything.

If only she hadn't been so stupid.

If only she was still alive.

I shiver, letting go of Mom's hand to wrap my arm over my stomach. The muscles harden beneath, and agony builds a bomb inside.

Don't cry, Becca. Don't you dare.

"You okay, sunshine?" Dad whispers, no doubt sensing my mood.

No, I want to say. *I'm dying inside*. But that's not what comes out.

"Uh-huh."

Without bravery, I'll fall apart.

My gaze wanders the congregation, searching for familiar faces. Those who loved Rose, those who might have hated her too.

Sienna's the first person I see. She's a girl I know from school, someone I hung out with at lunch if Rose wasn't there. A friend to me, a barely passable acquaintance to Rose. Her exposed cheek is blotchy and red, stained with tears I'm surprised she's shedding.

Beside her sits her on-again, off-again boyfriend,

3

Alex. His arm is draped around her shoulders and his head is tipped back, brown eyes half-lidded as he looks to the ceiling. He's either high or sleeping. Either option wouldn't surprise me

I look away, catching sight of a few nosy townspeople, some distant relatives of Rose's I barely know too. Overall, though, I don't see many familiar faces. Not Adam, her best guy friend. Not even Travis—though my ex not showing up doesn't surprise me. I think he hated Rose more than she hated him.

"And finally, I'd like to leave you with a few words from Rose's older brother, Ben," the minister finishes.

My lips part with shock. I move forward in the pew, my father's arm falling away. I can't believe he's actually here.

My best friend talked nonstop about Ben; hero-worshipped him even, despite the fact that he constantly ignored her. His achievements were *her* achievements. The awards he won, the trophies he earned playing football too. Rose treated her older brother like a king. A saint, really, who could do no wrong.

But then Mr. Perfect went away to college and turned his back on Rose and everyone else who loved him. That's when everything changed.

I search the room, eyes narrowing when I catch sight of his profile.

Head to shoulders, cheeks to hair, I take him in, inch by inch. It's been almost eight months since I last saw him—not since Thanksgiving. The Ben I knew back then was skinny yet cut. Six-foot-plus with a thick head of messy, blond hair. This Ben coming to stand before the congregation is nothing like that boy now, and I'm not sure what to make of it.

"So..."

His voice crackles when he looks up from the

4

podium. Red-rimmed blue eyes capture the crowd as he searches through faces. The mic squeaks while he adjusts it, and I notice right away how badly his hands shake.

"My sister was..." He sucks in a breath, exhaling harshly. "A monster."

Gasps sound from around the church. But instead of mirroring everyone's shock, I tuck my chin against my chest and sigh with relief. I may hate this guy with every fiber of my being, but I know exactly where he's going with this.

Rose *was* a monster. Just not in the sense that these people think.

My best friend was brutal, *a tell it how it is* kind of girl. She ranted with the best of them, standing up to everyone who she thought was in the wrong—even when they weren't. I loved her. God, did I ever.

But I'll never be as monstrous as she was.

I'm Becca and she was Rose and now I'm just...alone.

Ben furrows his brows as he looks at the podium again. "Sorry. Wrong choice of words for anyone who didn't know her, I guess." His lips purse. "More a top-shelf, grade-A beast."

Dad stiffens but makes no move to speak. Mom, though, glares at me like I'm in the wrong. I shrug her irritated stare away, breathing in through my nose and welcoming the change in pace.

"My sister was ferocious. All claws and bite," Ben continues. "She took stupid risks, never listened to anyone but her best friend, and that relationship was shady at best."

I blink.

Wait, what?

"I loved her, yeah," he keeps going, despite the increasing mumbles of the congregation. "But she was out of control."

5

I dig my nails into my palms so hard it sends a sting through my hand. I look down, spotting blood in the crevices from where I've pierced the skin. Ignoring it, I look at Ben again, waiting, wondering, hating...

"And this whole church thing?" Laughter spills from his mouth. "You really think that my sister cared enough about God and heaven and forgiveness to want any of this?" He digs his fists into his eyes for a moment before dropping them with a thump against the podium. "I'm pretty sure she never once stepped foot in a church for fear of being burned at the stake, honestly."

"Shut up," I whisper, drawing my parents' gazes.

Ben doesn't hear me, but even if he had, I'm sure he wouldn't care. To him, I'm nothing more than his little sister's sidekick—a glorified pain in the ass. (His words, not mine.)

"Becca." Mom touches my shoulder. "Did you know he was going to do this?"

"Of course not." It's not like Ben and I are besties.

"Screw this," Ben growls, crunching his paper into a ball. "And screw you too, Rose." He tosses the lined sheet up and over his shoulder, only for it to drop on top of her coffin.

"You cheated," he growls, eyes to the stained-glass ceiling above. "You hear me, little sister? You cheated!"

I narrow my eyes, unmoving, while the rest of the congregation grows even more restless, murmuring, objecting...

"Get him out of here."

"He's completely lost it."

"This is the most disrespectful thing I've ever witnessed."

Ignoring them, Ben cackles, his voice growing louder as he continues. "That's nothing new though, is it? Cheating's always been your way. Why the hell would I expect anything different?"

The minister rushes toward him, but Ben's mom, Ginger, gets there first. She tugs the mic out of her son's hands, placing a few fingers over Ben's wrists. Leaning up on the toes of her shoes, she whispers something into his ear.

Even that doesn't stop his rage.

"That was always your way, little sister," he yells without the mic.

"Ben, stop it. Right now," his mom pleads through the mic.

He shakes his head. "Your constant need for attention, then doing the worst thing imaginable just to get it." He turns toward the coffin, his upper body trembling. "Pretty sure I couldn't have helped you even if you asked for it." He scoffs. "And Becca, the one and only person you actually ever listened to?"

My heart jumps like it's bouncing on a trampoline.

Shut up, shut up, shut up!

"She sure as hell didn't keep you safe, did she?"

I'm on my feet before I can blink, the words burning my throat as I scream, "Shut up!"

Ben's gaze shoots in my direction, eyes widening a little. Guilt finds a home on his face in the form of a wince, while his cheeks darken to a shade of cherry red.

I lift my chin, thankful he feels the stab of my words. It's on the edge of my tongue to yell even more, but Mom tugs at my hand before I'm able.

"Sit down, Becca. Please. You're making this worse."

"*I'm* making this worse?" I motion toward Ben. "What about *this* asshat?"

She grips the bare skin of my forearm, her eyes going wide.

Maybe she thinks I'm on the verge of losing it.

Unfortunately for her, I think I already have.

I turn to Ben again, chin lifted in defiance. I'm not

7

going to let this go—ever. Not if it means he gets to bad talk me and my best friend's relationship. We worked, he and her did not.

His gaze lands on the podium instead of me, while his bottom lip seems to shake.

Good, I think, remembering the millions of times he'd made his sister cry.

Ginger stands even closer to him, an arm thrown over his shoulders as she whispers something into his ear again. The proverbial son—he could never do wrong in her eyes, and that fact disgusted me.

Seconds later, Ben nods, and she takes her position in the front row again, her gaze darting briefly to mine. There's a flash of desperation inside her stare, like she's asking me for help. If she'd been any kind of mother at all, we wouldn't be here, which is why help is the last thing she'll get from me.

"I'm sorry." He sniffs, wipes his nose with the back of his arm. "It's just...I loved her so damn much it hurts to breathe without her, and I don't know what to do." He inhales so deeply the sound echoes through the microphone.

Crackle.

Sniff.

Sigh.

"She was stubborn and reckless, yeah, but you all need to know this. Rose didn't kill herself, nor was her death some accident either. And as her older brother, I will clear her name and find out what really happened to her that night."

More gasps follow. Then the whispering begins—hands to mouths, gazes searching each other's faces like there's an actual killer among us.

I roll my eyes, completely disgusted.

Gossip is scary real here in Winston, Iowa. And

knowing my best friend's death has been the scandal of the century in this town only makes it that much harder for me to grieve. Nobody wants to believe something bad had happened to her—the sister of the Ben McCain, former superstar quarterback of Winston High who was undoubtedly destined for the NFL someday. Blah, blah-blah, blah-blah.

Supposedly an investigation took place. Nothing led to foul play, as all witnesses were accounted for and had alibis. The case is what my dad had called open and shut: a strung-out teen who'd jumped over the dam, then drowned in the Mississippi River not far from where she'd last been seen...at a party that I did not go to.

Some called it suicide.

Others called it an accident.

But not a single person said it was preventable.

Guilt twists my stomach, and my hands start to sweat. Unable to deal anymore, I turn toward my father, praying he understands because I doubt Mom will. I need fresh air. The room feels like a two-foot box. One I'm currently trapped inside. If I don't get out, I'll pass out.

"I need to go," I whisper.

Dad frowns, gaze still directed ahead. He's seduced by Ben's words. I can see it in the crinkles of his eyes, his hand as he rubs it over his mouth.

"You'll regret it if you do," he tells me.

"Yeah," I scoff. "I don't think so."

I stand and push around him, eyes locked on the middle aisle. My legs are too heavy, and the weight of them nearly pulls me down with each step I take. Behind me, Mom calls my name, but I can't look at her or anyone else.

Once I'm outside, the church doors bang shut behind me and the July heat smacks me across the face. In and

9

out I struggle to breathe, bending over, hands to my knees, eyes squeezed shut… Despair presses against my lungs. It's painful to the point of no return.

The memories I envisioned inside the church mix around inside my head like a milkshake in a blender full of knives. All the truths, lies, what-ifs, *what never will bes* are there, taunting me.

"Stop it," I tell myself, pulling at my hair. "Stop it, stop it, stop it."

Once I'm upright again, I quick make my way down the steps, inhaling the scent of the familiar farmland surrounding the church. The cow manure, fertilizer, and the dampness of an imminent summer storm. My trusty Doc Martens clunk against the gravel sidewalk as I move, matching the thudding of my heart. They were a gift from Rose on my sixteenth birthday, and other than my softball cleats and slides, they're the only things I wear. If I could wear them every day, for the rest of my life, I would. Now, especially.

My parents' car is where I need to be, the escape I'm desperate for as I yank at the handle. Thank God it's unlocked. Shaking from head to toe, I throw myself into the back seat and pull my knees to my chest. Like that, I wrap my arms around my shins, rocking back and forth, holding tight to my good memories. The ones that matter.

2

July
Present day

TWENTY MINUTES PASS before people start to pile out the church. I spot Mom first, her midnight-colored hair just barely grazing her shoulders. She stands in front of Ginger, awkwardly patting her arm. I know it's a challenge for her to console the woman. The two of them haven't ever gotten along. Ginger used to have it bad for my dad back in high school, and Mom doesn't like that fact, despite how hopelessly in love he is with her.

I force myself to look away, stopping short when another figure catches my eye.

Ben.

He's a ghost in plain sight, hovering beneath the church overhang. His hair is even more disheveled than it was inside, and his hands are buried deep in his pant pockets. With his head bowed, he barely acknowledges my dad who wraps an arm around his shoulder. The

11

view has my upper lip curling. Part of me wants to pick the kid's brain apart because I don't know if this is for show, or if he's feeling grief instead of guilt. The other part of me wants to forget he's even alive.

Like he can hear my thoughts, Ben starts searching the lot, a hawk on the hunt who spots me through the glass seconds later.

"Crap." I lock the doors and crouch down.

A knock sounds on the window seconds later, no surprise there. If there's one thing about Ben it's that he's a *determined* asshole, not just *an* asshole.

"Becca. Open the door, please."

"No."

"Come on, I wanna talk."

I flip him off and look the other way.

Courtesy of Dad having the keys, I'm guessing, the locks click open. Seconds later, Ben flings the door open, sliding into the backseat beside me. *Dick.*

"Hey," he says. "How are you?"

"How do you think I am?"

"Stupid question." He slides closer and blows out a breath, the undeniable scent of alcohol filling the air.

I scrunch my nose. "Have you been drinking?"

No wonder he'd been such a charismatic jerk in the church. I wonder if my father noticed the smell—the minister or his mom, even. Not that anyone would so much as *think* about calling out the town's biggest fame and glory.

Ignoring my question, Ben asks, "So, can we talk?"

"No, we can't *talk*."

"Come on, Becca. Pleee—"

"I have nothing to say to you." I press my fingers against the base of my throat, willing the ache away.

"Just give me five minutes."

"According to your little speech in there, I'm one of

12

the ones who don't matter, remember? So, whatever I say shouldn't be important."

"That's not what I meant." He scrubs a hand over his face. "It's just that I was angry, and your name's the first one I could think of. I'm sorry."

"Apology *not* accepted."

"Seriously, Becca. I just..." He pauses, studying me, head tilted to one side.

I squirm in my seat, leaning closer to my door. "What're you staring at?"

His face softens. One side of his mouth lifts higher than the other, and I can't help but notice the dimple on his left cheek because of it. Rose had the same one.

"You look different," he tells me.

Heat fills my face.

Moving closer—the boy has never known the meaning of personal space—he touches the end of my hair. "You dyed your hair pink. Is that it?"

I still don't reply, though I do push his hand away.

"I like it." He scoots back, the side of his lips kicking up. "It's edgy."

"Stop talking about my hair and say what you came here to say." Unless it's one of his world-famous insults. The kind he's been throwing at me since the idiot first discovered I existed.

"All right, sorry." He sighs, leaning his head back and finding his place against the door. "I said things in that church that I've been waiting to get out for days, but I didn't mean to bring your name into it, I swear." He blinks and looks at me again. "It just happened."

Accepting his apology feels too easy. So...I don't.

"Who would've thought that Rose's brother, the guy she *worshipped*, would wind up being the jerk of the century at her funeral."

13

"That's not true." He squints at me. "She didn't worsh—"

"She so did." I cross my arms. "Your denial only certifies how clueless you were when it came to her."

"Come on, Becca," he pleads, no longer the snarky, flirty jerk I remembered. "I just want to prove to this stupid town, that Rose's death wasn't an accident," he says. "And I want to figure it all out before I go back to school in August."

"God forbid you have to miss school, am I right?" I scoff.

"That's not what I meant."

"Doesn't matter either way." I pat his arm a little too hard, tempted to punch him in the nose. "Rose is dead. Which means you can go back to your life and continue to forget everyone else in it, exists."

"Jesus, Becca. What happened to you?"

"*You* happened." In all the ways he shouldn't have.

Ben hurt Rose, pushed her over a metaphorical line she never came back from. And when he hurt her, he hurt me too.

"Look…" He hesitates, pinching the bridge of his nose. "I know my sister did some wild stuff, but—"

"Just let it go. *Please*." I fist my hands in my lap, trying not to cry. "Don't you think you've done enough damage already?"

He flinches, opens his mouth, then snaps it shut again.

Good.

We don't talk after that. Ben doesn't get out of the car either. And for some reason, I'm stupid enough not to make him. Deep down, I know having him here is the closest I'll ever get to being with Rose again, and it's that thought keeping me from pushing him out the door.

It's almost like Ben's waiting for something, though I

don't question what that something is. Probably because it's the same thing I want: to wake up and discover that this is all a dream.

Only, it's not.

This is an ugly, dark nightmare neither of us will ever wake up from.

"Was Rose dating anyone?" he whispers out of the blue.

"No." I swallow hard. The lie slides down my throat, nicking the skin like a pocketknife. It's painful and unnerving and everything I never wanted to stand for. I'm not a liar. But Rose unknowingly made me into one.

"That's the thing." He rubs a hand over his jaw. "I don't think she was single. Something was going down with her. And you're the only one I trust enough to help me figure out what that something was."

"I told you no." I look away, refusing to rehash this when I already know the truth—have just begun to make peace with the idea of her death. Rose died because she was reckless. She was *always* reckless. Whether she was seeing someone or not doesn't change the fact that she's gone.

"You can't believe that she'd just—"

"Stop talking, all right?" I cover my face. "I...I can't do this with you right now."

"I'm sorry." He places his hand on my shoulder. "I just—"

"*Go away*, Ben."

"Fine." He blows out a slow breath. "I can take a hint."

"About time," I mumble.

He reaches for the handle, opens it. "Whatever."

"Don't let the door hit you in the—"

It slams shut, cutting me off.

Once he's gone, I let go of a growly breath, watching him approach his mom through the window. Agitation weighs his shoulders down, and he tosses his hands in the air when they meet. Seconds later, she's crying and he's sliding into the driver's seat of their car, the door slamming in his wake.

Regardless of my need to keep distance from Ben, I can't help but wonder if that's the last time I'll ever see him.

"Are we going where I think we're going?" I leaned my head back against the passenger seat of Rose's car, totally not in the mood to do the whole late-night, tire-swinging thing at the river.

"Mayyyybe." She winked. "Just try and relax. I promise it'll be fun."

I rubbed my sweaty hands back and forth across my bare thighs. "I don't even have my swimsuit."

"You don't need one tonight."

"But you're wearing one." I pointed at her yellow bikini, sickened by how freaking skinny she was. Not unhealthy skinny but the exact opposite. A to-die-for body with curves in places I had too many rolls.

"It's fine. I've got an extra in the back if you need one."

I rolled my eyes. I was a double D. She was a full B. There was no way in hell I'd fit into her bikini top.

"Who's gonna be there?" I asked.

"Not telling," she sing-songed. "It'll ruin the fun."

"I swear to all entities, Rose, if this turns out to be some big hook-up fest like last time, I'll—"

"It's not gonna be. I swear." But the twitching of her lips said otherwise.

I sighed. This was becoming a common occurrence—Rose telling me we were going one place, only for us to wind up somewhere completely different. I'd mentioned earlier in the day that I didn't want to go out tonight. She'd begged me to change my mind. When I'd finally relented—only because it'd been the last weekend before school started up again post summer break—I'd suggested we hit the final drive-in movie of the summer. She'd told me she was in, no hesitation. That alone should've given me pause because Rose hated the movies.

We turned down Colton Road, the pavement immediately switching to gravel. Rocks dinged the side of Rose's sedan, clicking blindly against the windows. The corn stalks surrounding us fluttered in the late-night wind, opening the familiar fields just enough to where I could see lights from town in the distance. The moon was extra high, it seemed, glowing down on "the spot" like an alien was seconds from the sky. It creeped me out a little, to the point where goose bumps dance ominously across my arms. The closer we got to the dam and the alcove, the riskier it was for builders to put down roots. This area in particular where we were headed was deserted thanks to the spring floods, the risky rush of water from the Mississippi.

Trees eventually replaced the fields the closer we got. It was a constant reminder that eastern Iowa was a land full of mysteries and dark corners, only changing to something beautiful or lurking with every mile you drove.

"Oh good. They're here already."

I squinted toward the bonfire ahead, the land opening in a small half circle. We weren't supposed to be here. The land was private property. Danger Ahead, the signs read. But nobody listened. Especially not Rose.

"Who are 'they' exactly?" I asked.

Ignoring my question, Rose grinned, her car tires bumping through the dips and divots in the now open field. "Welcome to your number seventy, girl."

A chill ran up my spine. My mouth grew dry too. "W-what are you talking about?"

"I'm not stupid." She huffed.

We neared an old pickup truck with rust on the hitch that stood out in the dark, even against the black paint.

"Seriously. I don't know what you mean," I insisted, gaze shooting from the two shadows ahead back to my best friend.

"I get it," she mumbled. "You're embarrassed, not that there's anything to be embarrassed about. It's a natural thing that happens."

"Oh God." I leaned my head back against the seat and shut my eyes.

"The thing is, if you didn't want me to find out about it, then you shouldn't have left that piece of paper on your closet floor where I keep half my shoes."

Realization struck me square in the gut. Stomach? Meet toes.

Rose had found it. My number seventy.

Damn it, I knew I should've thrown the stupid piece of paper in the garbage where it belonged.

"What happened to our no secrets policy, huh?" she asked.

"This is different."

She put the car in Park. "Riiiight, yep. Totally different."

I turned to her and opened my eyes. "It is, and you know it."

"Because admitting that you wanted to bang a guy you've been crushing on is something you should keep from your best friend."

"Rose, stop." My face heated, and I covered it with both hands.

"No. I won't stop. Not when you committed the biggest friendship sin ever by lying to me, damnit."

As much as I hated to admit it, she was right. We didn't keep secrets from each other. And after creating our out-and-proud bucket list nine years ago, we'd decided this notebook of ours would be a confessional of our deepest desires, no matter what they entailed.

What had started out as simple kid fun had fast turned into something more than either of us had imagined. Together or separate, we'd write down our biggest desires, admitting

19

them with a pen and following through with them—always together, somehow—with our actions.

With each year that went by, our list had grown darker, more dangerous. At least in Rose's case. My numbers, on the other hand, had maintained a saner vibe...well, except for a few of them, I guess.

#33. Becca must cheat on a test.

Not one of my prouder moments.

#46. Skinny dip.

I'd thought it was kind of childish, but Rose had insisted it was a childhood rite of passage that I'd sorely miss if I didn't do it. Spoiler alert: it had been cold, miserable, and I'd regretted every second of it.

There'd been items on the list that I hadn't gotten around to, is the thing. Dying my hair pink, getting a tattoo... Oh, and egging Michelle Baker's house after she'd called me a fat cow last year. I also wanted to slash Liam Jackson's car tires because he was constantly slut shaming Rose.

There wasn't really a timeline to our list. We had the rest of our lives to complete it. That was one of the reasons I'd re-thought my number seventy and ripped it out in a panic a few seconds before Rose had walked into my room the other day. I'd been too embarrassed to admit it out loud to anyone, especially myself. And telling Rose would mean actually having to follow through with it. I just...I didn't think I was ready, even if my body was telling me otherwise.

#70. Lose my virginity to Travis Morrison.

It was the most insane thing I'd put down to date, for one huge reason: Travis didn't know I existed.

"I'm sorry." I reached over and touched Rose's wrist. "Please don't be mad at me."

She didn't respond right away. Instead, she looked down at my hand, then out the windshield, lips twisting like she'd tasted something sour. "Look, I'm not going to say it's fine

20

because it isn't. But I am going to help you achieve your goal anyway because I love you."

"But I ripped it out for a reason," I told her. "I'm not ready."

"Liar. You ripped it out because you're scared, not because you're not ready. I know you, Becca. Probably better than you know yourself."

My heart skipped a few thousand beats, but I didn't disagree. The thing I loved and hated the most about my best friend? She never failed to call me out on things, especially when it came to my lack of guts.

"He's got a girlfriend," I said.

"They broke up before school ended." She rolled her eyes. "You of all people know that."

I tore at a hangnail, wincing. "What if he's not into me."

"A little birdie told me he thinks you're cute."

Despite the fact that her words sent my heart racing, I still wasn't convinced it was the right thing to do. It was one thing to crush on a guy but a whole other thing to have sex with him.

"Face it, young protégé, we're gonna get the ball rolling on Operation Bang Travis Morrison." Rose winked at me. "It's too late to back down."

I was thankful she wasn't mad anymore, but the cryptic promise in her eyes was definitely more terrifying than her wrath. I knew the things she was capable of, and it was always fine to view them from afar. But to be the person she wanted me to be, then actually following through with it at the same time? The thought made me a little sick to my stomach.

"I hate you so much right now." I sighed, letting my gaze stray to where hers had been. It took me less than ten seconds to find him, not that I was surprised. When it came to Travis, it was like I had superhuman vision.

He stood by the fire with a beer bottle in hand, his long, dark hair pulled back into a wavy ponytail. My heart leapt *like it always did when I saw him. He was just that freaking hot.*

"If I liked skinny boys with zero meat on them, I'd do the guy," she offered.

My lips twitched. I knew Rose was only trying to get a reaction out of me, ease the tension between us. But if I did react, she'd only add more fuel to the fire, doing something to humiliate me, no doubt—even unintentionally. I was embarrassed as it was. So I kept quiet and tapped down all of the forbidden thoughts running through my head. Thoughts that ended with Travis and me in the river, naked.

I bit down on my bottom lip and watched in fascination as he smiled at something Adam said—Adam being Rose's best guy friend and Travis's closest friend.

Without waiting for my reaction, Rose jumped out of the car and opened the back door, grabbing something, then tossing it at me when she leaned through the window of the driver's side again. "Here. Put this on just in case."

With unsteady hands, I lifted the tiny, black monstrosity called a bikini she'd thrown at me. "I am so not wearing this. My boobs will fall out."

"Exactly." She shook her head, laughing. "Now, get changed. Number seventy is waiting."

Before I had a chance to tell her off, she tapped the roof, shut the door, and skipped toward the fire, her wavy blonde hair looking almost white as it fell to the middle of her back.

My eyes were drawn to the flames again—more so Travis who stood closer to them than he had been before. He'd been new to our school last year. The quiet, bad boy type I'd always been drawn to but never bothered getting to know. He'd transferred from somewhere down south—Texas, maybe?—and now lived with his dad, who happened to be an English teacher at our school. The Jane Austin-loving nerd variety, apparently. I didn't have him as a teacher, but Rose did. She told me he was a widowed single father who wore bohemian-inspired male clothing and a fedora. A teacher who preferred everyone to call him by his first name, Leaf, instead of Mr. Morrison.

I hadn't seen Travis all summer. At least not up until that point. Apparently, he'd been at a military camp or something —so the rumors said. He didn't have social media, so everything was hearsay. But from the way his bare, tanned chest glistened with a sheen of sweat around the fire, I knew he'd become even hotter than he'd been in May—if that was possible.

Self-conscious, I found myself sucking in my gut and straightening out my frizzy, black hair. I was short and cursed with ginormous boobs that were too big for my frame, along with curls from my dad but clear, smooth skin from my mom. I worked with what I had, even if it wasn't ideal.

Rose's arms went wide in greeting as she approached the guys. But it was Adam she embraced, only for him to hug back like he hadn't seen her in months, not days. I frowned at the view. Rose claimed they were just friends, but moments like this gave me pause.

I looked at Travis again, back stiffening when I noticed him staring at me through the windshield. He lifted his chin in greeting, and I sunk lower in my seat, wishing I could hide.

Even from this far away, his face was beyond impressive, especially lit by the fire like it was. Full lips, strong cheekbones... God, how could one guy be that hot?

If I'd been Rose, I would've had no problems stripping my clothes and changing into a bikini. But I wasn't my confident, crazy, brave-like-nobody-else-I-knew best friend. I was me. Anxious and chubby. So, I slid into the back seat and crouched down, struggling to get out of my shirt and bra.

My boobs were sticky with sweat from the humid night and having no shower today. As subtly as I could, I lifted one arm and sniffed, thankful my deodorant was still holding strong. Had I known we'd be there, with him, then I'm pretty sure I would've tried harder to make an impression.

It took me three tries to push my boobs into the tiny bikini top. Even still, like I'd told Rose, they hung out of the sides.

"You can do this," I told myself, blowing out a shaky breath as my long bangs fell over my eyes. "He's just a guy and you're a girl, and..."

Yeah. Who was I kidding? I was definitely going to suck at this.

———

ROSE SAT cross-legged next to Adam, snort-laughing as he told her an off-handed joke that made zero sense to me. Her face was flushed from beer and exertion, mostly because the three of them had just gotten done on the tire swing Travis had set up. The tire swing I hadn't, in fact, gone on for fear of flashing my boobs and getting pulled deeper into the river.

Across from the fire sat Travis, a cigarette in one hand, a fresh beer in the other. He hadn't looked at me all night, not since he'd spied me through the windshield. I wasn't surprised. My face was pretty but unimpressive. Forgettable. Round, full cheeks, chubbier than most girls my age. My legs were short too and...I had zero butt. Like, at all—which all guys liked, according to Rose. My dark-brown eyes were my best feature, I think. Big and wide, doe-eyed, Mom often said. Innocent and sweet, a trait she swore would get me places in life.

I'd yet to find out what places she was referring to.

"You guys wanna play truth or dare?" Adam leaned back onto one hand, and I couldn't help but notice how his other was pressed against Rose's hip, sneaking up and under her shirt. She didn't try pushing him away, which was—yet again —really weird.

Travis tossed his cigarette into the fire and shrugged. "I'm down."

"You up for it, Becca?" Rose asked.

I bit my bottom lip, trying to keep my voice steady. "I dunno."

"Come on, Thompson." Adam groaned. "Don't be a stick in the mud. You already turned the swing down."

I swallowed hard.

"Shut your mouth, Adam," Rose shoved his shoulder. "If Becca doesn't want to play, then we won't."

He laughed but cut the taunting at least. I wasn't good with peer pressure when it came to Rose. Anyone else and I tended to fail even more.

The truth was, I didn't want to play truth or dare. I wanted to go home. Watch YouTube vids, maybe eat Takis until my throat burned... Number seventy had been ripped out of our bucket list for a reason, dang it: Travis Morrison would never give me the time of day; I wasn't ready to "bang" him. Tonight had most definitely proven both of those truths.

"You scared, doll?" a gruff voice asked.

My lips parted. Slowly, I swung my head toward Travis, half expecting him to be laughing at me. He wasn't though. Instead, his brows were furrowed, like he actually cared what I thought.

"'Doll'?" Rose laughed. "That is the stupidest nickname."

"Better than anything you've been called, don't you think?" Travis grinned. Adam did too. Rose, on the other hand, gave them both the middle finger.

I squirmed a little, uncomfortable. The tension in the air was ugly, and as someone who avoided it at all costs, I wanted nothing more than to run. But running would only make Adam's accusation true. I didn't want to be a stick in the mud. I wanted to be fearless, brave, strong, just like Rose.

"Fine. I'm in." I lifted my chin, feigning bravery when I was anything but.

"You sure about that?" Travis asked, dark brows lifting to the middle of his forehead.

I wanted to say no, to run far, far away, but instead I found myself nodding.

Adam released a loud whoop and Rose stood too, both fists pumping in the air. Their energy was contagious and electric, which helped me relax a little. Until I refocused on Travis.

His gaze slid over my body, tongue darting out at the corner of his mouth where he licked. I shivered, not used to being looked at so intensely.

This could've been the beginning of something very bad. But I was hopeless to stop it.

August
Present Day

"ALL RIGHT, young lady. You are getting out of this bed today, even if I have to drag you kicking and screaming."

I roll over onto my side, ignoring my mom as I face my bedroom wall. Yet again she's on a mission to get me functioning. The problem is, I don't want to.

It's been two weeks since the funeral. A month since Rose's death. The last thing I want is to face the world, even if my body odor is likely clogging up the air ducts in our house.

"I told you," I whisper, fiddling with the zodiac bracelet Rose got me for Christmas, "I need more time."

"Time? Rebecca Ann, it's been a month since Rose..." She pauses, likely catching herself. "I just think you've had ample time to grieve, sweetie."

I shut my eyes, wondering what planet the woman is hailing from today. Ample time? Is that really what she thinks? That she can just snap her fingers and force me to be okay again?

In a perfect world, maybe. Not this one.

"It's not like I'm missing out on anything," I say. "It's summer."

"You're missing out on *life*." She walks over to the window and spreads the curtains before yanking the rattling frame up. Dust motes fill the air, floating over my bed from the incoming breeze. They look like tiny sparkles dancing a misguided version of the tango.

I sigh, blowing a few away. Fighting with my mom is the last thing I want to do right now.

"Rose wouldn't want you to be like this." The bed dips when she sits beside me. I feel the heat of her hand lingering over my shoulder. Thankfully, she pulls away at the last minute. I don't want to feel *anything*. Not the physical touch of her hand or the emotional touch of her words. I'm handling this grief in the only way I knew how: by sleeping it away.

"I'm tired. Let me sleep." That's my only reputable excuse anymore. Since everything happened, it's all I want to do.

She starts in again, something about going to see a doctor, possibly getting on some meds to help me get "out of my funk". But this is no funk, that's the thing. This is my life now. My *grief*. Instead of telling her this, I study the photographs framed on the wall, losing myself in them for the third time today.

They're all of Rose and me—goofy, happy pictures spanning from years ago up until the end of May. Every time I compare the time periods, I try to find differences in them. A change in my best friend I hadn't noticed before, some sort of sign to prove she was unhappy or hiding something. But no matter how hard I study them I see no real differences. If anything, she almost looks

28

happier than ever in the last photo we took the weekend before Memorial Day. Like she could take on the world.

I smile at the memory, not listening to whatever Mom is saying. Instead, I continue to mess with my bracelet and scrutinize the image.

Our cheeks are both sun-kissed. My arm is around Rose's neck, while hers are folded at the waist. We're outside the barn, heads bent close mid-laugh. I'd forced her to come over for our annual picnic, regardless of the fact that she didn't like big family events. The only thing different I can see is that there were dark circles under her eyes. But that doesn't necessarily mean anything. We'd just finished school finals and had a lot of late-night practices at the batting cage. She was running on empty from end-of-the-year activities, that's all. But she was happy. So happy.

I hate how Ben's left me distrusting of her memory.

"You get ten minutes to shower. If you're not up and moving within those ten minutes, I'll be doing something drastic to get you out of here. You hear me?"

I roll over to yell at her, but all that comes out is an, "Ugh."

Ignoring me, she stands and walks toward the door, her hand lingering against the frame, fingers tapping wood. "We have company coming in an hour, so it's absolutely necessary that you put on some deodorant and dress in an outfit that doesn't have stains or holes."

I stiffen. "Company?"

"Yes." She huffs. "And if I'm expected to play nice, then so are you."

———

AN HOUR AND A HALF LATER, I'm in the kitchen, peering around the corner of the door frame and into the dining room. Sitting at our table, I find the last person I expect to see: Rose and Ben's mother, Ginger.

She's to the left of my parents, and across from her are two empty chairs. I blink at the view, sliding a hand down my neck when I remember the last time we'd sat together in this room.

Thanksgiving of last year.

Mom and Dad loved Rose like a daughter. But their love for Ginger never matched. They tolerate the woman on a level that says: *you gave our daughter her best friend who we love like our own child.* That's it. It's why I'm confused she's here.

Ginger isn't a bad person, so to speak, just drinks too much sometimes and can't keep a steady job for more than a month at a time. Even though she loves her kids, the woman is not about to win any Mom of the Year awards. Plus, she always favored Ben, and that pissed me off.

When it came to Rose, I'm surprised the lady even remembered her daughter existed most days. When they were together, it usually always ended with tears or an argument.

Like last year, when our softball team won State. Rose was MVP, pitching an almost no-hitter. Ginger, though, had been too busy to attend the game, claiming she couldn't get off work, when really, she'd spent the weekend at the bar with some random guy she'd been dating at the time.

I knew Rose had been upset about it. It was evident in her eyes when she scanned the stands for family members who wouldn't be there. But my parents were. Supporting us both, they'd held up signs in the air boasting how they were the proud parents of number sixteen *and* number five. It wasn't the same, but I know Rose appreciated it.

"So, how long is Ben back in town for?" Forks scrape across the plates as Mom speaks. I can tell she's on her last nerve already.

Ginger clears her throat. "Two more weeks. That's when pre-season training starts."

The tightness in my chest increases. God, I so do not want to do the small talk thing tonight. Especially not when it's about Ben.

"I see." Mom grows quiet. I can practically feel the tension from where I'm standing. She doesn't want Ginger here, which means this dinner was likely my father's suggestion. He's too nice for his own good sometimes. A little clueless socially too.

"Will he start this year or sit on the bench?" Dad intervenes. Lucky for Ginger, my father's hatred toward the woman doesn't span quite as widely as Mom's.

"I believe so," Ginger says, her voice thickening with emotion.

Curious as to what she's thinking, I bite down on my bottom lip, peer around the corner, and look at her. My throat closes off even more at what I see. Despondency in her blue eyes burning bright. The woman lacked parenting skills, yes. But I do feel bad for her.

"The pros are already eying him," Ginger says, looking at the table. "Given the chance, I know he'd draft up early."

"He needs to finish college first, don't you think?" Mom asks. "Get an education to fall back on. Football dreams are great, but they're not necessarily realistic."

Ginger's shoulders stiffen, but she doesn't respond. She's used to my mom always having a clapback. But she's never one to fight back either, kind of like my dad.

"Either way, he's got amazing talent." Still clueless, my dad pats Mom's hand and smiles, oblivious to the fact that she's gripping her knife like she's seconds from using it for reasons having nothing to do with the meat on her plate. "We should take a trip sometime this fall to see one of his games," Dad continues. "I think Becca would enjoy another tour of the campus."

"Oh, he'd love it if you did that." Ginger practically coos at my father.

Every nerve ending in my body electrifies at Dad's suggestion. I have *zero* plans to attend the same college as Ben now that Rose won't be going with me. Plus, I wasted enough of my time watching Ben play when he was in high school. There's no way in hell I'll be going to one of his *college* games.

Ginger turns to my mom, giving her a smile that borders on painful. "And I agree. Getting his degree would be ideal. But he's not much of a scholar. Quitting college and walking on to a pro team might be his best bet at succeeding in life."

I pull in a sharp breath. As much as I despise Ben, I know Rose wouldn't have liked listening to her mom rag on her brother behind his back. Yes, Ben lacks certain skills when it comes to school and learning, but it's not like the guy can help it or anything. Rose once told me he had a learning disability or something like that, I don't know. I never asked for specifics.

Regardless, to hear Ginger talk crap about him when the woman had been pro-everything-Ben for as long as I've known this family, it annoys me more than it should. Still, I'm not much in the mood to dip my toes into the battlefield tonight. Not when I'm as tired as I am.

Tired of grieving.

Of fighting.

Of living, even—not that I want to die.

"I plan on going to more games this year too now that Rose is..." Ginger trails off, those unspoken words breaking me more than the ones she did manage.

Why can nobody say it?

Rose is gone.

Rose is dead.

Say it. Say it, damn it. Say. It!

The room stays quiet. Even the sound of silverware and chewing is gone. I slip back into the kitchen, hands shaking with nerves as I slide down the wall to the floor. Now would be the perfect opportunity to escape back up to my bedroom, but I can't bring myself to move.

Thunder echoes in the distance outside, preceded by a flash of lightning through the window. Small drops of rain hit the roof a few minutes later, and I tilt my head back, almost expecting for it to fall through the ceiling. That'd be my karma for not going to this stupid dinner.

Before I can even stand to leave the room, there's a soft knock on the back door. I frown and push to my feet, praying it's not a friend from school. Not that I have many, aside from Sienna, and I've been avoiding her calls and texts for weeks.

Dad and Ginger begin to talk again. Mom, doesn't. I half expect her to be the one to answer, but when the visitor knocks again and no chairs budge, I realize I'm going at this alone. Wonderful.

With slow hands and feet, I move forward, unlatching the lock only to open the door to find the second-to-last person I expected to see tonight.

Ben.

"Aaaand she awakens from her pity-me coma." He snorts, then drops his chin to his chest like his head is too heavy to hold up.

I glare at him, my entire body like a lightning bolt ready to strike him down... until I see how bad he's wobbling.

"What the hell do you want?"

He reaches out and grabs the door frame—likely an attempt to keep himself upright.

"Came to eat." He looks around the kitchen, then sniffs the air like a dog.

I stare at his body, more so his clothing. His black-and-yellow University of Iowa Tee clings to his body from the rain, almost like a second skin. As much as I don't want to, I can't help but notice how it highlights his stomach muscles beneath the material. I can tell already the guy's got abs for days. I don't remember him having that many before, honestly.

Lips pursing, I look at his face again just in time to see water drip from his lashes; down his cheekbones; shadowing his glazed, hooded eyes. *Dangerous* would be the best word to describe him right now. Not to mention *annoyingly good-looking* too.

Before I can think of something witty to say, the stench of stale beer hits me in the face as he burps. "Eww. You're drunk again." I set a hand on my hip, waving the other in front of my nose.

"I was invited, just so ya know." Eyes unfocused, he sways a little.

"Sure, ya were." I roll my eyes and move to the side, allowing him in.

His arm brushes against the length of me—definitely on purpose.

"Can you not?" I push him away, hating how my stomach twists from his touch.

Instead of yelling back, he stops a few feet into my kitchen, a hand against the fridge as his body sways even more. His normal cocky smile is absent when he turns to face me. Words on his tongue linger but don't leave.

"You good?" I quirk a brow, not wanting to care.

Before he can answer, Ben drops to his knees with a

34

loud curse. Seconds later, almost comically, he face-plants onto the kitchen floor by my feet.

"Holy crap." I jump back, fingertips pressed to my lips.

What a douche.

"What in the world?" Mom gasps from the kitchen entryway a moment later. I'm pretty sure her love for Ben runs as deep as her love for Ginger does.

"He's shit-faced." I snort, only for Mom to approach my side and smack my arm with the back of her hand.

"Watch your mouth."

I roll my eyes.

"Ginger? Tom? You're going to need to get in here," she calls over her shoulder, making no move to do a single thing about the guy passed out on her kitchen floor.

Ginger saunters into the room first, my Dad just seconds behind. Their eyes widen at the view, but Ben's mom is the first to speak.

"Oh God." Her cheeks turn a bright pink as she approaches her son, yet I can't find it in me to reassure the woman. Mom doesn't either.

It would appear that the prince has fallen from the throne.

"You need to get him under control," Mom tells Ginger, her dark eyes intense.

I look at the woman whose son has obviously taken on his mom's coping mechanisms. For once, Ginger takes Mom's bait and barks back. "He's not your son so I suggest you mind your business."

"He came to his sister's funeral drunk!" Mom throws up her hands. "How can you see this as a nonissue?"

Huh. Mom knew. That's news to me.

"It is an issue, yes," Ginger huffs, "but not *yours* to worry about."

"I'd say it is, seeing as how he's currently passed out on my kitchen floor."

Dad steps between them. "Let's just all calm down. Fighting won't get us anywhere."

Annoyed with their bickering, I crouch down beside Ben's head, taking him in. His lips are parted, and I instantly gag when the smell of bile and beer hits my nose. I wonder if he puked before he came here. Worse yet, I wonder if he drove. That would just be the icing on the stupid cake when it came to this night. Or this *guy*, more specifically.

"You're such an idiot," I whisper to his sleeping form.

"That is *enough!*" I jump at the sound of my father's yelp, not used to his anger. "You are two grown women," he continues. "Shirley, it's none of your business or mine what's going on in Ben's life. Ginger's right."

Mom scoffs. "Like I said, it is my business if he—"

"If you've got that much of a problem with it, then why the hell did you invite me over in the first place?" Ginger yells back.

I blow out a long breath. Their back and forth has been like this for as long as I can remember. Mom hating on Ginger; Ginger on the defense while hating on Mom; and good old Dad, always jumping in as the—mostly clueless—martyr.

My mom and Ginger actually grew up together, went to the same school, hung in the same friend circle too. But the thing is, the two of them have never liked each other, even prior to my dad.

I tuck my knees under my chin as I continued to study Ben's face.

"*You're* the cheater," I say, quoting the words he used at Rose's funeral. He's not facing this any better than I am. The only difference is he's doing it drunk, while I'm doing it sober. That, to me, is cheating.

"She'd be so pissed at you, you know?" I whisper, laughing a little at the same time. "Then I'd have to tell her *I told you so.*"

"Just someone please help me get him to the car," Ginger says.

"No," Mom jumps in, surprising me. I look up, finding her sad gaze on me while she finishes. "He's going to stay the night. Then in the morning, he can pay for his idiocy by helping Becca with barn chores."

"What?" I widen my eyes. "No, no, no. I can do them alone."

"That's not a bad idea." Dad nods, neither of them acknowledging me as they look to Ginger. "I could use the help around here."

Ginger shakes her head, practically cooing at my father. It's kind of disgusting, really. If I was Mom, I'd slap the look right off her face. "I can't ask that of you, Tom." Then she looks to my mom with an angry scowl. "Especially if someone's going to be holding it over my head."

Mom turns away with an angry grunt and heads back to the dining room, her arms thrown into the air. "I'm done here. With you *and* your son."

I wince, wanting to follow her. Make sure she's okay. But what's happening in the kitchen affects me far worse, so I'm gonna be selfish again.

"Dad." I push to my feet, chewing on my bottom lip. "I'll do the chores on my own tomorrow. I promise." Anything to get Ben out of here so I don't have to wake up and see his smarmy face.

He settles his hand on my shoulder and squeezes. "Your mom's right, sweetheart. Plus, it would be nice to get an extra set of hands with the harvest coming." He pauses, glances at Ben, then refocuses on me. "If you don't need him to help you, then I'll find some other use for him."

I shake my head, willing my father to see how traitorous he's being. But other than Rose, nobody knows why I hate the passed-out guy on our kitchen floor so much. And it's not just because he abandoned my best friend.

Ginger walks over and crouches beside her son. Sighing, she places her palm to his cheek, shoulders quaking in a quiet sob. I try to look away from the private mother/son moment but fail—too entranced by the people with whom my best friend had always been abandoned by.

The view's weird. Makes me angry too. I want to throttle Ginger and ask why she didn't care half as much for her daughter as she does her son. But at the same time, it doesn't matter now.

Without speaking to anyone, I walk to the screen door, pushing it open because I need some air. My lungs squeeze with every inhale I take, but I refuse to cry when I only just stopped a few hours ago.

As I stand on the porch, hands clinging to the old, wooden rails, I tilt my head back and look at the lightning-filled sky. The rain, so warm on the back of my hands, continues to belt down on the roof in waves. I don't care about getting wet. Not when there are more important things to wish for. Like seeing, feeling, or seeing my best friend again, in a way that's not in memories or pictures.

"Becca?" Dad calls from inside. "Come inside. It's bad out there."

Throat tight, I say, "Just a minute."

He sighs but eventually lets me be, the echo of his retreating footsteps proof. When I glance behind me to see the screen door still open, I know this is Dad's way of saying, *Take your time—I'm here if you need me.*

It's that bit of time I both appreciate *and* hate. Part of me wants to be fought for, dragged out of my despair. But I know if he or my mom try, I'll only fight back. This is something I have to do on my own time and in my own way.

Inhaling through my nose, I head to the porch steps, needing to feel something besides the pain, even if it's the cold rain. Wetness drips from my lashes and trails over my cheeks with every step I take. The coolness does nothing to calm my heated skin, but the sensation of the water combined with my heightened emotions somehow keeps me focused.

The most glaring physical reminder I have of Rose is now passed out in my house like a sore that won't heal. With their identical blond hair and their coy smiles, their lone dimple most of all, I can't help but feel like I'm drowning in hopelessness whenever I look at Rose's brother.

Beneath my Docs, gravel crunches along the driveway, just barely audible over the claps of thunder. I spread my arms wide, hold my breath, and begin to wonder what might happen if I just left, or if I no longer existed.

What if it had been my life lost instead of Rose's?

Another crash of lightning crackles, pulling me in toward its bright, deadly promises. One step. Then another. The pain in my chest never easing, though I want it gone.

I want to stop feeling so much.

The wind picks up, and the pealing of my mother's favorite wind chimes slap against the barn, reminding me of my existence once more.

I don't want to die. I love my family too much to

leave them. Yet at the same time, I don't want to live this way either. Always re-experiencing my memories with Rose but never finding a future with her otherwise.

Haunting shadows appear before me as I stare out into the sparse land of my family's farm. Tall stalks of corn, practically black in the night, flatten with the angry winds. Every flash of lightning takes the breath from my lungs, mirroring my life as I remember, wish, and hate how the world I live in now exists without my best friend.

"Becca?" At the sound of Ginger's voice, I tighten my fingers into fists. "What are you doing out here?" Like mine did, her shoes crunch against the gravel as she approaches. "You're going to get struck by lightning."

I shrug, the words lodged in my throat. If I speak, I'm pretty sure I'll cry. And if I start to cry, I'm not sure if I'll be able to stop.

Moments later, when I'm sure she's gotten into her car, I hear her voice call out again. "She loved you, you know. More than anyone else."

A tear drips down my cheek, matching the pace of the rain. It's coming so fast now I can barely see Ginger's face when I turn to her. Still, I speak the only words I can. "I know."

But did Rose really love me like her mom says? We had a no-secrets policy, yet Ben insists she *did* have secrets. No matter how much I push the thought away, I can't stop thinking about it.

"IT'S JUST one more game. I promise." Rose chewed on her lower lip like it was a piece of steak, then lifted her paint brush back to my cheek.

"You say that every game."

Her light eyes pleaded with me from the driver's seat of her car. "I promise to buy you a party-sized bag of Takis for every game I've forced you to go to this season, okay?"

I scowled, ultimately relenting like I always did when it came to Rose. "Fine. Just know I'm not happy about it."

"Why, because you wanted to hang out with Travis tonight?" She rolled her eyes and began to paint what I guessed was going on one of my cheeks and tigers on the other. I knew this because I'd been forced to do the same thing to her cheeks five minutes ago.

"No, actually. He's busy tonight. I just really hate these stupid games and don't see the point in going now that your brother's not here."

"It's called a high school rite of passage." She twisted her lips and readjusted the paint brush. "Now, stop moving, otherwise this will be a huge mess."

"Whatever."

Since that night in August by the river, Travis and I had been talking. Then about a week ago we'd decided to make it official. We weren't having sex or anything yet, but that was because I wasn't ready.

Rose had been pissed about our official "relationship status", constantly asking why I had to go and ruin a good thing by turning it into something serious. When it came to relationships, Rose and I always held a different stance. She hated commitment—and most boys in general. I, on the other hand, had a romantically, desperate heart.

A group of guys walked in front of her car bumper, stopping when they saw us. The ringleader, Liam Jackson, made a V in front of his mouth and stuck his tongue through it as he focused on Rose. His idiot buddies roared with laughter, slapping him on the shoulder at the same time.

Rose dropped her brush against her lap, reaching her hand out to flick them off—which only made the guys laugh harder when they finally walked away.

I rolled my eyes and grabbed my zippered hoodie from the floor. "They're a bunch of idiots," under my breath.

My best friend snapped her paint kit closed. "They're just bitter because I won't give them the time of day."

"They'd never be good enough for you anyway." I grinned.

"Damn straight." We slapped hands in midair, then started to laugh.

Pride for my best friend's kickass attitude never failed to embody me. No matter what went down in her life, she'd never once let the rumors around town get to her. The promiscuity of her mom; the woman's drunken, late-night endeavors; and talk of people thinking Rose would wind up just like her, when, really, she was the opposite of that.

My best friend always strived to be a bigger and better person than that woman. And as her best friend, I was going to make sure it stayed that way, even if it meant rehashing the once-forbidden number seventy-one from our list.

"I think it's time," I said from over the roof as we stepped out of her car. My hands shook at the thought, but Liam had been giving her crap since eighth grade—since his mom had found Rose's mom in bed with his father.

"Time for what?"

"Seventy-one." I shrugged in attempt to play it cool.

"Seriously?" She clapped her hands together and squealed.

"Are you ready to break multiple laws to enact revenge?"

"Oh, hell yes, I am." She rubbed her hands together. "Now, spill. What's the plan?"

"We need supplies." The problem was I had zero clue where to get said supplies. It would take us forty minutes to get to my house, and Rose sure as heck didn't have what we needed at her place. To top it off, neither of us had any money to buy anything right now at the hardware store down the road, which I was pretty sure had closed for tonight's game anyways.

"Giiiirl. I love it when your dark side jumps out." Rose squeezed my arm. "It's a good thing I've got a certain some-one's number on speed dial who knows just where to get the crap we need."

———

"A CERTAIN SOMEONE" just so happened to be Adam, who pulled into the lot beside us ten minutes later. He drove this clunky, rusted blue Chevy, a hand-me-down from his grandma, apparently.

When he got out of the car, I could see the box filled with all the things we'd need to complete the job in his arms. The silver handle of a box cutter, feathers, peanut butter, and several large plastic spoons to do the spreading with. Each item reflecting the moonlight felt more like murder weapons instead of materials for a prank that could possibly get us kicked out of school.

"You're a god," Rose breathed, taking the box from his hands.

Adam laughed, rubbing at the back of his neck. I could almost bet that he was blushing. "Wanna tell me whose car we're planning on messing with now?"

I opened my mouth to tell him there was no "we". That this was Rose's and my thing. Unfortunately, my best friend jumped in before I could get words out.

43

"Liam Jackson's."

"He didn't touch you again, did he?" Adam frowned, lowering his voice like he was trying to hide it from me.

I set my hands on my hips. "What do you mean by 'touched you'?"

Rose shrugged, avoiding my eyes. "It's nothing. The guy's just an ass, and now because of your genius brain, he's going to pay for it."

Despite the cold air, I could feel my face growing hotter with shame. How had I not known he'd touched her? I wanted to ask more questions, get the tea, but Adam jumped in first.

"Where's his car?" he asked.

Rose motioned her head to the row behind us.

"Give me the blade." Adam grinned.

I wanted to argue, tell him that it was my job to slash the tires. But before I could, Rose grabbed the front of Adam's shirt and led him away like a puppy on a leash.

My throat burned when I swallowed. I refused to be jealous. I did. But this bucket list thing was for me and Rose, not me, Rose, and Adam. Still, I didn't call them out and instead kept watch while I followed them, weaving in and out of the rows like the soon-to-be stealthy criminal I was not.

The crowd from the field house roared behind us, and the announcer said something I couldn't understand. Rose and Adam walked side by side, laughing louder than I probably would've done for a pre-crime scene.

They stepped up next to the forest-green Mercedes belonging to Liam, and only then did fear began to truly take hold. I cracked my knuckles as I watched Rose. She didn't hesitate to drop the box with a thud by her feet. I looked around, eyes widening when I noticed several adults close by walking toward the stadium. They looked at us but went about their business seconds later, thankfully.

"You're so not doing the tires, Adam," Rose said.

Adam stood in front of her, holding a box cutter above his head. "You don't have the muscles to do it, champ."

She shoved at his chest, grinning. "What did I tell you about calling me that?"

He laughed. "And what did I tell you about—"

I folded my arms. "You guys need to keep it down."

Adam rolled his eyes. "You're too paranoid, Becca."

I wasn't paranoid. I was terrified. Getting caught could mean getting into huge trouble. Not only would we get suspended or possibly expelled from school, we'd likely lose our spots on the softball team too. And don't even get me started on the possibility of getting arrested.

There again, if I backed down now, Adam would inevitably make fun of me like always, and Rose wouldn't get her revenge.

"It's gonna be fine, Becca," my best friend said, swiping the box cutter out of Adam's hands when he wasn't looking. She held it out to me instead, like it was some sort of award. "Now, come on. You've got number seventy-one to tackle."

I licked my lips, hesitating a second before closing the distance between us. After taking the blade from her, I stepped back just enough to admire the tires on Liam's fancy sports car. They looked brand new.

Rose and Adam kept laughing, and soon they were both taking turns spreading the peanut butter on the hood of the truck as they traded banter.

Knowing this was my shot at making things right for Rose, I took a deep breath and walked closer to the front right tire before crouching down next to it. I set the blade against the rubber, opened it with a click. Then with shaking hands I held it against the rubber and . . . pulled it away at the last minute.

I couldn't do this. I couldn't. It was one thing to let the air out, but to slash the tires altogether?

"Hey, what's going on over there?" someone yelled in the distance.

Rose and Adam both started laughing louder before coming around to my side.

"Becca, we gotta go!" Rose whisper-yelled, yanking at my arm.

My stomach twisted as the voice grew angrier, and thoughts of Liam's face flashed through my mind. That's when I took the blade and stabbed as hard as I could...only for it to bounce off and onto the concrete instead.

"Damn it," I whispered, reaching for it, stabbing, stabbing, stabbing some more...until finally I got through.

I grinned wide, only for Rose to yank me to my feet. "Let's go, killer," she whispered with a quieter laugh.

That was the first time I'd tasted danger. And it was delicious.

4

August
Present Day

MY DOOR OPENS, banging against the wall. I moan, rolling over to see my worst nightmare come to life and currently approaching me.

"Damn," he says, taking a seat on the end of my mattress, bouncing a little. "You're looking like a before picture this morning, Becca."

I flip him off, pull the blanket up and over my face...only for him to rip it off my body completely.

"Leave, asshole!" I screech and sit up against the headboard, hiding all the places on my body I can cover with both hands.

He freezes, and instead of running out of the room like I'd hoped, his gaze sweeps lazily over the length of my body. My body warms, despite my irritation with him.

"My Dad's gonna kill you when he finds out you

47

snuck in here." I yank the covers up to my chest again. This time Ben doesn't stop me or pull them away.

The slight flush on his cheeks leaves me wondering if he's that disgusted with my body, or just embarrassed by his mistake of exposing it. Not that I care either way.

Snapping out of his mood, he falls back onto the end of my bed, one arm tucked behind his head as he stares at the ceiling.

"Your dad loves me." Without permission, he sets his arm on top of my foot over the blanket, turns my way, and winks.

My stomach tightens, betraying me again. I should be kicking him in the head, not feeling stupid flutters. This is Ben, Rose's brother. A guy I've hated for years. A guy who's now casually snuggled up to me like we've done this a million times before.

I swallow hard, attempt to get a grip on reality, but fail miserably as the heat of his arm on my foot sends invisible flames up and down my leg. Seconds pass. Seconds that are too long and too intense. A funny feeling builds in my chest in turn, and when his head falls to the side and his gaze snaps up to my face, I have to fold my arms to try to push it away.

"Cat got your tongue?" His smile grows a little more, showcasing the side of him I know best. The dickhead, cocky, know-it-all, too good for everyone else, part. Yet at the same time, there's something else behind this look. Something I can't decipher.

"No." I push my thoughts away, ready for battle. "But there's this nasty unwanted bug in my bed at the moment, and I can't seem to get rid of it." I kick him in the shoulder, not the head. Hard, but not bruising either. He grunts and moans like he's internally bleeding, a hand over his ribs rubbing.

I was nowhere *near* his ribs.

48

"Jeez, you're cranky." His bottom lip puffs in a pout.

"Because *you* showed up in my room uninvited." And snuggled up to my foot too. For sure I thought he'd be snuggled up to the toilet, puking this morning. But *Ben* is even too good for that.

"I wasn't uninvited." He sits up again and faces me, one leg folded beneath him. "Your mom told me to come upstairs and wake you." Like before, his gaze slides casually over my face, then lower, then higher, faster this time. Still, I don't miss the chance to call him out.

"Your eyes are going to explode." I smirk.

He smiles even wider, blinding and bright. His teeth are too white, and his eyes are too blue and he's too...pretty. I hate him.

"What are you looking at?" I grumble when he continues to stare at me.

"What do you think I'm looking at?" His eyebrows shoot up. "You're half naked in a bed, and I'm a man."

"You're not a man. You're a boy."

He laughs, standing from the bed. "I'm *too much* of a man for you."

"Whatever." I snort. "You're the last thing I'd ever want."

"Do you really believe that?" He stares at me from over his shoulder, brows furrowing a little.

"Absolutely, I do." I lift my chin. "Your reputation precedes you." I tap my lips and pretend to think. "How many girls did you sleep with in high school again? And I'm sure college hasn't been any different. Big *football* star, killin' it with the groupies."

Aaaand now I sound like a jealous brat. Which is so far from the truth that it's not even funny because I don't even like the guy. Not one. Stinking. Bit.

I mean, okay, maybe *once* I liked him.

A little.

49

And, yes, there might have been an incident between the two of us when I was a freshman and him a junior. I haven't thought about it in years. Until now of course.

Ben was almost seventeen. I'd just turned fifteen. At the time, he was basically the most popular guy at Winston High School. I'd been staying the night at Rose's and needed a drink of water. In the kitchen, I grabbed a bottle from the fridge, drank it down, then turned to find Ben at the breakfast bar in their kitchen, watching me.

I'd jumped when I noticed him, dropped the rest of my water on my toe, only for him to rush over with a towel and help me clean it up. When I looked at him to say thank you, I noticed tears on his cheeks.

The two of us had never really spoken back then, other than his teasing. At the time, I'd been kind of clueless about how to respond to his weird playfulness. But I'd also harbored a stupid crush on him and, somehow, managed to use my crush-skills to work up the nerve to ask him if he was okay. I blamed it on my under-romanticized heart.

He told me no, how he wasn't okay, no hesitation.

I asked him if he wanted to talk about it and, much to my surprise, he said yes.

We sat together at the island counter, side by side, just close enough for his knee to brush mine. And just like that, Ben became a waterspout, flooding me with his words and confessions. He told me things that night that I didn't know how to deal with. Stuff about his mom's drinking and her constantly sleeping around. How he was worried about Rose's reckless behavior too. I'd never considered Rose's behavior to be reckless until he'd pointed it out. She was just Rose to me. She was a daredevil tomboy with an affinity for breaking the rules without getting caught.

That was the first time I'd ever known Ben to care about someone other than himself. That was also the point in time when my harmless crush on my BFF's older brother fast turned into the warm and fuzzies...something that went beyond just a crush.

I thought he'd been feeling it too. For an hour we talked about our lives after that, comparing and contrasting, and he listened to me as much as I did him. His blue eyes bored into my soul, it felt like, and he looked at me in a way no other boy had before—like I mattered. Like I was a real, honest-to-goodness person. So, when I leaned in and took the chance, ready to kiss away his worries, and even some of mine, I'd been expecting fireworks.

Unfortunately for me, Ben wasn't in a Fourth of July mood.

What I thought had been the beginning of something had actually been nothing at all, just me just being stupid and clueless and reading every positive sign wrong. When Ben turned his head away, only for my lips to hit his chin instead, I immediately got up and ran from the kitchen, crying myself to sleep on Rose's bedroom floor.

Ben tried to apologize the next day, but I was so embarrassed—and so stupid—that I sassed him with the first clapback I could manage: *I'm really freaking jealous of all the people in life who have never met you.*

That was the beginning of our insult game.

Pushing my thoughts away, I lean over the bed, grab my yoga pants off the floor, stand, and quickly slip them on—careful to stay mostly covered as I do.

"You're still keeping track of my reputation all these years later?" Ben clicks his tongue against the roof of his mouth, "I'm touched, B."

B. He hasn't called me *B* since I was *twelve.*

I shake my head, regroup the best I can. His ability to

51

frazzle me is just as unnerving as ever. "Unless, of course, it's all been a cover. That you really *can't* get girls like you say you can."

Before I can even blink, I'm backed against my wall, a gasp climbing its way up my throat. His body hovers close, our stomachs press together too. Everything about Ben's sudden move says I've just hit a button he didn't want pushed.

"What's the matter?" I curl my upper lip. "Did I hurt your fragile little *ego*?"

A soft laugh falls from his mouth as he stares at me. His breath smells like mint, as if he'd taken the time to brush his teeth. But the hungry and haunted expression in his eyes has me faltering.

"Let me tell you something, *little girl*. I'm a man who likes women. There's no shame in that. *You* are nothing but a kid to me. You've always been that way. Nothing but Rose's little *friend*. So, do yourself a favor and quit thinking you know me when we both know you don't."

"Little girl?" I cross my arms and look down at the fair amount of cleavage I've got going on. "If you haven't noticed lately, I am so far from being a little girl that it's not even funny." I drop my arms and move in closer. So close I can't feel where his chest ends and mine begins. I'm hyper aware of him, his warmth, the way his breathing seems to quicken. But I'm determined to let him feel just how *not little* I am, which means I need to refuse to acknowledge my own rampant needs.

"Stop that." His eyes narrow.

I press my lips together to fight a grin. "Stop what?"

He shuts his eyes and grits his teeth, but it's the desperation in his words that gives me pause.

"Becca." Doing the last thing I ever expect for him to do, he lowers his forehead to mine and whispers, "Stop, please."

I pull in a sharp breath, blinking in surprise when he finds my right hand and interlaces our fingers. Neither of us move. I'm not sure I want to, either. Having him so close to me is warm and comforting, slightly unfamiliar but familiar at the same time. I like it. So much more than when Travis was ever this close to me.

It's the first time in a month where I can just let myself think and feel something other than the heartache in my chest. The squeezing...

We stand like that for a long while, his hot breath fanning over my neck, foreheads touching, bodies pressed close. Even my heartbeat stops, restarting only to thud harder against my chest like a warning or something possibly demanding more. For a moment, I'm almost positive he's gonna kiss me.

Until he pulls his head away and looks at me dead on.

His blue eyes are lost. Filled with unshed tears. It's as though he's unzipping his broken heart and laying it on display for me.

Ben is hurting. Maybe even more than I am.

Tears gather in my own eyes, and I pull my hand out of his to press it against his cheek. "It's okay," I whisper, terrified of my vulnerability, but knowing this moment between us is important for healing. "I...I hurt too."

He shuts his eyes, shakes his head, then presses a soft kiss to my forehead, lingering there for several shuddering breaths. My throat closes off, trapping a sob inside. Just before I can let my arms wrap around his waist and pull him in for a bone-crushing hug, he backs away and runs from my room.

———

I CAN'T GO BACK to sleep—not with that incessant knocking happening outside my window. Not when I can still feel Ben's lips on my forehead either.

With a huff, I'm resolved to the inevitable and sit up, this time throwing a bra on under my tank. I stay in my yoga pants, then pull on my boots, tugging both over low-cut socks without tying the laces. With the stretch of a hair tie, I tug my hair back and pile it all on top of my head into a messy bun.

"Good as it's going to get," I tell my reflection before leaving the room.

Tiptoeing around Mom in the kitchen, I head out the front door, ready to raise hell with my dad about the noise. But the second I'm on the porch, a sweaty, blond Greek god steals my attention—has my knees weakening at the same time.

"Sweet baby Jesus." I press my fingers to my lips, using my free hand to hold on to the railing for balance. I'm pretty sure I've never seen Ben shirtless before. I'm also pretty sure my heart can't take the glory of it.

Back muscles bunch when he moves, bends over, rakes... Every second longer I stand watch, my face grows hotter for reasons not caused by the August humidity.

"Good morning, sunshine." Dad moves into of my line of vision, and I jump back with an embarrassed yelp.

"Don't scare me like that." I step off the last few steps of the porch to meet up with him. Thankfully he didn't notice my Ben gawking.

"Sorry about that." He wraps his arm around my shoulder. "You sleep okay?"

Up until this morning's disruption, I slept like a baby. "Yeah. Fine." I curl my nose—"You stink though,"—and twirl out of his hold, careful not to let my gaze linger on Mr. Shirtless again.

"Hot day already." Dad laughs. "Thankfully I've got a part-time farmhand to help me out before things gets too steamy."

Feeling a gaze on my face, I look up again, finding Ben watching us. His cheeks are pale, which surprises me. He's even sweatier than my dad.

"I thought today was just a one-time thing?" I frown. *Part-time* sounds way too permanent for my liking.

"I figured he could stay on for the last few weeks until he heads to school. He needs a little pocket change, and I'd like the help."

My skin prickles. One day is bad enough. Anything beyond that should be illegal.

"Seriously." I tuck some hair behind my ear. "I'll pick up the extra slack. We won't need him after today."

Dad's eyebrows lift. "*You?*"

"Yes, *me*."

My father's right to be hesitant. I've always hated everything having to do with working on the farm, except for when it comes to the horses. But when the choice comes down to working chores I hate versus having Ben here, the answer to me is simple.

"Prove it, then." Dad shrugs. "Go give him a hand."

I wince, hearing Ben curse from inside the barn a minute later. "But we have people who—"

"Every job has to be done around here, no matter what it is or who does it. Remember that." Dad's face grows serious, proof that I don't have a choice.

Being a farmer's daughter really sucks sometimes.

Shoulders slumping, I head toward Ben like he's my executioner on death row. When he sees me, he sets his rake against the side of the barn and rubs his hands along the thighs of his jeans. His eyes, lighter now than they'd been upstairs, meet mine.

"You here to bust my balls, B?" His chest rises and

falls, capturing my attention first. Sweat slips between his pecs and travels down the ripples of his tanned abdomen.

My face begins to boil, and I jerk my head up, noting the smirk on his lips.

"You don't need to help. I'll do the chores."

I reach for the rake, but he leans over, grabbing it again. He lifts it and holds it above his head, his arm muscles straining. That stupid dimple is the first thing I see when I look at him again. It's so big that I find myself scowling at it.

"Nope. Gotta work off my rent for using your family's spare bedroom last night."

I jump, trying to grab the rake end. But he doesn't let go, just lifts it even higher. "That is not. Necessary."

"It is." His grin widens even more. "Especially now that I know I'll be ogled while I do it."

Oh, for the love of God. I cover my face with one hand and groan. Having him here is freaking torture. Not just because he drives me nuts but because he's also a reminder of Rose. If I want to move past her death, then how am I expected to do it with him around so much?

"This is a bad idea, you being here. That's all I'm saying." I huff.

Lame, Becca. So. Lame.

"Wellll," Ben drawls, losing some of his playfulness, "according to your parents, it's a very *good* idea, seeing as how your dad's been doing most of *your* work *and* his too."

I crouch down to tie my boots just for something to do with my hands. "Fine. Then if you're going to be here, you have to do whatever *I* say. And you can start by helping me feed the animals."

He points to the pile of horse crap in the corner. "But your dad said I need to—"

56

"You were told wrong." I brush my hands against my thighs and stand again. "We have another farmhand who takes care of the horses. They'll be here tomorrow. Dad was just playing you."

"Oh." He frowns and looks to his feet.

Awkwardness settles between us. I'm not sure what to say. And from the way he shuffles his feet back and forth, I'm thinking Ben doesn't either. It's weird how one second we're teasing each other, then the next neither of us can communicate.

The humid wind blasts me in the back of the neck, tossing bits of my pink hair into my mouth. The summer heat is killer—the sweat already dripping down my neck and back proof. I can't help but watch Ben when he rubs an arm over his forehead to wipe away his own sweat. I'm guessing he's been working since he got up this morning—maybe even for hours now. He's likely dehydrated from drinking too much last night, and I'm guessing Dad didn't bother to tell him where to get water either.

Deciding to tuck my irritation away for the sake of his health, I walk to the red ice chest Dad keeps outside next to the barn and grab him a bottle of water.

"Drink." I shove it against his bare chest when I return, hating how his damp muscles feel against the back of my hand. "You're probably dehydrated."

His face falls in relief as he twists off the lid and guzzles it. Water drips down his chin and onto his neck as he drinks, and I watch, oddly enthralled by the bob of his throat when he swallows.

"Thank you," he says with a harsh whoosh, wiping at his mouth with the back of his hand. "I'm used to practicing in heat worse than this, but not usually after drinking."

"You think?" I smirk. "I can't believe my mom and

57

dad..." I trail off, grinning to myself, trying to hide it by looking away.

"What?" he asks.

It all makes sense now. Today's horsecrap flinging, not telling him where the water is, letting him work and work and work until he's nearly dead on his feet... This is Ben's initiation into the world that is Thompson farm life. If anyone chooses to work on the land—even for a day—they have to pass a series of rigorous tests brought on by my dad. One being horse dung flinging, another being heat toleration.

I kind of, sort of feel sorry for the guy because he obviously has no idea what's going on. There again, after last night's stunt, then this morning's, he kinda deserves it.

Doesn't matter either way. He won't make it. Which means his new part-time job working on the land won't last after all. Big strong football player or not, Ben is *not* a farmer.

With my bottom lip pulled between my teeth, I turn back around to face him. "Nothing."

"Doesn't look like nothing." He scowls.

Ignoring him, I grab the chicken feed from the corner and motion for him to follow me. Seconds later, he stumbles over a pile of hay, falling flat onto his knees with a low, "*Shit.*"

I press my lips together, trying not to laugh.

Ben gets back up and follows me away from the barn and over to the coop. The crunch of his feet along the gravel is the only sound signaling he's still hanging on. I like that I can fluster him as much as he does me...even if said flustering isn't the same kind of flustering.

I show him what to do, where to toss the feed, how to change the water, normal stuff that's always been on me.

Helping him is a welcomed distraction, despite the fact that his presence still bugs me.

I finish before he does about an hour and a half later, taking a seat on a stack of hay in the barn. My gaze keeps wandering to his back, his shoulders more specifically, but somehow, I resist the temptation to look at his butt. For the most part.

"I'm sorry," Ben says out of the blue when he's finished feeding the horses. He places the last of the unused hay bales back onto the ground beside me, then takes a seat.

"For what?" I cross an ankle over my knee.

His brows push together, and he seems to think about his answer for a moment. "For not being here when it happened."

I drop my chin to my chest, releasing a long sigh. One of the horses comes up behind me, nudging at my hair. I turn, finding the brindle who's too small for his breed. His name's Calypso. I brush a hand over his nose, remembering, ironically enough, that this horse was Rose's favorite. When Dad let us ride them, Calypso was the one she always picked.

I shut my eyes, and memories yet again flood my mind.

We're riding the back roads, Rose ahead of me, laughing when she puts her hands up in the air. Her long hair drifts behind her like a superhero cape, and she squeals when Calypso automatically picks up speed without even a kick. He's unpredictable just like she was. I think that's why she loved him so much.

It's easy to forget what hurts me when I'm busy out here, brushing the horses, feeding the chickens, piling the hay. But the memories, when they do hit, hurt. Which is how I know it's time I go inside.

"I don't want to talk about it." I stand, intending to

run into the house and away from reality. I've gotten good at it.

"Of course, you don't," Ben snorts from behind me.

I glare at him from over my shoulder. "What's that supposed to mean?"

His lips press into an angry frown as he stands and moves toward me.

"You're always avoiding things, never willing to face anything head on." Ben runs a hand through his hair and leans against the inside of the barn wall in front of me. "You know, Rose always did hate that about you. How undecisive you can be."

My lips part, but any smart-mouthed remark I have gets caught in my throat.

He's right. In our friendship, Rose was the adrenaline junkie, while I was the rule follower, the chicken, the girl who struggled with decisions—even the good kinds.

"You can fix that now though," Ben tells me. "Prove her wrong. That you're tougher than she thought you were."

I glare at him, a sob lodged in my chest. I know what I was like, what I'm still like. A scared little girl, always hiding behind her best friend... Now that Rose is gone though, I have nowhere to hide, and Ben's using that vulnerability against me.

Asshole.

I lift my chin, holding his gaze. "The answer is no."

His eyes flash with both anger and sadness. "Come on, Becca. All I want to do is clear her name. Once that happens, you can go on with your life, and I'll do the same with mine."

I step around him and head toward the house again. "The answer is no."

"I just need to know, damn it. And if you were any

60

sort of friend to my sister, then shouldn't you be feeling the same way?"

I flinch, hold my breath, swallow. "What good will it do if there was something going on, huh? She's dead, Ben. Finding out won't bring her back."

He jumps in front of me, his face a mask of fury. "It'd do a hell of a lot of good, actually."

"Alright, fine. Say we did discover something we don't like," I tell him. "Something that hurts us even more than we already do. Would it be worth it then?"

"Yes," he breathes. "Because we'd know the truth. Then we'd be able to deal with it *and* move on." He moves in closer, sets his palm against my cheek. "Isn't that what you want? To move on?"

I stiffen, not expecting the touch. The tenderness in his eyes. The way his words bring out unwanted feelings.

"Is this some sort of prank? Are you messing with me, Ben?" A tear falls from my eye, and he quickly brushes away with his thumb.

"No." His eyes narrow. "Never. Why would you think that?"

It's apparent right then that he doesn't remember our night in the kitchen. How he pretended to care for me, led me on and then...

"Never mind." I shake my head and give him my back, make my way toward the front porch.

Enough is enough. I don't want to go digging for secrets when it comes to Rose—for multiple reasons. I'm terrified of what we might find if we do. I'm also terrified of *not* finding anything at all either.

Ben races after me, his hand flinging me around by my wrist when I reach the bottom step. I look over his shoulder, past his face, trying to find my dad. He's nowhere though.

"Don't you even care that people are talking crap

about her? Saying stuff like she was just a spoiled, teenage chick looking for attention? That she was no good anyway and won't be missed?"

"She didn't care what other people thought of her, so why should we?"

"Because she *did* care. She just never let anyone know this." He lowers his voice. "Don't you want people to remember her like we do? The funny, brave monster who'd do anything for us?"

Tears and sweat mix together against my cheeks. I wipe both away the best I can, catching sight of dirt and gunk on my fingertips when I finish.

"I do care. So freaking much. She was my best friend, and I was the one person who knew all of her secrets. More than you knew, more than your mother... I knew her pain. I knew her weaknesses. I knew her future." I stab a finger against his chest with a hiss. "And if anybody is knocking her memory, then I'll handle it in my own way. You got it?"

With a heavy sigh, Ben tucks his hands behind his neck and closes his eyes. The line of his jaw flexes, like he's both internally raging *and* on the verge of sobbing. I know that state of mind well because I feel it all the time anymore.

Maybe I should apologize, accept his proposition because he's Rose's big brother. But I'm grieving, and I need more time to do so. This may be how Ben wants to deal with his sister's death, but it's not the way I want to.

CHRISTMAS HAD NEVER BEEN *my favorite time of the year, mostly because I hated the whole extended family thing. But Thanksgiving, on the other hand, was awesome because we got to spend it with Rose and her family.*

This year, though, it was especially epic to wake up to, seeing as how Travis was there in my room with me. He'd officially helped mark off bucket list number seventy-two the night before: spend all night with a guy in my bed.

"You're sure you can't come for dinner today?" I chewed on my bottom lip, watching as he pulled his shirt over his head. His long, brown hair was messier than normal, and his eyes were tired from staying up all night. I'd made him watch movies on my laptop with me, which I didn't think he was happy about, but after messing around a little—and me telling him no for sex again—there wasn't much left for us to do.

Travis wasn't a huge talker, and I struggled to find things to say sometimes too. I figured we were kind of made for each other in that sense.

"Yeah, doll. Dad's got a strict set of rules when it comes to holidays. He's got all these siblings and shit that come over." He grabbed his jeans next, sitting on the side of the bed to yank them on. Leaving them unbuttoned, he stood and pulled his pack of cigarettes from the left pocket.

Eyes wide, I looked toward my door, then at him again when I heard the click of his lighter. "Travis. You can't smoke in—"

He cut me off with a hard kiss, his tongue sliding against my mouth, tasting like ash. Before I could get into it, he pulled back, saying with a smirk, "Relax. I ain't gonna light up in here." But the scowl he wore when he put the pack and lighter back into his pocket said otherwise.

Whenever we were getting ready to say goodbye, it was like he was sliding away from me emotionally as much as he did physically. I freaking hated it because I was always worried that this might be our last time together. Rose told me I was paranoid, that I had no reason to be insecure. But Travis was my first relationship, so I had zero clue how they were supposed to work.

"Can you come by later tonight, then?" I watched when he yanked on his leather coat, then attached his wallet to the chain he always wore on his jeans.

"Don't know what I got planned for tonight," he told me, eyes flitting over my chest.

I swallowed and nodded, then looked at the bed. "Sure, right. Totally understand."

"I'll call you," he said, the scrape of my window sounding throughout the room when he opened it. The sun had barely risen, and a cold gust of wind blew inside. I shivered, but not just because of the temperature this time. With Travis, most days I couldn't help but feel like an afterthought.

Tears filled my eyes. Tears that mortified me. I didn't want to let him see them so I feigned nonchalance the best I could and laid back down on the bed, pulling the covers up to my chin. "Okay."

"Hey," Travis called from outside the window.

Slowly, I rolled onto my side to face him, holding my breath at the same time. God, I was pathetic for hoping that he might change his mind.

"Yeah?"

He studied me a second longer, then said, "You should think about growing your bangs out. They might make you look less like a little doll."

I blinked, taken back by his comment. I'd always thought

64

him saying I looked like a doll was a compliment. "Oh. Um...okay."

He winked, climbed out onto my roof, and jumped the five feet to the ground.

Only then did I start to cry.

————

"HEY, YOU." Rose hugged me the second she walked into the house that afternoon. "You okay?"

On instinct, my bottom lip began to quiver, so I hugged her closer and shut my eyes, refusing to be selfish. "I'm good, just tired."

Rose pulled away and frowned. "Liar. What did that asshole do now?"

I hesitated, not wanting to give her any more ammunition against him, but the sound of footsteps behind her distracted me.

Looking up then, I found Ginger coming into the house first. In one hand was a bottle of wine, and in the other was a container of whatever she'd attempted to make for a side dish to share. Her cheeks were flushed, eyes unfocused too. Even from ten feet away, I could smell the booze on her skin.

"Is your mom okay?" I whispered.

Before she could answer, two more figures walked up the gravel drive outside my front door, their loud laughter cutting through the air. A scowl touched my lips at the sight of Ben and his guest—some pretty redhead who was in no way a relative of theirs.

"Who's that?" I jutted my chin toward the girl. She was tall and thin compared to my short, frumpy state. Truly gorgeous. Not that I was actually comparing myself to her.

Rose turned to face them at the exact moment Ben's gaze shot up to meet mine. A funny feeling hit the pit of my stomach when our eyes locked. Something twisty, something sharp, something like my guts were being ripped from the insides.

Before Rose could answer, Ben inched closer, forgetting his friend completely.

"Becca." His smile was genuine enough to anyone around us, but I recognized it as the beginning of our stupid game. "You're looking..." then he eyed me in that annoyingly lecherous way he knew I hated, "a little under the weather today."

I balled my hands into fists. "I don't know what makes you so stupid, but whatever it is, it's really working."

His lips climbed higher on one side, those blue eyes I hated turning darker, it seemed. "Is that so, huh?"

I nodded, lifting my chin in challenge. It was like the entire world evaporated into nothing but a pit of fiery rage then, existing only for Ben and me in a cage, battling till death.

"You've always been a pain in my neck." He tsked, close enough now to where I could feel the coolness coming off his skin from the outside air. "But I gotta say, every time I see you, that pain moves a little more to my ass, if you know what I mean."

Rose snorted, and I smacked her arm from behind. "Stupidity is not a crime, so you're free to go." I winked at his friend, whose eyes were wide and filled with confusion.

He grinned and pulled his friend to his side from behind, spreading an arm out toward me as he spoke. "Carly, this is Becca Thompson, Rose's friend. And also, living proof that God doesn't have a sense of humor."

I growled low. "I'm gonna kick your—"

"All right, you two." Rose yanked me back by the end of my shirt, dragging me from the room, laughing along the way.

"Let me at him. I swear, it won't take me a second to rip his tiny brain from his head."

Behind me, Ben told his friend, "It's better to let someone think you're an idiot than to open your mouth and prove it, am I right?"

The girl laughed. I hated her instantly.

Once we were out of ear shot, Rose whispered, "God, you two just need to screw already and be done with it."

My eyes widened. "Uh, no. I will never, ever hook up with that guy. Barf."

"Sure. I'll be dead and gone and you'll still be arguing with him instead of screwing him, but neither one of you will be married because you can't think about being with anyone but each other."

I gasped at her suggestion, face heating at the same time. She rolled her eyes. Before I could tell her where to shove her thoughts, Rose lowered her voice and changed the subject. "Now. I've got some serious tea to spill."

I frowned, intrigued—hating, too, that the first thought running through my mind was: Does it have to do with Ben? "What's that?"

"I met someone." She grinned so wide her eyes turned into tiny slits.

"What? Who? When?"

"I can't say much." She licked her lips. "He's, um, not ready for us to come out yet."

"Why not?" I frown. "Does he have a girlfriend, or something?"

"No, he doesn't have a girlfriend." She laughed. "I'm not that stupid."

"Well, who is it? Why does he want to keep you a secret?"

Rose shrugged and looked at her feet. "It's complicated."

I nodded, suspicious already. "Can you at least tell me his name?"

Rose's face fell. Then she licked her lips, seeming nervous. Her gaze flitted from the living room to over my shoulder, back to the floor.

"Rose?" I touched her elbow. "What's up?"

"It's nothing." She relaxed again. "I'll show you a picture later, okay? Promise."

Something was up, though I wasn't sure what it was. Rose wasn't a secret keeper in the least—that was my job—so I knew she'd tell me, even if it wasn't right now.

"Sounds good. I can't wait to meet him."

Her smile grew wide again. I was pretty sure I'd never seen her so happy before. Whoever this guy was, he'd better be worth it.

"Come on. Let's eat." She took me by the elbow and guided me to the kitchen. "I'm starved."

"Okay. I just need a sec."

She left the room, giving me time to compose myself. Between what had happened with Ben just now and my guilt over Travis staying the night last night, I was more on edge than ever. I rarely lied to my parents. When I did, it made me feel like crap. If either one of them found out that I'd let him stay the night, then they'd probably ground me for life.

What I needed to do was repent. Do something to make myself feel less guilty. I'd start by going into the dining room and helping my mom get through the next couple of hours when it came to dealing with whatever version of Ginger had decided to show up today: the drunk Ginger, or the Ginger who ignored her daughter and focused only on her son.

Mom insisted on hosting Thanksgiving here, with them, for the sake of Rose—maybe Ben too. But inviting Ginger over was a line I didn't think Mom had wanted to cross. Regardless, ten years later, she kept crossing it, growing more annoyed with every passing Thanksgiving since—though she never actually said the words out loud.

I finally made it into the dining room, stopping just short of the table. It was filled with all the things that made Thanksgiving delicious, and if I was hungry, my stomach would no doubt be growling. But at the same time, how could I be hungry when there was only one empty chair left? A chair that was seated directly next Ben.

"Got a chair for you right here," he told me, an arm outstretched over the back of it.

I rolled my eyes, grabbed it from his hands, then yanked it as far from him as I could get.

Happy freaking Thanksgiving to me.

5

August
Present Day

MY MOTHER HOVERS over the stovetop a few nights after
Ben's and my argument. She's cooking something that
smells surprisingly sweet, which is an immediate red
flag. Mom is *not* a dessert person. Like, at all.

The radio she's attached under our kitchen cabinets
is all the way turned up, something early eighties. I told
her she'd be better off playing music over a Bluetooth
speaker, changing up her playlist on the phone through
an app, but she prefers the regular radio and old CDs to
everything else.

She taps a toe against the floor, keeping time with the
music, her hips swaying like a twenty-one-year-old club-
goer trapped inside a forty-year-old's body. It's embarrassing as hell. But every time I tell her to stop, she only
does it more...and by more, I mean obnoxiously faster.

There's a serious amount of white powder on the

counter and floor surrounding her, like a flour-bomb has exploded in our kitchen—it's the second red flag of the night. I pause for another long minute in the doorway, taking it all in, not sure if I should walk away or ask what's up.

Deciding on the latter, I enter the kitchen as quietly as I can. Having forgone dinner earlier, I'm starved and in desperate need of something savory or, in the case of the cookies she's baking, maybe something sweet.

"Don't. Touch. A thing," she calls over her shoulder when I reach for goodness on the cookie sheet. I take it anyway because if she doesn't want them eaten, then she should have hidden them better.

"I'm hungry," I grumble through crumbs.

She frowns but doesn't yell at me. Hello, red flag number three.

I slouch onto one of the barstools by the counter, watching her.

"Did you see the article yet?" she finally asks.

"What article?" I frown.

She nods toward the paper just inches from my fingertips. Nobody buys an *actual* newspaper anymore, other than my parents and the old people who live on the farm just up the road from ours.

"The article about Ben, in the paper."

I tug the flimsy black-and-white *Winston Times* close to me, scowling when I see that it's the front page of the sports section. Precious *Ben* smiles back at me from the front page with a headline that makes me want to hurl.

Local football star Ben McCain gives back in the name of his deceased sister

"What's this?" I spread the paper out flat, hating how my curiosity always gets the better of me.

"Read it," Mom encourages with the dip of her chin.

So, I do.

It's not so much the words that have my hands trembling the longer I stare at it, but more the pictures instead. Ben smiles like he hasn't recently just lost his sister. His hands are plastered on top of the heads of two grinning boys. They're wearing baseball jerseys and holding bats, while Ben wears a hat on his head that says *Coach*.

Gag me.

"It's really great what he's doing, honestly," Mom says, surprising me with her #TeamBen mentality.

That's doubtful. Ben's never been the charitable type —not that I mention this to my mom. Still, as I read on, take in the words I want to read, I can't help but wonder what Ben was thinking when he signed on for this.

Winston football alumnus Benjamin McCain can't help but see his deceased sister's eyes in every child he comes across now. On July 8, Rose McCain's life was lost in a tragic accident. Initial reports say she drowned after jumping into Lock and Dam 12 along the Mississippi River...

The words burn my eyes like fire. It's a reminder I'll never be able to shake.

I skim the rest, only stopping here and there when something stands out. In the end, I get the gist of the stupid article. Ben's been collecting money for the local little league team to help underprivileged kids get the things they need to play baseball this season.

Though I know deep down it is a good thing, there's a bitterness on my tongue I can't swallow away. The rest of photos, aside from the main one with him and those unnamed boys, are mostly of him and Rose when they were younger. She's in cleats and sliding pants while Ben is carrying her gear bag and wearing a football helmet. I know for a fact that my mom is the one who took the picture because I was rolling my eyes beside her at the time.

Throughout the article, Ben speaks of his sister like she was a hero to him, instead of the opposite. Other than to taunt her and torment me, Ben rarely hung around us growing up. He really has zero right using his sister's death as a way to gain popularity points in a community that already adores him but disliked her.

My jaw locks so tightly my ears begin to ring. The *nerve* of this idiot.

Mom stands across from me now. I hear the grin in her voice as she speaks. "His mom had a hand in it, surprisingly. Apparently, she got the fire battalion and paramedic department to help raise most of the money. Not gonna talk about how Ginger pulled that one off. But according to the article, it was Ben's idea and all of Ben's hard work and planning that made it happen." Mom's still smiling when I look at her. "I didn't think the boy had it in him."

"He doesn't." I shove the paper away. "I'm guessing this is just his way of trying to earn sainthood."

Mom doesn't deny it. But her response isn't one I wanna hear either. "At least he's not wasting his life away."

If I wasn't afraid of getting a hand to the back of my head, I'd flick her off for the dig.

"He's living *for* her while you, Rebecca, are the epitome of hopeless," Mom continues to rag on me, stabbing her knife in my back. "You live like a hermit, you don't eat, you rarely shower, and all you do all day is mope in your sweats. I absolutely hate that my once lively daughter has come back to life as a zombie."

"Talking about Ben isn't going to help matters," I hiss, digging my nails into the skin of my palms.

"All I'm saying is that maybe Ben's not as bad as you thought." She shrugs. "I keep thinking about the things he did for you and Rose in the past. Like last year at your winter formal, remember? When you couldn't get a hold of anyone after that that idiot Travis—"

"Stop it." I snap my teeth like a tiger unhinged, every bit as unsteady as I sound.

Instead of saying something I'll later regret, I stand from the chair and start to leave.

"Rebecca," Mom calls after me. "I'm sorry, that was insensitive of me."

Despite the genuineness of her words, I swipe the keys to her car off the counter. "I'm going for a drive."

"But—"

"I'll be back." I push through the kitchen door and quicken my pace down the sidewalk, then the gravel drive. When I'm safe inside Mom's car, I slam the door shut with a loud grunt, hands at ten and two, not yet starting the car.

Instead of crying, my eyes stay dry, while my body grows cold. Numb. When it comes to thinking about the memory Mom was referring to, that awful night six months ago, I'm not surprised.

"PLEASE, doll. Don't tell me no again," Travis pleaded, lips to my neck, tugging the spaghetti straps of my dress down over my shoulders.

We were in his car, in the school parking lot, ice on the windows forming like gatekeepers, allowing us privacy. The winter formal was going on inside the gym, and the two of us had yet to make it out of his back seat. Any second someone could've walked by, but Travis was determined to make this happen.

I, on the other hand, wasn't feeling it.

"Travis..." I chewed on my bottom lip, eyes going wide when he slid a hand up and under my dress. "Maybe we should wait."

"Why?" he whispered, lips trailing down, down, until I pushed him away by the shoulders.

"Because our friends are waiting for us inside the school, that's why."

He pressed his lips flat but didn't immediately move. "Come on. Don't make me wait any more than you already have. It's torture."

Something burned in my throat then—anger mixed with fear; an abundance of confusion, most of all. This was coercion at its worst, completely not okay as far as relationships went. Yet a part of me—the part that loved the way Travis made me feel when we were together—still couldn't tell him no.

"Soon, okay?" I lifted my hand and tucked a piece of hair behind his ear, wishing he'd look into my eyes and tell me I was worth the wait.

"I don't see why we have to go to this stupid dance," he mumbled, pressing his lips against my neck again. "Why can't we just go to the alcove so we can be alone?"

"Because I promised Rose that we could all hang out tonight."

We were going to take group pictures together, capture the image of four friends, remembering their junior year formal. My first dance with a boy. My first dance ever, in fact. Since Rose's new boyfriend didn't go to Winston—the boyfriend she hadn't actually shown me a picture of—she had decided to go with Adam as friends. This was supposed to be a night to remember.

A smack sounded against the window over my head before Travis could say anything. I jumped in place, ramming my forehead against his nose.

"Son of a bitch," he groaned, finally sitting up.

"Becca," Rose hissed through the glass, smacking it with her palm. "I know you're in there. Open the door."

"Oh my god. I'm so sorry. Are you okay?" Ignoring my best friend, I reached for Travis's hand.

"No, I'm not okay." He leaned his head back, blood tricking from beneath his palm. "What the hell does she want?"

I looked around, spotting an old T-shirt on the floor. When I offered it up, he jerked it from my hands and held it to his bloody nose.

"I-I don't know. She's probably looking for me," I whispered.

"Did you plan this?"

"Plan what?"

"That." He pointed to the window, where I could see Rose's shadow outside, pacing.

"Open the door, Rebecca," she growled.

I jerked my head back a little, unsure what he meant. "Planned as in I asked her to come out here and interrupt us?"

"Yeah, that." He jerked his free hand through his hair.

"N-no. Of course not."

"Whatever." He huffed, the bleeding finally stopping.

My belly twisted when I looked into his angry eyes—eyes that were locked on the window, not me. "Please don't be mad," I pleaded.

Sometimes, Travis made me feel like everything was my fault. I knew that wasn't okay. That anyone else would kick him to the curb. But he was my first boyfriend ever and, well...I was pretty sure I was in love with him. The good parts, at least.

"Not mad at you." He grunted, loosening his tie. "I'm pissed at your little bitchy best friend."

Rose knocked again, louder this time. "Open the freaking door before I break it in."

"Just a damn minute," Travis yelled, grabbed his wallet chain from the front seat, then shoved it into his pocket.

I fought to reposition my pale-blue dress over my chest, then tugged it back down in place over my thighs. Travis jumped out, not bothering to wait for me, and starting yelling at Rose.

Like always, my best friend fought back. "What the hell was going on in there?"

Rose hated Travis. But the thing was, her hatred had come out of the blue just three weeks ago. We'd been at the alcove, hanging out. I'd left to go pee in the woods and when I'd come back, she'd been hovered over him, fist clenched, Travis lying on his side in pain. She'd punched him.

When I'd asked what happened, Rose had told me he was being a dick, that she had to put him in his place. When I'd confronted Travis about it later that night, he'd denied everything, saying how my "supposed best friend" wasn't who I thought she was.

Right then, I'd done what any best friend would do. I'd ended things with Travis. When it came to my friendship with Rose, nothing else came before it. Sisters always before misters.

But then a week later something changed. It was like a light switch had gone off in my best friend. Rose had said she'd been lying about things with Travis, claiming she was just jealous that I'd been spending so much time with him. Then she'd insisted that he and I needed to get back together—something about her being stupid. She'd told me Travis and I were meant to be, fated, and all that romantic stuff she'd never believed in.

When Travis apologized to me a few days later and begged for a second chance, I'd said yes, with a condition that he needed to be nice to Rose at all times.

Unfortunately, Travis wasn't keeping up his end of the deal.

"Screw you, asshole," Rose barked. "I wished you'd just die already."

I cringed and dragged myself from the back seat, standing between them, facing Rose. Travis tried to grab my arm from behind, but I pulled away and told him to go inside.

"Whatever." *He lit a cigarette and took off toward the school.*

When it was just the two of us, Rose clutched me by the elbows and hissed, "Tell me you did not just give him your number seventy in the school parking lot."

I bristled. "You're the one who's been pushing for it."

Her shoulders slumped, and she looked at her feet. "God, Becca. I just wish..."

"Wish what?"

"Nothing." *She sighed, meeting my eyes again.* "I'm sorry for being a bitch. Let's just go enjoy the rest of the night, okay?"

Instead of prying for more info like I should have done, I nodded and followed her to the front door. Something was obviously bothering her, but Rose was the type who didn't tell you things until she was ready. So, I decided to give her time, like always.

"Ben's here, by the way." She bumped her shoulder against mine when we stepped in line outside the front entrance.

I gritted my chattering teeth. "So?"

"Soooo, my brother has the hots for you, if you haven't noticed."

"No, he doesn't." I shuddered. "Ben's gross." Okay, so he wasn't gross in the physical sense. In fact, Ben was the definition of an all-American boy. I just so happened not to be very patriotic.

Rose glanced at me from the corner of her eye, a knowing smirk lighting up her pale face. "You really hate my brother, don't you?"

"I have never hated anyone more."

"But he's never actually done anything to you, which is why this is so weird." Her lips pursed and she tapped them with a finger.

"Um, yes he has." Not that I'd ever tell her about our almost kiss in her kitchen. "He abandoned you when he left for college, therefore he hurt me because he hurt you." Oh, and there was the little fact that he constantly insulted me whenever we were together—though Rose insisted our dumb game was more like foreplay than actual hatred.

"He hasn't abandoned me, dork. He went to college. There's a difference." She tucked her arm through mine as we walked up the stairs leading to the doors.

"He never comes home for anything unless it's going to benefit him." I rolled my eyes. "The guy is completely selfish."

"Not true." She scowled. "He brought that girl home from Thanksgiving because her parents were assholes who traveled out of the country and left her home alone. Now he's come home to take Andrea to the dance. Apparently, she and her boyfriend just broke up. He didn't want her to miss her senior formal."

"I bet he's only doing it because he thinks she's going to have rebound sex with him." I harrumphed.

"Maybe." Rose laughed. "But it's still nice, right?"

"Your nice and my nice are not alike."

"Potato, tomato, dork."

I rolled my eyes, hip-checking her. I was right. She wasn't. End of story.

Bits of snow fell from the sky, and I shivered, bouncing on the toe of my high heels. It was freezing out, and I'd left my sweater at the restaurant. Travis hadn't wanted to waste gas to go back and get it, insisting that he'd be there if I needed warming up. Some good that did me now.

We made our way through the front doors and handed over our pre-purchased dance tickets. The second we headed down the hall toward the gym, we were bombarded by the bass from the speakers coming through the doors. Streamers of blue and yellow hung from the ceiling, with huge balloons lining the way. It looked like a party store had puked its guts up in there.

"I thought Sienna Cartwright was dating Alex Lopez," Rose said, catching me off guard.

"She is. Why?"

"Looks to me like she's got the hots for teach." Rose motioned her chin to the left toward a set of stairs.

"Wait," I whispered, eyes narrowing when I took in the man's profile—more so Sienna's hands as they gripped the lapels of his suit. "That's Leaf, Travis's dad."

"Sure is." Rose picked up speed and took a sharp left, leading me toward the cafeteria instead of the gym.

"Hey, where's the fire?" I laughed, glancing back at the pair from over my shoulder.

"In that man's pants, from the looks of it."

I shook my head, trying not to laugh.

I'd only met Travis's dad in passing once when we'd swung by his house to grab a pack of cigarettes. Travis had told me I had to stay in the car, that his dad wasn't home—something about him having issues with his son bringing girls home when he wasn't there? I didn't know. Either way, I thought it was

80

kinda cool how he'd respected his dad's rules like that. Not many guys I knew did so.

But then I'd seen Leaf coming out of the house behind him a few minutes later, yelling something I couldn't hear over the radio. When I'd asked Travis why he'd lied to me about his dad being there, he'd said he hadn't lied. That he'd had zero clue Leaf would be home. Regardless, I'd never forget the look on his father's face as he'd watched us pull out of the drive: terror mixed with disgust. A locked jaw and the tiniest bit of blood dripping from the corner of his mouth. I'd known Travis had hit him, but I'd been so freaked out, I hadn't asked why.

The memory sent a chill down my spine, and I blinked it away. Like clockwork, Leaf lifted his head, narrowed eyes locking with mine when he spotted me from over Sienna's head. My stomach twisted, and I quickly looked away.

"There you are!" Adam announced when Rose pushed through the cafeteria doors a second later.

"I need a drink," she said, running straight into his chest, winding arms around his waist like she hadn't seen him for days.

I watched the scene play out. Adam rubbed a slow hand down her spine—up again, down once more—finishing with a soft kiss to the top of her head.

Wait...was Adam the new boyfriend? If that was true, then I had zero clue as to why he'd want to keep their relationship a secret when everybody knew he was totally in love with Rose. Part of me wanted to pull her aside and ask, but Adam was taking up all her attention with something shiny he pulled from the pocket of his suit jacket.

"Anything the queen desires." They guy wore a lazy smirk and handed it over, his skinny face so soft for her it made my stomach swirl with something I refused to call jealousy. Not that I wanted Adam. More so I wanted Adam to give his best friend some lessons in how to be a little nicer to girls.

I sat in one of the cafeteria chairs, yanking out the stomach *of my dress so as not to rip the seams. Like that, I watched Rose uncap the top of Adam's flask and guzzle it down like a dying person in the Sahara. That wasn't the first time I'd witnessed my best friend drink...but it was the first time she'd ever done it on school property.*

Surprised, I was not. Worried? Maybe a little.

"Hey, Adam?" I glanced around the dark cafeteria. "Do you know where Travis went? He came inside before me and—"

"Bathroom."

"Oh." In other words, he was likely smoking a joint.

"Thank you." Rose recapped the flask with a sigh and turned to face me. "Want some?"

I shook my head. She shrugged and gave it back to Adam, then took a seat beside me.

"We should probably go look for him." I messed with the corsage on my wrist. The one mom had bought, not Travis. "Then maybe get in line for pictures before the line gets too long."

"Pictures are twenty-five bucks," Adam grunted. "I'm not gonna spend that kind of money on a night we won't even remember."

"That's kind of the point." I frowned. "Having pictures will help us remember."

He rolled his eyes.

"I'll pay for them," I told Rose. We'd talked about this. "I have the money from my mom and dad for it."

"Of course, you've got the money." Adam looked at his phone, releasing a jerky laugh.

I opened my mouth to ask what the hell his problem was, but the cafeteria doors flew open, bringing with them a stream of light, the sound of a slow jam, and two arguing voices.

"Just leave, damn it. I don't want you here." Travis.

I stood from my seat to greet him—see if he was okay, most of all—but stopped short when I saw that his dad had followed him in.

"I'm just trying to help you, son, that's all. Please—"

"You're not helping. Nothing you ever do will help me."

Rose stood too, looking at me with raised brows. I shrugged, twisting my hands together in front of me.

Adam cleared his throat, drawing both Travis's and Leaf's gazes our way. The two of them wore an identical, cool expression. Leaf seemed less tense and even smiled, his gaze lingering on me a second longer than Adam or Rose. Chills skated down my spine as thoughts of him and Sienna under the stairs bombarded my head.

Did he know who I was? Would Travis introduce us finally?

A moment later, Leaf strode closer, leaving Travis behind— Travis, who was too busy staring at his phone to even pay attention to me. The man's smile grew wide in greeting, perfectly composed. Perfectly Travis on one of his rare, good days. He greeted Rose first with a hug, whispering something in her ear. She giggled like it was the funniest thing in the world, and something about the interaction had bile forming in my mouth. But then he moved on to Adam, embracing him in the same way—holding on a little longer, a little tighter.

Before I could put a label on what I was seeing, Leaf was in front of me, gaze searching my face as though he were memorizing me.

"Hi there. I don't believe we've been introduced properly."

"Um, no, sir. We haven't." I fidgeted with the front of my dress some more, palms sweaty.

He stuck his hand out, taking mine without permission. "I'm Leaf. Travis's father and an English teacher here at Winston High."

His voice was soothing and genuine, so much so I couldn't help but smile back. He had a way about him. Like everyone's bad mood could be irradiated with his sincerity and charm.

"It's nice to meet you, sir," I said. "I'm Becca."

"Please. Call me Leaf." The man didn't have a single wrinkle, and his eyes . . . they were intense. A dark-green shade nearly identical to Travis's, but minus the bitterness. It was hard to decipher the man I'd seen screaming at his son from the front door of his house to the person standing in front of me now.

He winked, dropping my hand before looking at Travis. "And I know exactly who you are."

"You do?" I asked.

"Of course." He nodded. "You're the young lady who's ruined all future women for my son."

———

THE ODD INTERACTION in the cafeteria with Travis's dad had left a bad taste in my mouth. Not because of Leaf but because of Travis. His mood was high and happy after we'd left. He laughed with me, danced with me, and even managed a few nice words to Rose—who was just as dumbfounded by the personality change as I was.

But the thing about perfection is that it was never meant to last.

Somewhere along the way, Rose had ditched out on us. In my ear she'd told me she was going to go to the bathroom and would meet me inside the gym on the bleachers when she was done. Something about finally wanting to talk about her new boyfriend... I'd offered to go with, but she told me to stay. That I needed to eat up whatever goodness I could get from Travis for as long as I could. The thing was, five minutes later, Travis and Adam left after she did, claiming they were going to head to the car to smoke a joint.

What fast turned into ten minutes of me being alone in the gym had turned into a half hour. Rose wasn't in the bathroom when I'd gone to look for her. Adam and Travis weren't in their cars. And nobody answered my texts or calls either.

On the way back from searching the parking lot, I ran into

Ben and his date, who were leaving. It was the first time I'd seen him all night.

"Becca?" He frowned at me, not that I blamed him. I was a mess of angry tears, shaking from the cold air too. "You okay? What happened?" He bent at the knees just so he could meet my eyes, smelling like mint gum. With his fingers on my elbows, I'd met his gaze with watery eyes and began to shake even more.

"Andrea?" he said to his date, "I'll meet you guys at the car, okay?"

She nodded, glanced at me with concern, then took off with her friends and their dates, leaving us alone outside the doors of the school. I didn't know her very well, other than the fact that she used to date Ben, but she was nice.

"Talk to me." He yanked me to his chest, hugged me tight with his chin on my head. It was weird but also welcomed. "What happened?"

Through my sniffles, I questioned whether or not he'd seen his sister. He told me had, about forty minutes beforehand, leaving with Adam. Betrayal hit me like a hammer to my stomach, and I'd nearly puked at his statement. For the first time in our friendship, Rose had officially ditched me.

When Ben asked if I needed a ride home, I ignored him and took off inside, despite the fact that he'd called my name...begged for me to talk to him. I didn't need Ben's ride or his pity when I knew he'd likely hold it over my head later.

Outside the gym doors, I'd found Travis standing there with his hands buried in his pants pockets. I asked where he'd been, and he told me he'd been inside looking for me. As annoyed as I was with his disappearing act and obvious lies, I realized right then that he was the only person I could stomach spending time with. In turn, we left together and wound up at the last place I wanted to be.

In the back seat of his car along the river alcove.

Travis's hand moved up between my legs. Before I could

breathe, he positioned himself over the top of me, lifting my dress. I winced when the fingers of his other hand accidently yanked some of my hair, but he didn't seem to notice, so I pretended it didn't hurt, too worried he'd change his mind. Or vice versa.

"God, I can't wait to be inside of you," he said, pressing his mouth to mine in a sloppy, wet kiss.

The scent of liquor and weed both invaded my nostrils and taste buds. I almost asked him if he'd pop a mint or chew some gum, but I didn't want to be a buzzkill. So, I kissed him back, moaning into his mouth in that way I knew he loved.

A minute later, he pulled something from the wallet that was in his pants. "Gotta get a condom, doll."

My smile was wobbly, my eyes wet. Why was I even crying in the first place? It wasn't like I didn't want to have sex with him. We'd been dating for four months. I loved him. He said he really cared for me. Plus, I was seventeen. It was time.

"Okay," I whispered. "We can."

He fumbled around with a foil packet, and I felt him moving to put it on a few seconds later. I didn't ask to help like I probably should have because I was worried the view might freak me out. I'd only touched him down there, like, one time.

"You ready?" he asked, squeezing one of my thighs with his hand.

I was pretty sure it'd leave a bruise.

His eyes were hazy through the dark, and pieces of his dark hair fell over his forehead. For a second, I wanted to tell him no. Say that I'd rather do it in a bed and be fully naked like we were supposed to be. But it was kind of too late, and I really fell in love with how he looked at me right then. Like I was suddenly his entire world. Which I so wanted to be. It was the first time anyone had ever looked at me like that.

And unlike Rose, he hadn't ditched me.

With that thought in mind, I closed my eyes and nodded. Then I clung tightly to his elbows. With one more deep breath,

I opened my legs a little more and finally said, "Yeah. I'm ready."

Travis was gentle enough. He moved slow, even as I felt something burn. My body tensed around him, and stars filled my vision behind my closed eyelids once he was all the way in.

It didn't feel good.

It hurt. A lot, actually.

But I didn't tell him to stop.

Travis didn't seem to notice the tension in my body. How both of my legs shook instead of just one, and how my heart nearly beat out of my chest too.

Instead of asking me if I was okay, he buried his face into my neck and hair and took big, deep gulping breaths. "Damn, doll. Just damn."

Wetness spilled down my cheeks.

I was crying.

I squeezed my eyes closed even more, not wanting to see the roof of Travis's back seat during my first time having sex. Instead, I envisioned a tropical island, beaches, the sunny sky, and the blue clouds too.

But everything around us was too dark and cold for the vision to stay long. Plus, my shoe fell off, leaving one of my feet bare. All I could think about then was how much I hated having cold feet, how I wished I was wearing socks.

This was all normal though. It had to be. The emptiness I felt doing this, as though I was standing outside of my body looking in. It was likely because I was so nervous and that it hurt. There was nothing wrong with the situation or the guy I was doing it with. I mean, yeah, sure, it felt more clinical than anything. Like my first trip to the OB-GYN when Mom had taken me to get on birth control to try and regulate my periods.

I winced when Travis began to move faster. That burning sensation only getting worse. It felt like sandpaper against my insides. That probably wasn't normal. But I wouldn't tell Travis. I couldn't.

I swallowed the bile building inside my throat and wrapped my arms around Travis's skinny shoulders, holding him there to try and stay warm. His grunts had grown louder, and his damp skin was sticky with sweat. When I tried to inhale, to keep from passing out, all I could smell was sweat and liquor. In turn, my stomach grew harder, the bile thicker.

Oh God, if I puked right now...

I turned my face away, gasping for more air as my cheek hit the cloth seats. They were torn and started to scratch at my face, and soon the tears were rolling down them too.

I couldn't relax, but I wouldn't stop him.

There was something oddly sad about losing my virginity this way. There again, Travis and I were an unusual sort of couple, so it fit. A round peg in a box would eventually work with some adjustments, right? The only reason I was crying was because it hurt. All first times did. I was sure of it. Positive.

And I was happy. That's why I was crying.

I refused to let my tears mean anything else.

———————

I WAS COLD NOW. Too cold. It was snowing a lot, and I decided, right then, that winter was the time of the year I hated the most.

Next to me in the back seat was a passed-out Travis. Five minutes after losing my virginity to him, and I couldn't even keep him awake long enough to experience post-sex cuddling.

I was such a freaking loser.

My phone was almost dead, and my curfew was fast approaching. Rose hadn't responded to my SOS calls or texts yet, and neither had Adam. I was too worried about getting home on time to be mad, but there was no way I'd be able to walk in these heels, in this snow, wearing this dress.

The last thing I wanted to do was call my mom and dad

and explain where I was and why I was there. And since I didn't have a lot of friends besides Rose, there were very few people I could call for help. Still, I scrolled through my tiny list of friends anyway, stopping on the last name I'd ever wanted to call for help—or call for anything, actually.

What choice did I have at this point?

I pulled in a slow breath, deciding it was better to ask him for help than anyone else. He might judge me, but he wasn't a snitch.

Surprisingly, he picked up halfway through the first ring.

"Becca?"

I wasn't sure why, but the soft concern in Ben's voice and the way he said my first name instead of Thompson or B, I began to cry.

"Jesus, what's wrong? Is it Rose? Talk to me."

"N-no. N-not R-Rose." I looked to Travis, who'd yet to move. "I j-just..." My teeth started to chatter; goose bumps broke out over my arms and legs too.

"You just what? What is it? Are you hurt or in trouble?"

"I-I need a ride," I managed. "Rose isn't...answering." I hiccupped. "I can't call my mom or dad, and it's so cold out—"

"Tell me where you are." I heard the squeak of a mattress, the shuffle of blankets.

"The river alcove."

"I'll be there in a few."

——————

BEN SHOWED *up about fifteen minutes later, his headlights lighting up the sparse land and reflecting off the now frozen river. Seeing him there made this even more real, to the point where I wanted to cry all over again. Still, I kept myself together, somehow.*

He put his car in Park and jumped out of it at the same time I jumped out of Travis's car. The first thing I noticed was his state of dress—sweats, a hoodie, and a baseball cap. In his arms there was a huge coat too.

"What's going on?" He ran to me, immediately wrapping the coat around my shoulders. Seconds later, like he'd done earlier at school, he pulled me to his chest, hugging me.

At least I'd stopped crying.

"Nothing, it's fine. Thank you for picking me up."

He pulled back and scowled, keeping his hands on my shoulders. "You don't look fine."

"I am. Please, just take me home."

A second later, he looked over my shoulder toward Travis's car, likely trying to see who was inside...though I was guessing he already knew because his next words were, "Did he hurt you?"

I shook my head.

It was fifteen minutes past midnight. My phone was officially dead. I was cold. And I could almost bet my mom was up and pacing the floors, panicking and thinking the worst. It was fine that I was late every once in a while, mostly because I always called to let her know. But I hadn't been able to tonight.

Ben's jaw clenched, and I could tell he wanted to say something else. But my teeth began to chatter some more, despite the warm coat, and his entire face softened. "You're shaking."

I shrugged.

Frowning, Ben wrapped an arm around my shoulder and guided me to his car. "You're still wearing your dress."

I nodded, careful not to speak, mostly because I didn't want him to notice the shaking of my voice or the chattering of my teeth anymore. It always felt weird being vulnerable in front of him.

My body ached in ways I wasn't used to, and there was a cramping in my belly that felt like someone was twisting a knife inside. I was also pretty sure I was bleeding because something wet was dripping down my thigh. Regardless, I kept

90

my focus on each step I took, the back of my high heels rubbing blisters against my feet.

"You're hurt." Ben stops us at the bumper of his car. "Did he..." I watched as his Adam's apple moved, studying his hard jaw when he looked toward Travis's car again.

"I'm okay." I smiled in reassurance—or at least I tried to. "Promise. Just cold and tired."

He faced me again, opening his mouth, studying me a second longer. Thankfully he let go of whatever else he was about to say.

"Let's get you home."

He settled a hand on the small of my back and led me to the passenger's side. Once I was inside, I stuck my hands in front of the vents to warm my fingers. It smelled like a guy in there, deodorant and aftershave and something like old fries. Normally, I'd think it was gross, but right then it felt safe. Everything about Ben felt safe actually. And for a second, I wondered if maybe I'd misjudged him all these years.

He didn't get in the car right way and instead pulled his phone from his pocket and put it to his ear. It took him all of three minutes to get through the conversation he had, with whoever it was. When he finally got in, he didn't offer up any details on who he'd been talking to. And I was too worn out to ask. Or care.

6

August
Present Day

I FIDDLE with my charm bracelet, watching Dad and Ben interact on the couch the following afternoon from the entryway of the kitchen. All morning, the two of them had been outside working to replace a few pieces of siding on the barn. I'd scrutinized Ben's every movement while doing my own chores, hating how mesmerized I'd become with his muscular back whenever he moved.

It annoyed me that he insisted on doing his work shirtless?

What I hate the most, though, is that my father seems to have become #TeamBen like Mom, laughing at everything he says—even when most of it isn't funny.

There's a Cubs game on the TV, and I'm tempted to join them because I love the Cubs, but Ben's and my argument from the other morning still weighs on me to the point where I turn around and head to the kitchen instead.

The scent of charcoal fills the air through the screen door as Mom moves back into the kitchen from the front porch. I want to ask what the occasion is. But I can't find it in me to put a damper on her one-woman parade. Not when she's whistling.

I watch her from where I stand, struck by a bout of guilt over last night when I'd taken off. I should apologize for running away like I did, but my pride's got other ideas and, instead, I do the only thing I can: offer up my non-existing kitchen skills.

"Need any help?" I scoot in beside her at the counter, watching while she chops and rinses potatoes.

Mom's voice is light, if not a little tentative. She's not mad at me, I can tell, but she's not one hundred percent forgiving either. The two of us are equals when it comes to our inability to discuss emotions, and Mom holds grudges almost worse than I do.

"You can peel a few potatoes, if you'd like."

I reach for the peeler and nod while she moves to grab mayonnaise and relish from the fridge. Just like that, I know we're okay. We don't need huge declarations of forgiveness or apologies. It's not us.

I bite down on my bottom lip. "Making potato salad?"

"Yes. Since Dad and I have Cousin Rachel's wedding in Chicago next weekend, and then we've got school shopping to get ready for the following weekend, he and I figured it'd be a good time to give Ben a little send-off dinner."

A send-off dinner. For Ben. I don't know what planet she's hailing from lately, but I don't like it there. Regardless, I'm not in the mood to fight about it today either.

I clear my throat. "Are you and Dad excited to get away?" This trip of theirs has been planned for a few months now, and I know the two of them are pumped to get away, mostly because they need a break from me. Still, I can't help but wonder how she feels about leaving me all alone for a weekend. Any other time they took off, I stayed with Rose, but now...

"We are." She pauses for a moment, then says, "And I have good news. I've spoken to Rachel. She says there's room for you on the guest list now. So, I'm even more excited because we get to make it a family fun weekend. I figured we could go to Navy Pier, do a little shopping..."

I cringe at the idea of spending even a single night hauled up in a hotel with my parents. I love them, but I like my privacy more. "No, no. You and Dad should go alone. I'll be fine here by myself."

"But—"

"Seriously, Mom." I stop peeling and reach over to touch the back of her hand. "You guys deserve time away together." A lump fills my throat as I speak. I'm not sure what I'm getting so emotional about. They've left me home alone overnight before, and now that I'm a few months from turning eighteen, it's even more plausible for them to do so.

"I'm gonna be honest, honey." Mom inhales a heavy breath through her nose, then releases it quickly to speak. "I'm worried about leaving you."

My belly twists, regret taking me on a roller coaster of feelings and emotions.

I did this to her. To my dad too. It's been over a month since Rose's death, so it's time I try and fix it, even if it's all a mirage.

"I'm sorry I've made you feel that way." I swallow hard. "But I'm okay. I swear."

She doesn't look at me, but I can hear the hope in her words. "If you're sure you're going to be okay..."

Before I can say yes, shoes skid to a stop from the

entryway of the kitchen. I know who it is right away and can't help but scowl at the peeler in my hand.

"Anything I can help with?" Ben asks.

"You can go play in traffic," I mumble.

Mom smacks my arm, but when I look at her, I notice she's smirking. She's well aware of the game Ben and I play, mostly because I've been complaining about it for years. She once told me he teases me because he likes me. I told her that is one ideal that should be immediately banned when it comes to guys.

Ben laughs, but before he can get a comeback in, Mom shoots off a request. "Actually, do you think you could run into town and grab some ketchup? I ran out."

"Sure," he says, and I can hear the smile in his words. He's always been so good about doing what's asked of him, even if it's just to build a quality reputation with adults. "But *only* if Becca takes me. My car's almost out of gas."

I shoot him a nasty glare over my shoulder, ready to tell him to go get gas, *then* go to the store, but Mom jumps in before I have a chance. "Good idea. Becca needs to get out of the house. Why don't you go ahead and take my car?"

I sniff my non-runny nose, then chew on my lip too. Saying out loud, *I'd rather eat a hive full of bees than spend time with Ben* would upset her. So, I pull a different card instead.

"I, um, actually don't feel so good. Think maybe I'm coming down with something. I should probably just—"

"It's likely allergies. Pollens bad right now." She butts in. "Haven't you been taking your nasal spray like I told you?"

"Mom, seriously?" My face heats, and I steal a quick glance at Ben again, whose lips are currently twitching.

Oblivious to my mortification, Mom shakes her head

and continues. "You know what will happen if you haven't been keeping up with the regimen. First the neti pot, followed by all that snot and—"

"Fine. I'll go." I drop the potato peeler into the sink with a bang, wipe my hands down the front of my jean shorts, and reach for Ben's wrist, yanking him out the back door.

I could *kill* my mother and not even blink an eye right now.

"I'm driving," Ben calls from behind, racing to catch up with me in the driveway.

"Absolutely not." I huff, arms swinging as I head to my car. He cuts me off at the driver's side door, his face pinched with restrained laughter. "It's my mom's car, so *I'll* drive."

"Hold on." He frowns suddenly, and it's so abrupt that I can't help but wait for whatever crap he's ready to spew. Slowly, he lifts his hand and touches my face.

My breath catches. "W-what are you doing?"

Fingers trace over my cheekbones, my chin, until I feel them caressing the bridge of my nose, then down to the spot between my nose and lips. It's so sweet and gentle that I don't see his next words coming.

"Did you hear?"

I blink, my throat drying. I'm not sure what's going on, but I'm not altogether sure I dislike it either. "H-hear what?"

"Allergies are getting so bad that people are turning their meth back into Sudafed."

I shove him when he starts to laugh, so hard he nearly falls—but doesn't actually, of course. He's Mr. Athlete Extraordinaire, with the balancing ability of a freaking tightrope walker.

Ben keeps laughing, bent over at the waist like I've

96

just told him Santa is real *and* that there's millions of dollars at the end of a rainbow.

"I hate you," I say out loud this time, turning to get into the car—the driver's side—then locking all doors so he can't get in.

"Come on, B. I was kidding," he says, still laughing through the window.

I start the car, ready to go get the stupid ketchup on my own. But when I look up and notice Mom on the front porch staring at us, I realize that the last thing I want to do is upset her again, especially after last night.

"Open the door," he says, losing some of his fire as he yanks on the handle of the driver's side. He groans, running a hand through his blond locks. "And I'm definitely driving because there is no way I'm putting my life in your hands today. I have goals," he lowers his voice, "unlike some people who want to wallow away in their self-pity all day."

I tip my chin up, rolling down my window just enough so he can hear me. "What are these goals you speak of?" I ask, my inner snooty girl coming out to play. "Screw every girl within a hundred-mile radius?"

The second the words are out of my mouth my stupid throat tightens. Why the heck do I keep bringing up his sex life? Thankfully, he takes my insult with a grain of salt, grinning instead of calling me out like the other morning in my bedroom.

When I finally unlock the door, he surprises me by relenting his need to drive and gets in on the passenger side. "There, was that so hard?" he asks, buckling.

"The only thing hard in this car is your over-inflated ego." My tires squeal when I pull out of our drive. I'll catch hell for it when I get home, but whatever. It is what it is.

"Yeah, well, have you felt my arms lately?"

I put a hand against my forehead. What an idiot.

———

THE RIDE to the grocery store is silent, other than Ben's need to dominate my radio. I let him, only because I'm too annoyed to argue. But the second I shut off the car in the parking lot and reach for my purse, he touches my wrist and drops a ginormous bomb on me—one I'm not sure how to respond to.

"Let's hang out. Do stuff together while I'm still here in town. I need the distraction, and I think you do too."

I clutch my purse handle tight. "Like, what, as friends?"

"Well, yeah. But I also think maybe we should do some research together on Rose's accident."

"Not this again," I snap back, opening the door.

Of course, he has an ulterior motive.

"Come on, Becca," he groans. "What about the people she was with that night? Your ex, that Adam dude, anybody from school. Maybe they drugged her? Maybe they pushed her into the river? Did you ever stop and think about that?"

I grit my teeth at the mention of my ex, inhaling from my nose, exhaling through my mouth. I told him before that I needed to leave this in the past, yes, but the more I think about it, my memories of Rose and those last few months of our friendship, along with her secret boyfriend I never met, the more I realize I likely won't rest either until I do know the whole truth.

And that scares me more than anything.

"I told you I'm not comfortable with talking about this."

"A week and a half. That's all I'm asking for," his voice softens with his plea.

I sigh, feet hanging out of the door. "You've always been such a jerk to me. Why should I help you?"

"Seriously?" I feel his sharp gaze on my profile, but I don't look at him. "You're so clueless."

"No. Not clueless. More like self-aware over the fact that you were a big loser who ditched the people who loved you the most."

He groans, and it's so loud I can't help but look at him. But it's his words that catch me off guard—a simple truth I'm not expecting.

"For the millionth time, I didn't ditch Rose, damn it. I was just busy at school—focusing on getting through college, then making it into the pros so I could earn enough money to get her out of Winston."

I frown. "Why would you need to get her out of Winston?"

"If you haven't noticed, our mother's a pretty big loser." He rubs a hand over his face, gaze locked ahead.

"I know she had an alcohol problem. But did she, like, *do* something to Rose?" I cringe at the thought, lowering my voice. "She didn't hurt her, right?" I would've known. She would have told me. Rose told me everything because I was her supersecret keeper, for God's sake.

"Not physically hurt her, no." Ben blows out a long breath, hesitating. "Our mom...she nearly ruined both of our lives with her drinking. You know that. But she also brought multiple creepy assholes in and out of the house without me there, so there's no telling what Rose might've seen or heard. Been through."

"Rose would've mentioned if something happened."

"Would she though? Really?"

I look at my lap. Had I really missed something? Rose was at my house constantly over the last year and a half, claiming she didn't want to be alone with her mom or

99

her mom's boyfriends. I never questioned it. But maybe I should have more.

Ben leans his head back against the seat with a loud sigh. Something about that noise has my heart skipping.

"What?" I ask, still not able to look at him.

"It's just...Mom hasn't had a steady job in almost two years. And because of that, she was barely able to make ends meet at home."

I know this. Mostly because my parents paid for a lot of things for Rose. School supplies, clothes, even food. They didn't mind. Never thought twice about it either, as far as I remember. But maybe they knew something I didn't when it came to Rose and her family.

Ben slouches lower into his seat, kicking his feet up on the dash. I don't even have the energy to yell at him about it.

"I was constantly sending money home to pay bills. And when I wasn't playing ball, I was working two jobs." He purses his lips. "Kinda made it hard to come home."

"Rose didn't tell me any of this."

"I told her not to," he says.

I scowl. "Why would you do that?"

"Because it's embarrassing, that's why."

It wouldn't have bothered me. If anything, it makes me look at Ben in a different light. But I'd never walked a day in his shoes—or Rose's—so I have no right to say anything.

"Is that really why you never came home?" I ask.

"Yup."

A sinking feeling hits my belly. Rose always told me I judged Ben too harshly, and for the first time in years, I'm seeing that.

"I'm sorry," I tell him. "I didn't mean to belittle you."

"Yeah." He rolls his eyes. "It's not like you ever cared enough to ask *why* I never came home."

"I did, that's the thing. All the freaking time, actually."
I perk up, face him. "Rose just told me you were always busy. I assumed—"

"I was partying it up, sleeping with multiple women, and ignoring my family?" He lifts one brow.

I shrug, feeling my face heat.

"Rose was probably embarrassed anyway."

"But she never acted like it. I told you. She hero-worshipped you."

He flicked an invisible piece of something off his thigh. "Not with me. But with our mom. She didn't want the world to know just how crappy Ginger is, though I'm ninety-nine percent sure the entire town of Winston already does."

It's true. Rumors swirled constantly once Ben left town, taking not only Ginger down but Rose too. Yet my best friend never seemed to care. Or so I thought.

Guilt eats away at my insides, twisting me all up. I've treated Ben like crap, and I can't help but feel awful about it. The thing is, I'm not sure who I'm mad at more: Ben, for being good but hiding it with his jerky side, or Rose, for hiding Ben's good side all this time.

"You really asked about me, Thompson?" he asks.

"Uh, yeah." I huff, my heart skipping a few beats. "But not because I liked you or anything."

"Well, you know what they say about hating someone, right?"

"No. I don't." A bead of sweat dribbles down the base of my spine under my shirt. "Enlighten me, wise one."

"Hating me is basically the same as loving me. Those emotions tune in on the same wavelength and—"

"Ugh, stop it." I jump out of the car, slamming it shut behind me.

"You're in love with me," he calls out to me through the parking lot. "Don't deny it."

I flip him the finger and pick up speed.

———

"I'M gonna go get dessert from the bakery section," I say when we step into the store. "You get the ketchup."

"Sir, yes, sir." He salutes me. *Loudly.* And once again, I find myself rolling my eyes, while wearing a stupid smile at the same time.

Despite the truth bomb he just dropped on me, I'm weirdly relaxed. I don't want to admit that it's because of the company I'm keeping, but at the same time, I really don't have much of a reason to hate him anymore—other than our miscommunication that day in his kitchen. Even still, that wasn't necessarily his fault.

Elevator-like music plays from the store speakers as I make my way through the aisles. Though Mom baked cookies last night, I need something more chocolatey after Ben's declaration.

I wind up settling on brownies. They were always Rose's favorite. She'd insist we make them every time she came over. Sometimes to eat like normal. Other times to plant her weed in.

When I turn to go find Ben, I run smack dab into a wall—a tall and very familiar walking-talking wall.

"Becca?" Adam stands before me, smile personable, if not a bit sad.

I take a small step back. "Hey, um, it's good to see you."

"You, too." He sticks his hands into the pockets of his shorts, the tension thick and awkward. "How are you?"

"Fine. Good." My own hands start to shake, and the plastic container with brownies ticks as they do. I'm nervous for some reason, and I don't know why.

"I tried to find you after the funeral," he tells me.

I narrow my eyes. "You were there?"

He nods. "Travis and I both were. So was Leaf."

"Oh." I'm not sure how I'd missed them back day, but now that I know they were there, I'm kinda glad I did.

Adam lifts his chin. "He's tried to call you, ya know."

The brownie container shakes a little more. I have a dire urge to drop it and run when I realize who Adam's talking about. I don't, of course, because the last thing I want is to look a freak who's barely holding it together. Even if I kinda am.

"I, um, changed my phone number."

Adam runs a hand over his jaw and nods. "Listen, Bec, there's something you should know. Travis never..."

"He never what?" I snap, blood now boiling in my veins. "Never meant to turn into a giant douchebag after I gave him my virginity. Is that what you mean?"

Adam takes a step forward, running a hand through his hair. He lowers his voice, looking around us. "That's not it. I mean, not exactly."

"Yeah. Sure. I've got to go." I turn to leave.

"Wait." He grabs my shoulder and holds me in place.

"What?" I look to the aisles ahead of me, already on the hunt for Ben.

"I...I miss her." He sniffs. "A lot."

Red flashes through my vision, anger and rage the cause. I face him again, hating the unfairness of the world as I poke his chest with my finger. "What right do you have to miss her, huh? She was my friend first."

He flinches, then stares at the tile, sniffling. "You're right. I'm sorry."

Guilt eats at me more than ever, like a festering wound that won't heal. Adam isn't Travis. Adam was always good to Rose. Adam is not to blame for his best friend's idiocy, most of all. I may not like him, but that doesn't mean I need to be cruel.

Slowly, I lift my hand to touch his, holding it briefly while I speak. "I shouldn't have said that. I'm sorry. I know how close the two of you were."

The soulfulness in Adam's eyes when they meet mine is heavier than I expect. Our grief is shared though, and two of us nod, no doubt feeling the same things, just on two different levels.

"I'm sorry we never got to know each other better," he tells me. "And I'm sorry for being a dick sometimes."

I shrug his dick comment away, then say, "I'm sorry too."

Adam was Rose's friend, and I was Travis's girlfriend. We were connected in a way but never as anything but acquaintances.

"Look," he says. "I'm having a party next Saturday. It's at my dad's garage in downtown Winston. You should come."

I smile politely, knowing I'd never go. The last thing I want is to see Travis, and I know he'd be there. Going back to school this fall will be hard enough. I at least need the summer to recuperate.

"Thanks, but—"

"Did I hear something about a party next Friday?" Ben sidles up next to me, wrapping an arm around my waist. I stiffen at his move, not sure if I want to elbow him, or snuggled closer.

Adam tips his head to one side, studying his face. "Hell, man. I didn't realize you were here too. It's good to see you again."

Ben narrows his eyes at Adam. "Do I know you?"

"Yeah. Rose and I were good friends."

"You two date or something?"

Adam laughs, and his cheeks go a little red. To save him the uncomfortable moment, mostly because I feel bad for what I'd said, I jump in and do the official introductions.

"Ben," I say, motioning with my right arm. "This is Adam. He and Rose were good friends."

"Yeah. We were, um, good friends." Adam rubs the back of his neck. "I'm really sorry she's gone."

"Wait..." Ben pauses, eyes narrowing. "Are you the one who's friends with Becca's ex?"

"Travis, yeah." Adam clears his throat.

It all happens in a flash—a blink of an eye, really. Before I can try to intervene, Ben takes two steps forward and shoves Adam back against the shelves full of baked goods. "You're a dirty son of a bitch, you know that?" Ben roars.

I gasp, reaching for the end of his T-shirt. "Ben, stop it."

Before I can pull him back, he slams his fist against Adam's nose.

I yip and cover my mouth with both hands. Ben lands on top of Adam, knocking him to the floor and letting another fist collide with his cheek, then his eye...

"Ben! Stop it," I yell. "What are you doing?" I reach for his arm, but he still doesn't listen.

Blood pools out of Adam's nose, dripping over his lips. The poor guy doesn't fight back—just lies there and takes Ben's punishment. Feet thunder down the aisle behind me. I know we need to leave, otherwise the cops will be called, but Ben's out of control. Angry and wild like I've never seen him.

Somehow, I draw up all the strength I can and yank him back by the neck of his shirt. He stumbles just enough that he rolls off Adam and lands on his butt, chest heaving, hands slapped over his face like he's trying to push something from his mind.

Adam takes the free pass to jump up and wipe his

bloody nose with the back of his arm. Seconds later, his shoes slap against the tile floor as he rushes through the store, then out the front door.

I gape at the floor, blindsided, confused. It's a mess of homemade breads and cookies, and soon the manager comes into view, hands on his hips.

At the last minute, I make a rash decision and tell the man, "Some guy attacked my friend. He just took off."

The manager blinks at me, then studies Ben with narrowed eyes. "Does he need medical treatment?"

"No. He'll be fine." Physically, maybe. Mental stability is a whole other story here.

"Okay. I'll call the police. You two sit tight."

Several other customers and employees gather around us once the man leaves, but nobody makes a move to help Ben. Maybe they sense he's on the verge of cracking. Or maybe they all saw what really went down but are too afraid to say anything.

Taking a deep breath, I crouch down beside Ben. Blank eyes meet my stare, and I swallow at what I'm seeing. He looks so broken. Worse than I've seen him before.

My fight-or-flight instinct eats away at my nerves, but I go with my gut, ignoring the manager's orders.

I manage to get Ben to his feet and whisper, "Let's go."

He complies with a quick nod, then laces our fingers together as he stands. I let him, needing to stay grounded, mainly because I have no idea what just happened.

7

August
Present Day

SITTING in the parking lot of the store, hands clenched around the wheel, I let Ben have it. "Wanna tell me why you just attacked one of Rose's best friends for no reason?"

He leans back in the seat and sighs. "If you know what's good for you, you'll drop it."

"Oh, no. No *freaking* way. As long as you're in this car, you *will* answer my questions."

"Fine." He knifes a hand through his hair. "I'll explain everything. But not now."

"Then *when?*"

"Soon."

"Not good enough."

He growls. "Whatever. I'll come over tonight. Late though."

My jaw burns from clenching it so tightly, but it's

107

enough of an answer to satisfy me...for now. Whatever secret he's holding onto is obviously bad, so maybe taking an afternoon to prepare for it is for the best.

"Whatever. As long as you tell me everything." I lower my voice. "I can't handle any more secrets, Ben."

His nod is silent, eerie, to the point where I can't help but feel like he's lying already about not lying.

Since we'd traded the ketchup and brownies in favor of a quick getaway, I tell him we need to swing by a gas station to pick some up, at least. Ben's voice basically goes extinct the rest of the trip back to the farm, and with the quiet, I can't help but grow more irritated by the second.

We pull into my driveway twenty minutes later, and I'm so emotionally messy that I don't even care when he drops another bomb on me.

"I'm gonna head home. Tell your mom and dad I'm sorry."

"Just like that, huh? You're gonna ditch out on..." I almost say *me*, then think better of it because that would sound clingy and, well, I'm *not* clingy. I also don't care if he leaves. "My family? On my mom, who's gone to all this trouble today to fix a good meal that's meant for *you*?"

Ben's winces before looking at my house. Still, he says nothing.

"And to think my mom was actually starting to like you too." I shake my head. "Now you'll just set her back."

"How can she not like me?" He grins just the slightest bit, face softening, gaze meeting mine. "I'm amazing."

"You're a loser is more like it, especially after that stunt you just pulled."

His smile falters. "I've got my reasons to be mad at Adam."

"You care to share them yet?" I quirk a brow.

With a heavy sigh, he unlocks the door, pushes it open to get out. "You'll know soon enough."

I frown, staying put for another second, even after Ben shuts his door. I'm not sure if it was Adam who pushed him over the edge or something like a tether that's been latched from Rose's grave, leading to Ben's heart, that finally snapped.

Since his sister's death, he's taken on several roles in his life, but not one of them have stepped toward grieving. I think he deserves that. We all do, really. Maybe this is his beginning.

Eventually I get out of the car, avoiding his gaze in favor of the gravel under my boots. From the corner of my eye, he closes the distance between us, until he's before me, lifting my chin with a finger.

My chest squeezes at the soft touch, the way he searches my face feels too intimate, almost. It's the kind of stare he's never used with me before, and I'm not sure how to feel about it.

"I'm sorry for what happened," he says. "And, please, tell your parents I'm sorry for leaving. Tell them I got sick, or something." He hesitates. "Or just tell them I'm an asshole who doesn't appreciate good things until they're out of my reach."

Part of me wants to tell him to man up and come inside, that he should tell them himself. But I also know what it's like when you want to be alone.

"It's fine. I'll cover for you." I purse my lips, pretending to be mad, when really, I'd do anything to find the escape he's aiming for myself. "As long as you don't do it again."

"Do what again?"

"Grocery store box."

He chuckles, dropping his hand from my chin before kicking the gravel with the toe of his sneaker. "It's too bad I have to leave." Ben sighs, looking at me through those dark, inky lashes as he takes a few steps backward. "I prepped for a battle of wits with you today, and it seems *you've* come unarmed."

"Huh?" I jerk my head back, completely confused.

"Victory is mine!" He punches the air with a fist, miming a crowd roar as he spins in a circle.

"You are so freaking weird."

He winks at me. "See you tonight, Thompson."

———

LAUGHTER ECHOES from the living room when I step back into the house. The scent of unfamiliar cologne fills the air too. I frown, wondering who's here. Dad's not a cologne dude, nor does he shave enough to use that stuff. Plus, I didn't even see any other cars outside.

Curiosity leads me forward, and the second I step inside the living room door and spot our new guests on the couch, I wish I hadn't been so inquisitive.

Dad's there still, but he's not alone. Ginger's on the love seat across from him, and next to her is Leaf Morrison.

Travis's father.

Unease races up my spine and I look around, half expecting Travis to be here too. But he's not.

"Hey, there you are." Mom steps up behind me in the kitchen, and I quick scoot back out of the doorway so as not to be seen by Ginger or Leaf. She frowns. "Where's Ben?"

"He's, um, not feeling good." I lower my voice. "What is Travis's dad doing here?"

Mom rolls her eyes. "Apparently he and Ginger have been seeing each other for a few weeks. We invited her over, thinking it'd be good to have her here with Ben, but

110

then she shows up with him. And now Ben isn't even here."

"That sucks," I say, but only because I don't know what else to say.

"I know it's going to be awkward, but it's only dinner." Mom chews on her bottom lip. I'm pretty sure she's trying to convince herself. She's likely thinking the same thing as me right now: this isn't awful; it's a freaking disaster.

"Yeah, sure." I wonder if she'd change her mind if she learned the truth. That Leaf's son was an absolute moronic dick who ruined my first—and only—time having sex.

She knows Travis and I broke up and that it didn't end well. But if she knew the details behind it, I'm betting she'd junk-punch Leaf, then demand his son's head on a platter.

"Come on." Mom touches my elbow. "The faster we get dinner on the table, the sooner they'll leave."

I help Mom serve up the food, trying to stay calm. Small talk is the last thing I want to take part in, but if Mom's got to deal with Ginger, then I'll buck up and deal with my ex's father.

"Dinner's ready," Mom calls out minutes after we set the last platter of food onto the table. She pulls a chair out besides hers, patting the seat. I take it, thankful there aren't any empty spots around me.

I keep my gaze trained on the plate when everyone begins entering the room, my heart racing a little faster. I have no idea what Travis told his dad about us. I'm not sure if I want to know either.

"Where's my son?" Ginger asks first thing, sitting across from me. Leaf takes the chair next to her, staying quiet. I can't stomach looking at him anymore than I can actually talk to him.

"He's not feeling good." I shove a strawberry int my mouth. "Went home."

"I should call him." She pushes back, like she's about to get up.

"No," I blurt out. "He's really okay. Just went home to nap is all."

She purses her lips, hesitates, then scoots her chair back in. I blow out a relieved breath, not sure why it matters anyways.

Mom begins to pass the food around the table. Dad makes small talk, Leaf laughs, Ginger too. Meanwhile Mom and I are silent, barely touching the food on our plates. Thankfully, nothing about Travis is brought up. Instead, the three adults discuss the weather, Ginger's job hunt that never seems to end, and Leaf's job as a teacher—though he doesn't stay rooted in anyone's conversation for long.

Throughout dinner, I feel his gaze on me once or twice. It's unnerving enough that I want to flip him off *and* ask what he's thinking. But I do neither.

Ginger is the first one to draw me into the conversation. "So, Becca, are you still looking into the University of Iowa next year?"

I lift my head, open my mouth to tell her, *no, I don't think so*, but my gaze stops on Leaf, who's staring at me with veiled interest. I don't want him to tell Travis what I'm about to say, which is why I end up lying.

"I think so. With Ben there, it might make things easier for me." I give Ginger my most sincere smile, noticing how Leaf's is holding her hand on top of the table. It's weird to see.

"Travis applied there too," Leaf offers. "Perhaps you two will be close to each other on campus."

"Yeah, no. I don't think so," Mom barks out of the

blue. "My daughter and that *son* of yours are no longer allowed to see each other."

I pull in a fast breath and jerk my head her way. Mom's face is fierce with a capital *F*, and my god...she knows somehow what happened between me and him.

"Really?" Leaf tips his head to the side. "I'm sorry to hear that. They were very good for each other."

I scoff. It's more like I was good for Travis, and he was the *ick* in *toxic* for me.

Mom continues to run interference. "Did your son ever tell you about the time he passed out drunk in the back seat of his car after the winter formal, leaving my daughter alone, without a ride, in the middle of a snowstorm?"

I turn to my mom fully, face hot. "Mom, please. Not right now."

Her eyes narrow at me, but she doesn't push. I'm thankful for the reprieve, mostly because I'm to the point where I want nothing more than to forget that crappy night ever happened.

THINGS BETWEEN ROSE *and me had been pretty tense since the night of the winter formal. And the fact that she never actually apologized didn't help matters either.*

"Travis told Adam he wants to get back together with you," *Rose said, leaning against the locker beside mine.*

"And let me guess: You think I should give him a second chance?" I laughed. It was déjà vu, really, just like it'd been the last time I'd broken up with the idiot.

"I don't know, Becca. He seemed sincere this time."

"Sincere or not, it ain't gonna happen." I gritted my teeth and yanked open my locker.

Silence passed between us while I gathered my stuff—extra pencils and my notebook too. It wasn't uncomfortable, but it was weird for me and Rose. There was a distance between us that hadn't been there before, and I half wondered if it had to do with the secret boyfriend she'd yet to tell me about.

"You're not still pissed at me, right?" she asked.

It was on the tip of my tongue to say, Yeah, duh. But I didn't. More like I couldn't. Confrontations sucked, and honestly? Despite everything, it had been hard to hold a grudge against her. I just wished she'd apologize and realize what she did wrong, then this would be so much easier.

"Just..." I pulled in a slow breath and finished with, "don't suggest that Travis and I get back together again, all right?"

Had she not ditched me at the dance, then maybe I wouldn't have gone with Travis to the alcove in the first place. I was the one who'd made the stupid choice to have sex with the guy, but that didn't mean I wanted to reconnect with him.

She stood and brushed a hand down the side of her jeans. "Are you sure? Because he loves you, and—"

"Yes, Rose, God. Can you just stop trying to interfere? I'm done with that asshole this time."

She nodded, cringing a little, but stayed silent on the matter. For the first time in all of our friendship I was questioning whose side she was really on. She knew what had happened. I'd told her everything. Yet she didn't see anything wrong with it, other than him passing out. That, out of everything, bothered me the most.

With a sigh, Rose put a hand on my shoulder. "How about we have a girls' night? Hair, makeup, nails, movies, pizza..." She wiggled her brows. "I'll even buy the facemasks."

I wasn't sure if I was ready for a night of just her and me, hanging out like everything hadn't happened. But the pushover in me struggled with denying Rose anything.

I crossed my arms. "When?"

"Tonight?" She held her hands together and pressed them to her chin before dropping to one knee and saying loud enough for everyone around us to hear, "Becca Thompson? Will you do me the honor of wearing my face mask?"

I groaned, throwing my head back at the same time. "Fiiine."

She stood, grabbed my hand, and shook it. "I'll even throw some Takis into the mix."

"Bribery is not becoming." I rolled my eyes, then kicked my foot back against the locker.

"A girl's gotta do what a girl's gotta do, am I right?"

"Whatever."

The door across the hall opened. We looked over at the same time, finding Travis's dad standing there, laughing with another teacher—a pretty woman who apparently had grabby hands because hers were all over his chest. Tie hanging haphazard across his neck, his hair wild, like someone had been running their hands through it...I wasn't stupid. I knew exactly what they'd been doing in there.

"Desperate much?" Rose snort-laughed.

I shrugged and watched the pair, curious about Leaf Morrison. He seemed so real and down to earth compared to his son—a high-class jerk-off with zero human decency.

"He's hot though," Rose continued with a longing sigh. "I heard Sienna banged him, which is why she and Alex broke up."

"What?"

She nodded.

"Wouldn't he be fired because of it?"

"Maybe." Rose tapped her chin. "If anyone found out about it. Besides that, she's eighteen."

"But he's a teacher. It's...wrong." I shuddered.

"I bet I could do it."

"Do what?" I jerked my head her way, not liking where this was going.

"Get a teacher in bed with me."

"Rose," I hissed, looking around, praying nobody heard her. "You can't say crap like that."

"Oh, please. I know what I'm doing, Bec."

That was the thing. She did know what she was doing—too well, most times. And when it came to challenges, Rose got high off them. "Seriously. You have a boyfriend. Why would you even think something like that?"

Rose sunk her top teeth into her bottom lip and twirled a lock of her blonde hair around her finger. "Because it'd be fun, don't you think? Older men are far more experienced." She finally looked my way, a gleam filling her gaze. It was one part wicked and one part challenging. It meant she had plans —likely of the reckless variety.

"No. Older men are wrinkly and gross." I shuddered, looking back at Leaf. The teacher he'd been with was gone,

116

leaving him surrounded by a group of girls who all seemed to
fall over the guy for attention. It was gross.

Rose yanked something out of her Chromebook bag. A pen.
She motioned a hand toward my hand, fingers wiggling as she
asked, "You got that list of ours handy?"

"No." I shook my head, already knowing her plans.

"Give it, or I'll tell my brother you have sex dreams about
him."

"What the hell, Rose? That's not true."

Ignoring me, she started unzipping my bag and tugging out
the notebook. Once she had it opened, she turned away from
me and flattened it against the locker.

"Seriously?" I asked.

She laughed and wrote something down with her pen.
From over her shoulder, I watched as number seventy-five on
our list was born.

"Done." She slapped the front of the notebook closed and
shoved it back into my hands.

"Do I want to know what you just wrote?"

Her answering grin was slow. Wicked, even. "Oh, you do.
Trust me."

———————

I DIDN'T SEE Rose at lunch today. She'd texted, saying there
was a test she had to make up in World History. The teacher—
who was a real dick, apparently—demanded Rose come to his
room during the noon hour to do so. I'd had Mr. Lavender last
year and knew this wasn't odd for the old man. But what was
odd was that fact that he was also on lunch duty today, which
meant my best friend had been lying to me. Again.

I sat at a table with a couple of acquaintances, the most
recognizable being Sienna. It wasn't ideal, but it was better
than being alone.

"Did you see her? I mean, how much more obvious can the woman be?"

I took a bite of my carrot stick and looked to where Sienna was pointing, stiffening when I realized it was Leaf standing with the teacher from earlier. She was just as eager and touchy as before, only this time, her hand sat on his bicep instead of his chest.

"I heard they got caught screwing in a classroom," Sienna said, her lip curling. "Stupid bitch," she whispered under her breath.

"Yeah, but can you blame her? I mean, look at the guy. He's like Timothée Chalamet all grown up." Another girl mumbled, fanning her face.

"Yeah," Sienna sighed, almost longingly. "It's really hard to imagine that someone like him would have such a jerk son like..." Her wide-eyed gaze slid to me, like she forgot I was sitting with them today.

"It's fine." I poked through my uneaten food with a spoon. "We broke up."

A few ohs and sorrys sounded from around the table, but I pretended not to care. Instead, I refocused on Leaf, who was now alone and frowning at something on his phone.

I took in the full expanse of his outfit then, trying to see the appeal. He wore a pair of khaki slacks with chocolate-brown patches at the knees and a white shirt that looked more like a woman's blouse with how it cuffed and flowed around his wrists. It was very Shakespearian. He also wore his curly hair in a low-slung ponytail, tied back with what looked like a piece of twine. Totally weird, though it did make him look younger, I guess. Even so, I still couldn't see what made all these girls go googly eyed over him.

"I heard he was fired from his job in Texas because he tied up another teacher for sexual pleasure in his classroom," another girl said.

I rolled my eyes, trying not to laugh at that. The guy

wouldn't be teaching at all if that were the case. Rumors were ugly, yet nobody ever stopped trying to spread them.

Another girl, Blake, tugged on the sleeve of my sweater. "I mean, you dated Travis. Are any of those things true?"

"Oh my god," I mumbled, no longer hungry. Sienna met my gaze from over the table, an apology in her dark eyes. "I'll see you in Spanish," I told her, picking up my tray and leaving the lunchroom.

I sat in the hallway for the rest of lunch, texting Rose. She answered right away saying she was so bored and that she hated how Mr. Lavender's room smell like tuna. I started to type a text to call her out on the lie, that I'd just seen the dude in the lunchroom, but decided against it, mostly because I wasn't in the mood to argue. Instead, I pocketed my phone and rummaged through my notebook, pulling out our list to see what she'd written down. I'd been avoiding it all day, too scared to know exactly what it said—though I had a pretty good idea already.

Once it was opened, I shifted through the crossed-out numbers. When I finally got to number seventy-five, my stomach took a nosedive. There, in Rose's familiar handwriting, was an impossible task that didn't make sense but scared me all the same.

#75. Sleep with the forbidden.

8

August
Present Day

IT WAS ALMOST midnight when I heard the knock against my window. Three soft and consecutive thuds, all of which match the beat of my heart. Why he chose that way to get my attention instead of texting, is a mystery. The kind of mystery I was way too amped up to question.

I wasn't excited in the sense that I like him and want to spend time with him or anything. At least that's what I told my racing heart when I first saw his smile from the other side of the glass. He'd been crouched on his belly on the roof of our porch like a stealthy spy, and the sight was something I'd never forget.

I'd thrown a hoodie on over the Tee I'm dressed in, pairing it with some denim cutoffs. Then I tossed my hair up into a messy bun and slid on some cherry Chapstick—but only because my lips were chapped. That's it. No other reason whatsoever.

Once my Docs were on, I slid out my window and met him head on, the two of us jumping the five feet off the low hanging roof. I'd giggled uncontrollably when he landed on his butt instead of his feet, and he'd nearly pulled me down with him when he tried grabbing my laces. That would be the last time I'd ever not tie my boots.

"Guess what?" he whispered when we started to walk away from the house. "I researched your family tree today and found out that you, Becca, are the biggest sap." He ended that statement with a tap to my nose. My freaking nose, for God's sake.

He'd *booped* me.

My response—one which had been paired with a hard thump to his equally as hard abdomen: "You're so dumb, you planted a dogwood tree and expected a litter of puppies."

We both laughed at how stupid we sounded, yet at the same time it felt good to just be goofy. Or dare I say, normal. Though that word—*normal*—was a bit of a stretch when it came to the two of us anymore.

After that, Ben took my hand like it was the most natural thing in the world and proceeded to lead me to where we are now: the middle of the cornfield.

I trail my fingers over the silky corn stalks, marveling at their height and the way the midnight moon reflects off the green color. Nothing about this spot eases my frazzled nerves, of course. It doesn't give me peace of mind like it once had when I'd come out here with Rose either. It's kind of like the alcove in that sense—a spot tainted by a bad memory, despite the many good memories trying to override it.

Ben moves closer, our shoulders brushing.

"What are you thinking about?" he asks.

"Stuff." That no longer matters. A time and a place and a memory that's long past.

"Rose said you guys used to hang out here a lot."

I shrugged one shoulder, unwilling to indulge in what happened the last time she and I had been out here. It's not a huge thing, smoking weed and all, but for some reason, I don't want Ben to know that it'd been my bucket list item, not Rose's. It shows my age—how I'd been so young and inexperienced.

Not that I care what he thinks.

"It's nice," he continues. "Quiet too. I can see why you liked it."

"We did some of our best thinking out here." *Thinking* that was more along the lines of Rose smoking joints, while I stood by to keep watch.

"Hmm." He nods, kicks the toe of his foot into the dirt. "I'm gonna go to that party on Saturday," he tells me out of the blue.

I frown. "You think that's smart after beating up Adam like you did?"

"Yup."

"Why?"

"Because Adam's gonna be there." He looks away, but I don't miss the flex of his jaw—not even in the dark. "I don't trust the guy."

I turn him around by the shoulders, forcing him to stand in front of me. "What's there not to trust, exactly?"

"Lots of things."

"Like what?"

"I've got facts that need exploring." His lips purse.

"Yeah." I roll my eyes. "Because you're suddenly a detective now. I forgot."

Adam wouldn't hurt a puppy, let alone be behind Rose's

death. He used to talk big, but his love for my best friend was endless. Without a doubt, I know that's who her secret boyfriend was. I just don't get why they never went public.

"I'm more of a private eye, actually." He covers one eye and curls the corner of his upper lip, making an *argh* noise.

"That's a pirate, not a private eye, dork."

"Either way, they're both sneaky, right?"

I sigh, wondering if he's always been this weird. Cocky, a smartass, and a huge instigator—that's Ben. Not *funny*.

"Fine. I'll go to the party with you." The second the words are out I regret them. I also refuse to take them back. If Ben shows up there without me, and Adam jumps him out of retaliation, I'd feel like crap because I wouldn't be there to stop it.

"Well, *I* thought about it and decided you'd be better off at home," he says.

I put my hands on my hips. "Don't give me that crap. I'm going. You'll need me there to help deal with those idiots."

"I *deal* with idiots on football field all the time. I can handle some little high school boys." He lifts his chin. "Plus, I won't be able to concentrate if you go because all I'll be thinking about is Travis possibly messing with you."

I touch his forearm and lower my voice. "I can handle Travis."

"Right." He runs a hand through his hair, fisting it. "Like you handled him the night of the dance."

I flinch but refuse to back down. He has no right bringing that night up.

"I'm not the same girl I was back then."

I'm stronger. *Angrier*. Bitter. So very, very bitter.

He searches my face for another second, then sighs. "Sorry. You're right. I just hate that he took..."

"Took what?"

"You know..."

"Um, I *don't* know."

He groans and rubs a hand across his forehead. "Please don't make me spell it out for you."

"Wait." I put my hands on my hips and squint at him. "Do you mean, my v-card? Is that what you're trying to spit out?"

He nods quickly and looks at his shoes. It's almost as if he's embarrassed...which of course isn't right. This is Ben McCain. Mr. Womanizer Extraordinaire.

Regardless, it's confusing as to why he cares so much. Ben's not my keeper or my brother, so I don't owe him any kind of explanation. At the same time, I feel the need to stand up for myself—explain that what I did wasn't out of love, but immaturity and a huge mistake.

"Did Rose tell you what happened between him and I? Not that night, but after and before."

"I know enough." He squares his shoulders. "Hell, Becca. Why him?"

"You make it sound like I had a choice."

"Didn't you?" His lips flatten into a straight line, head tipped to one side.

"Not really, no."

"What do you mean?"

"I felt trapped. Like, if I didn't have sex with him, he'd...I don't know, break up with me?"

He scoffs. "That would've been a hell of a lot better."

"Not that it's any of your business," I tell him, "but, I agree. It's just that I was naïve back then and didn't understand how relationships worked."

"You're right." He pauses, surprising me with how

124

easily he relents. "It's not my business. But that doesn't mean I can't still hate him for how he treated you."

"I hate him too, just so you know. But back to the issue at hand here."

He groans.

"What?" I ask. "Adam's not bad, Ben." Aside from his need to tease me constantly. "I honestly don't think he would hurt Rose because I'm pretty sure he was in love with her."

"Love?" Ben laughs, head tilted back as he digs both palms into his eyes. "If that's your idea of love, then it's obvious you're not emotionally ready to handle what I'm about to tell you right now."

My spine goes rigid. "Handle *what*, exactly?"

He looks at me again, his face unreadable. I squirm, heart in my throat, body stiff.

"What is it?" I ask again, softening my voice. "Do you know something about Adam I don't?" If he does, then I'm not too sure I want to know.

Ben takes a small step back, looking away as he speaks, his gaze to the star-lit sky, face a mask of dark shadows. "My mom found Rose's phone at home the night she died. Saw these... these *texts* from Adam. Something about wanting Rose to change her mind. Saying it wasn't worth it. That if she didn't believe him, he'd take care of things on his own."

"But they were together that night." At least I thought they were.

"Yeah. Tell me about it. It's why the damn texts make no sense."

I stare at the flattened stalks, eyes pulled together. Some of Travis's friends from Texas were there that weekend. I didn't want to go because I didn't want to see Travis or deal with anyone associated with him. But Rose had been adamant about being there, almost desperate to go. I'd chalked it up to the fact that she just wanted to get away from her mom, who'd been drinking a lot more. But maybe I'd been wrong.

"What if Adam slipped something in her drink without her knowing?" Ben asks.

"Didn't they check for drugs in her system when she died? What's that called? A tox screen?"

He rubs a hand across his forehead. "Yeah. And I think they did. I don't know for sure."

"You *think*?" I bark. "You either know or you don't. Which is it?"

He looks at me, and I blink, waiting for his reassurance.

Only it never comes.

"Jeez, Ben How do you not know this?" My voice cracks. Everything swirls in my mind as I try to recreate that night, piece things together. The things Rose said when she'd messaged me. Her voice mail, begging me to come with her.

"I...I don't know." He finally relents, his shoulders slumping. "Mom never told me, I guess."

It's like the ground's been sucked out from underneath me and I'm falling so fast, so hard, I can't breathe or think or feel. If there were drugs in Rose's system, other than maybe weed, then that changes everything.

"I just wonder if Adam slipped her something," Ben tells me—or maybe he's telling himself.

"Ask your mom. Tell her to show you the police report." I'd watched enough crime dramas to know they have rights to this. "And find out which drugs were in her system if there were any. You have a right to know." I move in closer, needing him to see my face. To see, most of all, that I'm in this now. Deeply. Irrevocably so.

He sticks both hands into his short pockets and blows out a slow breath. "Okay, I will."

We both go quiet then, studying the fields, the moon, anything but each other. I'm not sure what to say or even do. Piecing things together, things I might not have noticed before she died, is growing harder and harder by the minute. The truths and lies are now blurring with added in facts that I didn't expect.

"Adam's a nice guy," I say, more to myself than Ben this time. "I can't see him slipping her anything. Not when I'm pretty sure he was in love with her." I'm not sure why I'm defending him. Maybe because I saw how they'd been together? Or maybe that was a huge cover-up for something else—or *someone* else, I should say.

Ben snort-laughs, the sound both angry and bitter. "Yeah, trust me when I say that even good guys do really stupid things when they're in love."

I frown, not sure why I ask what I do next. "Have *you* ever done stupid things for girls you've been in love with?"

He doesn't hesitate. "Yup. All the time, actually."

I bite the corner of my mouth, wanting to ask who those girls are. If there's someone now that he's making a mess of himself for. But it's not about him tonight, or my stupid curiosity. This is about Rose. What happened to her, most of all.

"Maybe she was scared of him," Ben adds, eyes meeting mine again.

"Who?"

"Adam. Maybe he threatened her or something."

My throat swells, nerves making my words crack. I need to tell him about the mystery boyfriend. How I'm pretty sure it was Adam. If we're going to go all Nancy Drew here, then he needs to know all the facts like I do.

"I have to tell you something," I say.

He tips his head to one side. "What's that?"

"Rose..." I swallow hard, not sure why I'm so nervous.

"She *was* dating someone a few months back, but I never found out who he was. He didn't go to our school, supposedly, but I think she was lying. I think it was Adam."

His eyes go wide. "And you didn't think to tell me about this when I asked?"

"I didn't see the point at the time, okay? She'd just died, and I was barely holding it together." Still am, though I don't mention this to Ben.

He's quiet. But his glare says what he doesn't, making my skin itch with nerves and regret. Still, I won't let him get to me. He has secrets too, I'm almost positive. This isn't a one-sided situation.

"Didn't the police question everyone involved?" I ask.

He pinches the bridge of his nose. "You can't trust the cops in this town."

He's right on that. Winston is known for peace and tranquility, which means the police want to keep suspicions low and calm at a high. It's hell to live in this tiny, conservative town sometimes.

"I just don't get why you didn't tell me," Ben continues, obviously not ready to let this drop. "I specifically asked you if she was seeing anyone. This is the kind of shit my mom would pull. I expected better of you."

My face grows hot. So do my eyes.

"Screw you." I turn away, intending to leave. I don't need to stand here and take his crap. He has no right to compare me to that woman. I did what I thought was right. That's it. Just like he does what he thinks is right too.

Feet rustle on the ground behind me as I rush back to the house, the humid air smacking, forcing my hair to stick to my now sweaty cheeks. Ben grabs my hand before I can make it to the edge, nowhere near as winded as I am, and I hate him even more for it.

128

"Don't go. Please. I'm sorry. I shouldn't have said that," he says, voice garbled, like he's seconds from crying.

I rip my arm away. "Yeah, right."

"I am, Becca."

"Then tell me this: Why yell at me when you did the same thing by keeping the drugs a secret?"

"I was going to tell you, but you've been avoiding me and the subject."

"For good reason, obviously."

"Come on, please?" He takes both my hands in his, pulling me closer. "I'm grabbing at straws here because I'm freaking lost. I'm sorry." Tears slide down his cheeks so quickly I don't have time to think about reaching up and catching them. Ben isn't in a place to stop them either, and instead he becomes a waterfall of words and feelings and regrets so deep I could bottle them away as my own if possible.

"I want to believe that Rose didn't jump into that river on purpose or that it was an accident. But what if I'm wrong? What if I screwed up and I missed something big because I was away at school? I wasn't there for her like I should have been, just like you said. But I'm here now and I don't make this right..." He bows his head. At the same time, his shoulders begin to shake.

My throat burns, the truth of his words so painful I struggle to breathe, let alone get my words out. "You wouldn't be alone if that was the case," I whisper. "It'd be my fault too." Because I'd been so wrapped up in myself, with Travis and that drama, I didn't have time to stop and really look at the signs...signs I couldn't even begin to pinpoint if I had to. Rose was happy. Rose was reckless. Rose was just...Rose.

Or was she?

I look down, and soon my own tears find freedom

and fall down my cheeks. This is why I've been avoiding the truth: because I didn't want to question who Rose was when she died.

"I really am sorry, B," he tells me again, tipping up my chin with his finger.

I sniff, wiping my nose with the sleeve of my hoodie. "It's fine."

He moves in even closer, so much so that I can smell his aftershave, even the mint of his toothpaste when he exhales. Without warning, he slides his hand to my cheek, holding it there as he searches my face, the moon our only light.

Warmth builds a path inside of me, from my chest to my stomach. It's so quick, so surprising, that my knees begin to shake. The coarseness of his palm is like the safety blanket I didn't think I needed but would suddenly do anything to keep.

Our eyes stay locked, but the knot in my throat chokes me to where I can't speak anymore. I want to ask what he wants...what he's doing and thinking. But the only thing I can do is blink and study his face like he's doing to mine.

It's always been hard not to be swept away by Ben's blue-eyed gaze and those soft pillow lips of his; lips so pink I can even make out the shading in the dark right now. But tonight, it's nearly impossible.

Everything I pushed away after that night between us in his kitchen when I was fifteen starts to resurface again. Only this time, I'm more cautious. Less open to possibilities because I'm terrified of being rejected again. There are a lot of things I expected tonight. But this feeling, this possibility, wasn't one of them.

"You don't have to go with me next weekend," he whispers, stroking his thumb over my chin. "I'm fine handling this on my own from now on. I'm sorry I asked for your help at all. You're right to want to stay out of it."

My shoulders slump. "Look. You can either drive me, or I'll call and ask *Adam* for a ride there myself because I'm in this now, just like I told you. No turning back. You've buried the seeds, Ben. Now I have to wait for them to bloom or die."

He sighs in resolve, drops his chin to his chest. "You're impossible."

I grin. "You shouldn't have been pushing me for help in the first place."

A gust of wind blows through the air, creating a whistling effect that sends more shivers down my spine. I fold my arms over my stomach, take a step back to get out of whatever spell he's put me under tonight.

"Before you do this with me, you need to know that there are rumors going around in town," he tells me.

"What kind of rumors?"

He motions me forward with his chin. "Come on. Let me walk you back to the house."

"Ben, just tell me. Please."

"It's late. Just...let me get you safely inside. I'll tell you. Promise."

I sigh, letting him take my hand again. I shouldn't like it. But I do, despite all the anger and hurt he's caused me tonight.

As we head back to my front porch, thoughts spin webs in my mind about what he means by rumors. People in our small town gossip, and I can only imagine what exactly they're saying about Rose, the star softball playing thrill-seeker who supposedly died a tragic death after jumping over a dam along the Mississippi.

Suicide. Stupidity. Reckless.

Ben's hand tightens around mine every so often as we move, as though he's thinking the same thing as me.

131

"People are talking crap," he finally says when we stop along side of the front porch. "How Rose..." he cringes, "*deserved* what she got."

"Deserved it?"

"We both know she was reckless." He drops my hand to tuck his into his pocket when we approach the porch. Ben looks up at the sky, his jaw working over. "People are saying it was only a matter of time before she got what was coming to her."

"They're really saying that?"

He nods.

Rose was wild, there's no denying that. She pulled pranks, had attitude for days with authority figures too. The parents of the Winston Varsity softball players never invited Rose over for after-game parties because she was loud and obnoxious at times, despite the fact that she was the star pitcher. I was used to it. Knew that was just who she was, which is why I never bothered going to those stupid parties either. To me, Rose was spirited with a side intensity—two traits that didn't always mesh well together. Yes, she pushed limits, but she was a good person, even if she didn't always seem like it to others.

"You know what this town is like. Church-going bible thumpers who can't see anything that's not straight and narrow."

"It's disgusting," I say.

"Yep. And it didn't help that Rose was in trouble all the time. And being raised by a single, drunk mom didn't help matters either."

I hate how I'm privileged in the sense that I have a loving and devoted set of parents. Nobody in Winston has ever looked at us any differently. That doesn't mean people don't ever talk, just that we're lucky enough not to hear them if they do.

"My sister and I were the best at what we did, sports

wise, and everyone *loves* an athlete," Ben says, mockingly. "But take that away and we're nothing but the trash everyone wanted to steer clear of." He shrugs. "Mom's never made enough money to keep up with the country club crowd, and what money she did have? It's always been spent at a bar."

"I'm sorry," I say, hating Ginger, the gossipers, everything that's ever hurt or tried to break my best friend and Ben.

"Don't apologize," he tells me. "It's not your fault."

"Yeah, but it's not right."

"It's the truth, isn't it?"

I want to tell him no, that it doesn't matter what people think either way. But that would be a huge lie. *I* care about stuff like that. Just like Rose and Ben likely did too, even if they both pretended not to.

"Your mother's issues shouldn't have anything to do with who Rose was as a person. If anything, people should be blaming your mom for this."

"They do, is the thing. Hell, B. They probably blame me too, just like *you* did."

"Ben." I touch his hand this time. "I didn't mean—"

He presses a finger to my lips, holding it there. "You didn't know, remember?"

But I wish I had. So much. I channeled all of my hatred into Ben for so long and not just because he'd pushed me away for trying to kiss him either.

He squeezes my hand. I let him, allowing our fingers to intertwine. We need each other for support. For friendship. And friends...they hold hands, right?

In the distance, lightning fills the sky. It's daring us to stay where we are or run, yet neither Ben nor I are in a hurry.

"Mom may have sucked as a parent," he says, "but she's not to fully blame on this. Rose was—"

"The best person I knew," I say, leaning back against the railing of the porch. I'm too exhausted to beat down her memory tonight. "She had flaws, but she wasn't the worst kid in this town."

"You sure?" he questions me softly.

I turn, staring at his profile when he leans against the porch beside me. "To me she was." But, then again, did I really know her like I thought I did?

I LIFTED the joint in my hands, hesitant as I stared at the unlit end. We chose tonight to do this because my mom was out of town. She was way more aware of the things Rose and I did than Dad. Still, weed had a distinctive smell, and I was worried he'd somehow find out if we did it on the porch roof.

Rose and I sat cross-legged on the blanket we'd laid on the ground. Since the snow had melted, the fields had grown muddy and gross. Mom would lose her crap if she found muddy clothes in the laundry, then question what every second of what we did when she was away.

"You're the one who wanted to try it tonight," Rose said, flicking her lighter on then off again.

"I know, but if my dad smells this crap on me, I won't live to see eighteen."

"So that's a for-sure no, then?"

I nodded.

"Alrighty." She kicked her feet out in front of her, ankles crossed. "I'll just have to smoke this for the both of us then."

"Sorry."

"Girl, don't be sorry. There's no timeline as to when a person's gotta get high for the first time." Rose snagged the joint from between my fingers and pressed it to her lips. With her free hand, she flicked the lighter on, and took a long drag.

"Maybe brownies would've been better." I laid down on the blanket and put both hands behind my head.

"Maybe." Rose did the same, only with the joint stuck between her lips.

Flat on our backs, we looked up at the cotton candy-

colored sky, my "getting high" experience shifting to an evening of R&R for her. It was one thing to invent number eighty-five on our list but another following through with it. I guess there were a few things in life I just wasn't ready, and weed smoking was one of them.

After a few more hits, Rose stubbed out the joint beside her, propping her head up on one hand as she faced me. "Has Travis tried to call you anymore?"

I winced. She knew not to bring up Travis, yet there she was, doing it again. "No. And even if he did call, I wouldn't answer the phone."

"Hmm."

I dropped my head to the side, staring at her. "What?"

"It's nothing."

"If it was nothing, then you wouldn't have brought it up."

"It's just that I talked to him." She folded both arms around her shin.

"At school?"

"No." She bit her bottom lip then said, "At his house."

I sat up, heart skipping at her confession. "What were you doing at his house?"

"Leaf's been tutoring me and Adam on the side. We're failing three classes, B. If I don't get my grades up, I won't be able to play varsity."

"As in your teacher, Leaf? Travis's dad?"

"It's no big deal. Leaf's chill like that." She bumped my shoulder with her own when she sat up too.

"Why didn't you tell me?" Better yet, why hadn't she asked me for help instead? I wasn't a genius, but I did get straight A's. And when it came to tutoring, I had a knack for it. Rose had told me I should become a teacher. I'd told her I didn't like kids. The point was, she always came to me when she needed help.

"You've been busy." She shrugged. "And Leaf offered when

he found me crying after class one day. Told me he tutored Adam on the side and invited me over too."

"I haven't been 'busy'. I've been home every night, grounded since the winter formal. You know this."

"Exactly." She scoffed. "It's not like your parents would've let me come over."

"Don't give me that crap excuse." I got to my feet, upper lip curled. "You practically live at my house. And school is way different. Neither of them would've cared."

"Yeah, well, sometimes it gets to be too much, okay?"

I narrowed my eyes. "What gets to be too much?"

"Being at your house all the time. Around your mom and your dad. Their rules and stuff."

I jerked my head back. "Since when have their rules bugged you?"

"Since always," she said. "I mean, I love your parents, but they're overbearing sometimes. It's not like I'm their kid or anything."

Where in the heck was this coming from?

Rose loved my mom and dad, always said she wished she could be their daughter, my sister. More often than not, she said she appreciated how protective they were of us both, saying nobody but Ben—who was hardly around anymore —ever cared enough to know where she was, who she was with, or what she was even doing.

"They love you like you are their daughter. You know that."

"I'm not though." She stood, avoiding my eyes. "And I'm going to be going to college soon anyway so it's not like they'll send me money when I don't have enough. Or pay for my tuition because Mom's spent that money at the bar."

I touched her hand. I wasn't sure where her anger was coming from, but the idea that she didn't feel like my parents would be there for her broke my heart. Time and time again

Mom and Dad had given her the world, yet she thought so little of it.

"Rose. They will always take care of you, no matter what happens. You know that."

She pulled her hand from mine and brushed off the back of her jeans. Her body relaxed a little at my words—or that could've been the weed's doing. Still, she seemed so lost right then—especially her eyes. Empty blue pools of nothing, like a light had been shut off.

I wasn't sure where this was all coming from. Just knew that I didn't want my best friend to feel like she wasn't a part of my family. Blood was great and all that. But love? That's what was real.

"Sorry," she said, looking me in the eyes. "I'm not making sense."

"It's probably the weed." I bumped her shoulder with my own, smiling softly.

"Maybe."

I grabbed her hand again and squeezed it, not letting go this time. "Wanna go eat something bad for us?"

She grinned at that, brushing hair from her eyes. "Say chocolate, and it's a deal."

I smiled. "Chocolate it is."

138

9

August
Present Day

I'M a wreck of nerves as I pace back and forth in my living room, eyes to the gravel drive out the side window, then the floor, then back to the window again. Saturday night has arrived, and though I claimed I was ready for it, my heart is suddenly saying otherwise.

Not only am I nervous about going to a party where the guy my parents forbade me to see might be, but I'm also seconds from seeing Ben for the first time in a week.

On Monday, Ben had to go back to Iowa City for some football stuff, so we haven't seen each other since last Saturday. We've been texting back and forth a bit throughout the week, mostly him checking in on me, and me telling him to mind his own business.

I'd never admit it out loud, but I did miss him, despite our misgivings. His annoyingness has grown on me, to

139

the point where I didn't know what I'd do when he wasn't there all the time.

No matter—I don't have the energy or the time to figure out what that means. And I am *not* about to mark out a place on my calendar to do so anytime soon either.

At least that's what I've been telling myself all day.

Or all week, really.

At eight, the sound of the doorbell has me jumping in place. I press a shaking hand to my heart, cursing out loud.

With slow steps and a deep breath, I walk toward the front door, praying I don't have armpit stains or anything. I double check, take a quick smell, catching the scent of my body spray and deodorant. After I wipe my sweaty hands along my thighs, I send a silent prayer out into the world, begging that he won't try and hold my hand or anything weird like that. Not because I didn't like the idea—more so I need to, like, draw a line between us from here on out. This is Ben, Rose's brother, after all. An annoying, cocky jerk I've known since fourth grade.

I pull at the door handle, freezing at the sight of him. Leaning against the door frame, Ben's looking all sorts of college-boy-preppy-hot in cargo khaki shorts and a zippered navy hoodie, with a white Tee underneath. I refuse to think about the fact that he's, well...he's freaking *beautiful* right now, especially with that lock of blond hair falling across his temple, but it's hard. Too hard for someone who's never been able to turn off her ability to crush on boys who are no good.

And Ben McCain is definitely no good for me.

Getting more dirt out of Adam is the point tonight. Which means I can't let Ben distract me.

"Hey, B." His gaze does a slow sweep of my body, over my short, tan-and-black plaid skirt and the long T-shirt I tied at the corner of my hip. My belly roll is hanging out on the side, but I don't care. I'm not out to impress.

"What's up," I say nonchalantly.

"Nice tan." He smirks and points to the fresh sunburn on my chest from working alongside Dad this week.

Without him there as farmhand, I've definitely had to pick up the slack, which is what I wanted all along. Though *not* seeing him outside every morning has left an annoying pang in my chest.

"Pink is my favorite color." He winks.

I roll my eyes, catching the slight scent of pine as he slides into the house. His chest brushes mine, and I'm pretty sure it's not an accident.

"This burn is *your* fault," I tell him.

"How so?" He watches me from over his shoulder as he makes his way into the living room.

"Because you haven't been here to help. I'm stuck doing *all* the chores now."

"Aww, poor B." He faces me, bottom lip puffed out. His eyes fill with mischief as they do another sweep of my body. "I'll make it up to you."

My face and neck start to burn. Any clapback I might've had is suddenly gone like the stupid breath in my lungs. Damn him for being so...so *Ben-ish.*

He sits on the edge of the coffee table, setting an ankle on his knee. "Penny for your thoughts?"

I fold my arms, realigning my mindset. "I'm just wondering..."

"Wondering what?"

"Did you eat paint chips as a kid?" I tip my head to the side. "'Cause I'm pretty sure there's something wrong with your brain."

A chuckle slips from his mouth, one that's just loud enough to make me smile. Soon all the initial weirdness disappears, and I find myself more and more thankful that this thing between us—whatever it's called—comes so easily now.

"You really sure you wanna go with me tonight?" Ben runs a slow hand through his hair, leave pieces standing on end. I see the fear in his eyes when they meet mine, hating that I'm probably the reason why it's there at all.

I reach for my zip-up black hoodie. It's hot out, but I need something to do with my hands. "We're not doing this again."

"Fine." He holds his hands up and sighs. "But we need to set some ground rules before we go."

"Liiiike?"

"As in tonight, we should be a couple."

I laugh at that, bending over at the waist... A couple? Yeah, right.

But then I feel his body, his presence hovering. Hands on my shoulders, he pushes me upright until our faces our only inches apart, and I can feel the heat of his breath on my face.

"I'm not kidding, Becca." He reaches forward and tucks a lock of hair behind my ear.

"Y-you're not kidding," I repeat.

"No." His smile is smooth, as are his fingers when he slides them under my chin. He settles his other hand along the side of my waist, like it's as natural as breathing to him.

I don't hate it either. Whatever that says about me, I don't want to know.

"We need to pretend that we're together so that Travis stays away. That way, I'll always be with you and people won't question why I'm at a high school party."

He's right. I do need Ben at my side at this party as much as he needs me. There again, people are probably going to wonder why *I'm* there instead. Rose is gone, and Travis and I are no longer together. I have nothing but a half-assed invitation from Adam to show I'm wanted there, and that's up in the air now that Ben's fist did a number to his face.

"Fine." It is what it is, I guess.

He lifts one eyebrow, moves even closer too—to the point where our chests graze. Where my heart races so fast I can hear it in my ear.

"Are you sure you can handle it?"

"About as sure as I want a hammer to the head."

Ben grins, knowing he's got me. Seconds later, he drops his hand from my chin and sets it on my other hip.

"What are you doing?" My breath catches.

He pulls me closer, sliding both thumbs up and under my shirt a little. "You're gonna need to relax a little if you want to make us look real. You're too tense."

Ben leans closer, warm lips pressing against my ear.

I shut my eyes, my entire body a flame I can't put out. "But—"

"Trust me." He lifts a finger, presses it against my lips. "I can handle this."

"That's what I'm afraid of."

He chuckles low, sending goosebumps down my arms. "The thing is, if I'm gonna be your pretend boyfriend for the night, then you're gonna have to *pretend* to like me."

"That's not possible," I lie, closing my eyes, feeling too much. Loving and hating every second of it.

"You sure about that?" Lips brush against my ear lobe again, fingers dig even harder into my hips.

"Yes." I tip my chin back, wishing he's press his lips there. I want to feel them across my skin, their softness, most of all.

He grins against my cheek instead. The jerk knows exactly what he's doing, I bet. "Then I guess I should warn you...I'm gonna need to put my hands on your body, especially if Travis is close by."

My stomach twists. The idea is...not hated. "Fine," I say, the word a little breathier than I want it to be.

"Lean against me," Ben tells me, all business now. He wraps both arms around my back, allowing his fingers to graze the top of my butt—it's definitely not an accident. And I definitely don't want him to stop.

My throat burns from dryness when I attempt to swallow. I'm a toy, the willing puppet to his strings.

"Wrap your arms around my shoulders, Becca," he insists, brushing hair off my shoulder with his free hand, then letting his fingers trail down my arm to my elbow.

I do as he asks, inhaling his skin, the woodsy scent nothing like I'm used to. Our chests are fully flush, rising and falling at the same pace.

"Now what?" I manage, meeting his gaze.

His eyelids are heavy, lashes grazing his cheekbones with every blink. "Lay your head on my shoulder."

I stare, full on confused.

"Come on," he says with a sly grin. "Don't question it. You have to trust me."

Trust is a hard word for me to wrap my head around. I thought I had that with Rose. With Travis too. But look where that got me. Still, in order to make this work, he's right. I need to relax. Not feel. Not *think*, most of all.

With a huff, I settle my cheek against his right shoulder, leaving my lips a little too close to his neck. The vein pulses, and I study it for a moment before I finally whisper, "Happy?"

He doesn't speak. But I feel him nod. And everything about that one movement has my entire body taking a sabbatical from humanity. I'm relaxed, otherworldly, and from the way his Adam's apple bobs when he swallows, I'm wondering if he's there too...maybe thinking about someone else. Forcing himself to pretend I'm not me but that girl in his dorm he sees in passing; someone he's seen or sat with in the cafeteria; or the girl in the stands at one of his games who's always there, cheering him on.

The thought has possessiveness running through me. It's unwelcome and pisses me off. Even still, my hands don't get the memo, and I can't help but grip him a little tighter. Pull him so close I can feel every inch of his hard abdomen.

Ben is either really good at pretending or feels the same way I do because the hand stroking up and down my spine is almost reverent. It's so real that I find myself snuggling closer, relaxing. Any second now, I expect him to pull away and crack a joke. Call me a good student or a fast learner. But he does neither.

Ben has never hugged me before.

Up until these past couple of weeks, Ben and I have barely touched, other than a noogie to my head or a poke of my finger to his chest when he made me mad. Being close to him like this is realer than my first kiss. Realer than the night I lost my virginity too. It's an addiction in the making, and for a moment, I'm not sure I'll be able to let him go.

All good things must come to an end though, and Ben's the first to make that happen. He pulls away...but hovers there, so close to my mouth that the heat of his breath grazes my lips. It's free of beer or booze, laced with that same minty toothpaste smell, and my stomach does dips and swirls like schools of fish have rooted inside. Gross, yes, but it's also peaceful because it reminds me of swimming in the alcove, smiling up at the sun, Rose's hand in mine.

Our space, our world.

I'm too scared to open my eyes and see what might be there on Ben's face. Another smirk, annoyance, possibly

145

disinterest. What if this really *is* a game to him? What if he's pretending only to tease me about it later? He's always been an ammunition holder, but I can only take so many shots.

I can't keep my eyes closed out of fear for forever. So, I open them. And what I see takes my breath away.

Ben's lids are half closed, downturned, and currently studying my mouth like he wants to taste it. "Becca," he whispers, leaning closer, his eyes shutting again, his voice crackling.

And just like that, I'm thrown back into time...to that night in his kitchen two and a half years ago, only I'm the one who breaks the connection, not him.

This isn't real.

Not real, not real, not real.

"I think we'll be fine." I take a step back, not bothering to look at him when I walk away to grab my purse in the closet by the door. I half expect him to be there behind me, making a joke, but he's not. Instead, when I turn to see him, I find him standing in the door frame of the family room, looking like he's just been kicked. Part of me wants to say *payback's a bitch*, but it hurts to even think it. I refuse to go down that road again.

"What?" I say, failing to keep my hands steady as I study his expression.

His eyes are wide and full of questions, his lips parted too. I hold my breath, waiting to hear him say what I've always wanted; that he likes me—always has.

But of course, it doesn't happen. That would be fairy-tale crap. Stuff that doesn't exist in my life.

Eventually, Ben blows out a breath and rubs a hand across the back of his neck, losing some sort of inner battle when he finally says, "Nothing. Let's go."

———

THE NIGHT AIR IS SCORCHING. Unfortunately for me, Ben seems to prefer to have the windows down in his truck instead of turning on the AC. By the time we make it to town, my neck is so sweaty I could soak a freaking towel. Still, I'm too bothered by what almost happened at my house to say anything.

The party's at Adam's father's autobody shop in downtown Winston, which isn't uncommon for Adam and Travis's crowd. I'm just thankful it's not at the river.

"You'll be okay." Ben breaks me out of my thoughts as we pull up next to the curb close to the shop. He settles his hand on my upper arm, squeezing lightly. "I won't let him bother you." We both know the *him* he's referring to.

"I'm not worried about seeing Travis. I'm worried about what he's going to do when he sees *you* with me."

Travis treated me like crap, but his possessiveness—post our breakup—was kind of creepy. It's been almost six weeks since I saw him last, so I'm not sure what he'll be like tonight. Anything's game when it comes to my ex.

"You worried about me, B?"

"No." I snort-laugh. "I'm worried because I didn't bring any money to bail you out of jail if you two get into it."

Ben lets go of my arm and taps his thumbs against the steering wheel, ignoring my dig. "Why did you even date him in the first place?"

"You already asked me that." The last thing Ben needs to know is that I'd wanted Travis to take my virginity because I thought he was hot.

Past me was *such* an idiot.

"But not full on details." He frowns.

"I was stupid. *That's* why I dated him." The thought of Travis ever touching me again makes me want to puke. He's greasy and doesn't shower, drinks far more than

Ben, smokes like he's begging for lung cancer, and cares little about everyone but himself. Total. Sociopath.

What I need is better standards when it comes to guys. Travis is the poster human being for what *not* do date. Still, I'm too bothered by what almost happen—

"Did you love him?" Ben asks, the question catching me off guard.

"Honestly?"

"Always." He leans back, gaze never leaving my face.

I sigh. "I thought I did at the time. But I think it was more lust than anything." And any love I might have thought I felt ended after the night of the winter formal. The sex between us might have been consensual. That doesn't mean it was smart.

"How about you?" I ask.

"How about me what?"

"Have you, you know, ever been..." Why can't I say the words?

"In love?" His lips lift on one side, like he's holding on to this huge secret I'm not allowed to ever hear.

"Yeah." I chew on my bottom lip, impatient.

His shrug is so fast I almost miss it. His words, not so much. "Yes. I've been in love before."

I force myself to look out the window toward the empty sidewalk. There's a gnawing in my stomach that's not from the Ramen I had an hour ago.

"In other words, you're just as stupid as me."

Ben's response is a small hum, which sends unwanted chills down my spine. I shift in my seat, fidget with my stupid skirt that's too tight on my thighs.

"Rose never liked him," Ben tells me.

I clear my throat, chancing another quick look at him. "Travis?"

He nods. "Every time we talked, the first thing out of her mouth was, *God, Becca's boyfriend is such an ass.*"

My chest tightens. Wordless, I open the car door for something to do—mostly to hold off on what I'm about to say. I need the time to process my thoughts. Rose's stance with Travis drained on me. Still does, especially since I never got a straight answer out of her as to why she was the way she was when it came to him.

"You went quiet on me," Ben says, meeting me on the sidewalk in front of his truck a second later. He holds his elbow out for me to grab on to, a gentlemanly quirk I've only ever seen my dad do for my mom.

I take it willingly. "You mention Rose hating Travis. But the thing is the two times he and I broke up, it was *Rose* who always pushed for us to get back together."

Ben takes a moment, likely thinking it over. "Maybe she wanted to distract you from whatever BS she had going on in her own life."

"Maybe."

He's quiet for another minute as we make the slow trek toward the autobody shop.

"Not to be a dick, B, but you were kind of dense when it came to that guy."

I stop in place, turn to him. "Excuse me?"

He cringes. "I mean, not that you could help it or anything."

"Are you implying that I was stupid for wanting to date him?"

"Yeah," He breathes. "I guess I am."

"Go to hell." I pick up speed, darting toward the front of the building.

I hate how right he is. But what Ben doesn't know is that I tried to break up with Travis even before we had sex. It was *Rose*—yet again—who always made it seem like I was being stupid for not working through things. Yes, I made some poor choices on my own when it came to the guy, but I don't need to stand here and be ridiculed by another person who barely knows me or the situation.

"Becca, wait." Ben's sneakers slap against the cement as he runs to catch up with me. "I'm sorry." He stops us at the corner of the building, a hand on my elbow as he draws me back around to face him. It's pure déjà vu—me running, Ben chasing. *Apologizing.*

I open my mouth to tell him off, to say I don't want him to be my fake boyfriend for the night—or anything even remotely close to that. I hate him and his good-looking face and his know-it-all attitude and the way he seems to know Rose better than I do.

But I can't say any of those things because none of them are true. And *that* hurts more than anything he could say to me about Travis.

For so long, I thought Rose and I were each other's worlds. Now, it's like she had an entire universe filled with people who were her main planets, while I'd become her Pluto. Yes, he's her brother, but nobody could hold a candle to our friendship.

Ben takes my hand in his, interlacing our fingers, and my insides instantly melt.

Damn this boy.

"I shouldn't have said what I did," he whispers, sad eyes meeting mine.

"But you did," I say. "In fact, you seem to be putting your foot in your mouth a lot lately."

He stares down at our connected hands. "It was an asshole way to put it."

"It was. And I'd prefer if you kept your *asshole* comments locked away. I know what I did wrong when it came to my relationship, and I do *not* need you there reminding me of them every step of the way."

He makes an X over his chest and says, "Cross my heart I won't. Swear it."

"Good."

⸻

A TENT SITS to the right of the building as we walk to the front of the shop. Ben's hand is now settled against my back, and I can't help but welcome the touch, especially knowing that Travis is probably close by. I may be annoyed by Ben's big mouth, but nobody makes me feel as safe as he does.

Everywhere I look, I see unfamiliar faces among the even more unfamiliar crowd. It's unnerving. Makes me wonder if Rose knew any of these strangers too. A stranger who could have given her drugs...worse yet, a stranger who might have actually drugged her. Someone who's not Adam. Someone who's *close* to Adam?

Ben leans over and presses his mouth to my ear. "You okay?"

"Yeah." I point toward the front door. "Start in there?"

"Lead the way."

We pop into the building, one right after the other. The music is so loud I can't hear myself think. Like sardines, everyone's packed together in the middle, the hardcore punk metal makes it almost impossible for actual conversations.

"Just say the word, Becca..." Ben's hand lingers on my upper arm, but I'm not sure what he means. Say the word, and we'll leave? Say the word, and we'll start questioning people?

Either way, one of us has to get through this without losing our heads, so with thoughts of Rose in mind, I take the lead of our two-person team and guide Ben to the back of the garage.

When we find a spot, he reaches for my hand, interlocking our fingers like he did outside. "You thirsty?" He motions his chin toward the keg on the left, his lips to my ears.

I nod, still eying the room.

"You sure you're able to handle your alcohol?"

I scoff and grab my own cup, filling it. "Yep." I holler over the music. "Can't say the same for you though."

I down my beer in less than a minute. Getting buzzed will make this a whole lot easier. And with my parents being out of town, they won't have a clue if I indulge a little.

Ben groans. "That was *one* time."

"Nope." I grin. "Funeral day too."

His lips purse, but he doesn't deny it. I know he's not going to turn into his mother, but he won't get a free pass for those situations in my eyes. Ben needs to keep himself together and in check. Rose wouldn't want him to lose who he is because of grief, just like I know she wouldn't want that for me either. Granted, I'm taking a while to get to that point, but still. My vices aren't toxic like Ben's have been.

I turn my head and burp. Ben laughs, and soon I'm forgetting everything, swaying my hips to the beat of the music, though punk doesn't necessarily have much of a steady beat.

Within a half hour, warmth has spread throughout my whole body and the numbing potion of the tapped beer is already working its magic. Ben watches me the whole time, eyes narrowing a little when I reach for my third cup.

"You sure that's a good idea?"

I open my mouth to say *absolutely* but instead spot a brown head of hair from across the room. My stomach instantly revolts what I just drank, and I turn away, covering my mouth because I'm seconds from puking on my Docs.

152

"I'll take that." Ben grabs my cup, obviously thinking I'm sick. I am—just not from the alcohol.

Travis is in the corner standing with a girl. Her hands are draped around his neck, while he stares at me from over her shoulders with curious eyes. I look away quickly, chest squeezing.

Like he's my human armor, I turn into Ben's chest. "Maybe this wasn't such a good idea," I say.

His arm comes up around me, his lips to my ears as he bends to get closer. "What is it?"

"He's here."

Ben stiffens. "Where?"

"Left corner, toward the front."

He looks casually, then grumbles something under his breath before lowering his mouth to my ear again. "He's not gonna bother you. I won't let him."

I pull back to meet Ben's eyes. Our gazes lock and hold, like they did at my house, and the longer we stand there like this, the faster my heart beats—for reasons other than fear. There's something in Ben's stare I haven't seen before. Several somethings is more like it. Determination. Sadness. Hope. Loss and—

"Hey, hey, Becca! You...came..."

I stiffen at the sound of Adam's voice. Like some sort of gorilla, Ben's chest puffs out and he wraps an arm around my waist instead of my shoulder, pulling me against his side.

Adam looks between us, his mouth twisting like he's eaten a box of nails and every single one is currently trapped in his throat. It's obvious he dislikes Ben, and I can't blame the guy. He's still got a bruised eye from that grocery store brawl.

I take a moment to study Rose's *other* best friend— her possible lover. It's like I'm a detective, profiling him

153

in my mind as killer, dealer, boyfriend, all of the above, or none.

"Hey, Adam," I finally say, waving, careful to keep my voice steady, my body casual.

"Glad you could make it." He takes a drink.

"Wouldn't miss it." Or maybe I *should've missed it* would be more accurate of a phrase.

Adam yells over the music, "Can we, uh, maybe talk for a few, Becca?" He motions his head toward the side door, eyeing Ben for a second before he finishes. "Outside and alone?"

My nod is hesitant but not enough that he seems to notice. This is the chance I need to get him by himself to discuss things.

Ben, on the other hand, isn't having it. "Where she goes, I go."

Adam shakes his head. "Uh, yeah, this ain't a conversation for three people." He looks to me. "Never mind. It was good to see you again, Becca. We'll talk another time."

Adam turns and sets off toward the front of the building, then out the door.

I look to Ben again, hissing, "What the hell are you doing?"

"You're not going to go with that guy alone."

"Stay here." I step up on the toe of my boots and smack an angry kiss to his cheek, whispering, "Watch the door, and makes sure Travis stays inside. I'll be okay. Adam won't hurt me." I smile, but even as I say the words, my throat jams up with fear.

Ben places a hand on my hip, squeezing as he lowers his forehead to mine. "I don't trust him."

My chest squeezes. "Do you trust me?"

"Yeah." He releases a long breath. "I do."

"Good." I squeeze his hand on my hip. "I promise you I'll be fine."

He nods. I pull away, but instead of letting me go completely, he wraps both of his arms around my lower waist, crushing me to him for another hug.

My eyes widen. The feel of his strong arms tight around me like this, mixed with the beat of his heart against my ear, calms me enough to where I'm forced to shut my eyes. His fear isn't a game this time.

"Be safe," he says, kissing the top of my head, making me forget that this is supposed to be for show. "And take this." He slips something from his pockets and presses it against my stomach. When I reach for it, he wraps my fingers around it, squeezing. "Just in case..."

In my palm sits a pocketknife. Warm and unnerving, safe and terrifying.

"I don't need it." An icy sensation fills my chest. Still, I pull it to my stomach.

"Keep it for my sake, then." His smile is faint. Soft. A little filled with terror and a lot filled with resolve. "It'll make me feel better."

"Okay," I manage, even though I don't look Ben in the eyes again before turning, then walking toward the front door.

Adam's sitting down and leaning against the side of building when I find him, pretty close to Ben's truck. Head back, eyes to the sky, he doesn't even look at me before he speaks. "Warden let you escape?"

I cringe. "Yeah, I'm guessing he'll be out here in, oh," I look at my imaginary watch, "five minutes or less."

"When did you two start hooking up?" he asks.

I hesitate, not expecting the question.

"That's what I thought," Adam laughs. "Don't worry, your secret's safe with me. But it'll drive Travis nuts thinking you two are an item. He's never gotten over you."

My face heats from being called out on the lie. I thought we were more convincing.

"Poor Travis." I snort-laugh, snatching onto the thing I can control. "Broken hearted all these months later."

"Good to see you've finally grown some lady balls, Becca." Even though his words are probably supposed to be funny, Adam's face stays emotionless as he lights up a cigarette.

I take a seat beside him on the cement. "You smoke now?"

"It eases the nerves." He inhales, and the crackle of the butt fills the dead air.

I'm not sure where to start or what to say. I know it's my duty to question him, but it also feels off handed to just bring up that night. Not when I don't have a starting point that doesn't seem suspicious.

"I still can't believe she's gone." Adam takes another drag.

"Me neither." I lean back against the building and cross my legs at the ankle.

"Are you okay? I mean..." He looks at me, his eyes sad.

"No." I shake my head. "I'm not okay. Don't know if I ever will be." Right now, I'm living my life the only way I know how. By breathing, surviving, and doing all the mundane stuff I don't want to do but am forced to do at the same time. But truly living? I don't know how to do that without Rose.

"I think back on that night every damn day, reliving it. The last hours we were together most of all," Adam says offhandedly.

My ears perk. The detective in me takes root as questions form, a truth that has everything to do with the drugs she'd taken, whether purposely or unknowingly, whatever they even were.

"What was she like that night?" I ask.

"Sad as hell." Adam doesn't hesitate. "Crying a lot."

"She was?" I'd spoken to her earlier in the day, and other than seeming disappointed that I wasn't coming with her to the party, she'd sounded fine.

"Yeah." He squints in the dark like he's trying to remember something. "She went to the doctor with her mom and got some sort of bad news." He frowns.

I remember her going, being tired all the time, and me pushing her to get the appointment. But she didn't say anything about it later in the day when we'd talk.

Adam scrubs a hand over his jaw. "I gave her a joint, and we smoked it together that night. Usually, that helped relax her, you know?"

"Did it?"

"Nah. If anything, it made her paranoid as hell."

My throat closes off. If only I'd gone with her...

"And just so you know, I gave it to her, like, three hours before she walked to the dam," he clarifies, his voice defensive.

"The weed?"

He looks away, nodding. "Got in trouble for that shit too. Cops found my stash when they searched my house."

"Do you know what they were looking for?" I ask.

"No clue."

Part of me wants to run inside, get Ben, and force him to leave. But for Rose's sake, now more than ever, I need to keep it together. Again, I'm in this deep, even if I hadn't planned on it before. I can't live through lies when one truth might be the very thing to set all the pain away.

"Rose was dating someone a while back," I prompt.

"Thing is, she never told me who he was." I swallow hard. "Do you know who it was?"

His body goes rigid.

"Adam?" I touch his arm and turn to face him full on, just in time to see his eyes close. His bottom lip starts to tremble, and he lifts his hands to cover it like he's afraid I'll see. Under his breath, he curses, then stands, and his long legs blur in and out of focus when he begins to pace.

That's all the proof I need right now to know.

Adam was the mystery boyfriend.

"Adam?" I try again. "Why didn't you guys tell me?"

"I'm not getting into this with you," he snaps, a vein bulging alongside his temple. He's like a livewire down on an open road, squirming and waiting to strike who ever passes by.

My hands tremble when I step in front of him. I lift them in the air, placating. "I'm sorry. I didn't mean to upset you. I just wanted to ask in case—"

"In case it was me?" He knifes both hands through his hair. They're both shaking by the time he lowers them.

I squint at him in confusion. "But it was you, wasn't it?"

He laughs, the sound so angry and bitter I can't help but step back. "Hell no. I was a cover-up. Someone to draw attention off who it really was." He runs another hand through his hair, his entire body practically trembling. "Rose never thought I was good enough. I never stood a damn chance with her."

Adam *was* in love with Rose. Rose wasn't in love with him. He was mad. Furious, even. But was that motivation enough for him to hurt her? I have to know.

"She did love you." I try to soothe his beast. "You were her best friend, beside me."

"Yay for me." He throws a hand in the air.

158

I flinch, determined to keep going. "Who was it, then?" I whisper. "Can you tell me?"

"What's that saying again?" He sneers at me, head cocked to the side. "Oh, I know. Snitches get fucking stitches." He gets in my face then, forcing me to take a few steps back. My head and shoulders hit the brick of the building as he hovers, two hands on either side of my head. The smell of BO, beer, and weed linger in the air. I want to gag but don't.

"Please," I whimper, not sure if I'm more afraid of him or what he's hiding.

"She didn't tell you or that pissant of a brother for a reason. So just do her *memory* a favor and leave it. The hell. Alone."

Fear eats at my emotions, forcing a lone tear to escape my eye. As quickly as I can, I wipe it away and lift my chin. "It's not your decision to make, what happens to her memory."

"Then whose decision is it, huh? Because it looks here like I'm the one who holds all the cards right now." He laughs bitterly, drops his hands away, and shakes his head. "Unless, of course, you'd like to take it up with someone else..."

I blink. "W-what?"

Adam smirks, takes a step back too, then motions his head toward something behind him.

I hear his footsteps before I see him. And by the time I'm looking, he's already five feet away. Travis.

"Hey, doll." He steps closer, his footfalls heavy like the ache in my belly. The first thing I see is the twirling of his wallet chain—though the wallet isn't attached. The second is his curled upper lip.

My body shakes, but I manage to keep my voice steady. "Travis."

"You come to see me?" He tips his head to one side,

taking me in from head to toe. "Change your mind about us finally?"

"I'll scream." I cling to the knife in my pocket, terrified to use it.

"You don't need to do that." Travis tsks, setting a hand on my shoulder, squeezing so tight I wince. "This will be quick. Painless, even."

I yank out of his hold and back up the sidewalk. "Stay away from me. Both of you."

Travis grins. Adam stays silent, lowering his head.

I get it now. This is some sort of setup. Adam asked me here tonight so Travis could corner me. *Threaten* me. But why?

"Ben will come out here," I warn.

"Counting on it." Travis winks. It's a wink I used to find charming. A wink that is suddenly the stuff of nightmares. "He's been snooping around too much. I need to put him in his place."

"You leave him alone," I hiss.

"Fine." He folds his arms. "Let's chat about that dead, bitchy friend of yours though."

"Don't call her that."

Ignoring me, Travis lurches forward, his rancid breath filling my nose. "She was pregnant, did you know that?"

My chest grows cold.

I blink.

"N-no."

"Stop, man." Adam grabs Travis's arm. "Don't go there right now."

"You're lying," I growl, fingers wrapping around the handle of the knife.

Travis's lips split into a huge smile. "You really didn't know?" Travis turns to Adam and laughs, jerking his

160

thumb at me. "She didn't know, can you believe that shit?"

"I said *stop*." Adam shoves Travis back against the building, getting in his face.

"The hell, man?" Travis pushes him away with enough force that Adam falls to the ground.

Jumping to his feet again, Adam looks up, at the road behind him, toward the front of the building, then back to Travis. "This ain't what this is about, remember? You just wanted to warn her off. That was the deal."

Travis laughs, looking at me from over his friend's shoulder. "Rose was nothing but a dirty little whore who couldn't keep her legs shut. She deserved what she got."

"Shut up." I hold my hands over my ears, trying to block him out, trying to make sense of what he just told me.

Rose was pregnant.

Rose was pregnant.

"You were always too stupid to realize what she was really like, Becca." Travis yanks my hands down, holding tightly to my wrists. "And you'll continue to be, especially if you're screwing around with her brother." His upper lip lifts in a snarl. "That whole family and their dark, little secrets. You've got no idea."

My stomach tightens, squeezing my insides.

Rose is dead.

Rose was pregnant when she died.

She lied to me.

Dark little secrets.

I slide down the wall, ignoring the scraping sensation of the brick against my back through my shirt. There, I pull my knees back to my chest, not caring if I'm exposing myself. I cry into my knees—sob, really. They don't matter. Nothing does. My grief was better off how it was before. *I* was better off before.

How could you, Rose?

"Now," Travis crouches down in front of me and grabs a lock of my hair, yanking it so hard I see stars, "if you know what's good for you, you'll back off. Just like Adam warned."

I blink back at him, nerves slicing at my stomach like machetes.

"You *and* that detective douchebag brother you're screwing."

My mouth dries up. Before I can ask why it matters, Travis is ripped away as a dark shadow appears above me. There's a slap, a grunt, followed by a moan. I bite back a scream as the sound of Ben's growls and curses. He sits on Travis, hissing whispered words into his face. Adam hovers over the two, eyes flashing with fear and anger. But he doesn't stop Ben. I'm not sure why. Maybe because, deep down, whatever secrets he's holding for Travis are not secrets he *wants* to be harboring after all. I know right then I need to get Adam alone, out from under his best friend's hold.

Ben stands, panting and hovering over Travis. His fingers are fisted in my ex's shirt as he growls, "Stay. The hell. Away from Becca."

Travis just laughs, even as blood slides down his nose, over his mouth, coating his chin. When he gets to his feet five seconds later, it's me he's looking at, not Ben.

"Stay the hell out of our business, *doll*," he warns, waving a hand between himself and Adam. "Otherwise, you might not like what you find."

Adam's ten or so feet away now, both hands in his hair. Pain and anguish twist his features, but he doesn't take Travis's side *or* leave. He simply stares at me. I want to tell him he's better than this, that Rose did love him, even if only as a friend. But Travis grabs his arm and yanks him away before I'm able to.

Then just as quickly as they got there, the two of them are gone.

And Ben does nothing to stop them.

"Jesus, B. You okay?" He crouches in front of me and set a hand on my knee.

"Don't touch me." I push his hand away, then get to my feet, no longer trusting him either.

His need to be kind to me, his need to have me help him too...? I'm positive, now more than ever, that it's all been a ruse. Something to get him closer to whatever answers he's seeking. Answers I didn't even know there were questions for.

Rose was pregnant.

I squeeze my eyes shut at the thought. The world spins around me at the same time. It's like I'm back in that church, staring at her coffin, yet Rose is sitting beside me, not my dad or mom, and she's laughing, her words on repeat: *I'm a liar. I'm a liar. I'm a liar.*

"Hey, hey. It's okay, it's just me. They're gone," Ben whispers into my ear, taking my hand in his. Our chests touch when he gets me on my feet, and as much as I want to shove him away again, I don't.

"I'm so sorry," he murmurs. "A girl I knew from high school was in there, and she distracted me for five damn minutes. I shouldn't have—"

"Did you know?" I ask, voice steadying, somehow.

He pulls back and frowns. "Did I know what?"

"That"—my throat burns when I swallow—"Rose was pregnant."

He flinches. It's just enough to reaffirm what I already know is true. Ben knew. Which means Ben *very much* kept that information from me on purpose. Lucky for him, I'm too exhausted to ask why.

"Take me home. Now."

Not looking him in the eye, I start toward his truck,

knees nearly too weak to carry me. My soul is weary and spirit broken. I want to go back to bed, lie there forever. I clench my hands while his deceit runs through me. How is it possible that the one person I'm supposed to trust is the one person who'd been hiding the most from me?

"Becca, please. Let me explain." He takes my hand from behind, but I whip it away. We're not doing this anymore.

"You don't get to explain. Or touch me either. Not when you've had over a month to tell me the truth." I grab the door handle, yank. It's locked.

Ben jumps in front of me, his hands on my shoulders. "Please, I'll tell you everything you want to know. I just need to make sure you're okay first. That he didn't hurt you."

I want to say yes, that I'm hurt—that I'm *broken*. I want to tell him I'm ripped into shreds. Like a pack of wolves named Travis, Adam, *and* Ben just tore me limb from limb.

But the words won't come.

My mouth is too dry to let them.

And my heart... God, it hurts. Too much to let me speak.

Ben keeping this from me is like a scissors cutting through my already aching soul, a pair that's too rusted and embedded inside of me already to be pulled out.

I stare at the zipper of his hoodie, tracing the zigzag lines with my gaze. Looking him in the eyes will only hurt me more.

"They didn't touch me," I whisper. "Now please, unlock the truck."

"Thank God." He blows out a slow breath, but does as I ask, opening the door for me.

Once he's in the driver's seat, Ben starts the engine.

He doesn't drive off right away, which really shouldn't surprise me. If there's one thing I hate about Rose's brother, it's his persistence. His stubbornness, most of all.

"Listen, B. I was going to tell you. I swear. But you've been hurting and—"

"Stop it." I sit back, finally looking at his face. Somehow, I've turned off my emotions because when our eyes meet this time, I feel nothing. No anger. No regret. No pain. Just... emptiness. It's how it should be. How it needs to stay until I can process everything I've just learned.

"Please," he begs. "You have to understand. I was going to tell you. You and your mom and dad. I was just trying to find the right time to do it."

"You don't get to decide what hurts us and when."

"Yeah, well, she was *my* sister, so I didn't even have to tell you at all."

My body grows cold. "Screw you."

He drops his forehead to the steering wheel. "Damn it, Becca, I'm not going to say sorry. I can't. Not when I was just trying to protect you." He pauses, takes a deep breath, then drops a new bomb on me that I in no way expect.

"I'm in love with you, all right? So much so that the thought of seeing you in pain physically hurts me." He sits back and slaps himself in the chest. "*That's* why I didn't tell you."

My tears come then, his admission making my stomach compress.

I can't breathe. I can't think. I can't move.

"No."

The streetlight shadows half of his face, but the look in his eyes is of both adoration and regret. They don't match. Kind of like his words. Because Ben doesn't *actually* love me. This is just him trying to find a way to heal.

165

A way to smooth over his mistakes too. Possibly a way to get me on his side again. Ease his conscience.

It won't work.

"Yes." He reaches for my hand, but I pull it away.

"No, Ben. You don't love me." I shake my head. "Love means being honest. Love means not keeping secrets."

"Don't you dare," he hisses. "Don't you God damn *dare* try and pretend I don't know how I feel about you." He leans closer, reaching for my face this time. I let him, but I'm not sure why. I think I hate him though. More than anyone.

"You've always been more than a friend to me, you know that?"

He's lying. They all lie. Ben, Becca, Travis, Adam... Beneath their skin and smiles and fake personas sits liars of the worst kind.

Tonight is not about love confessions, and I won't be distracted. Sweet words won't make deceit any less significant.

"Take me home." Leaning back in my seat, I stare out the front window, tighten my fists around the hem of my skirt.

"That's it?" He laughs. "That's all you're going to say?"

I nod once, then hold my chin high.

I've been tricked into loving someone before. I'm not about to do it again.

THE BELL RANG ALREADY, *signaling the beginning of sixth period. By all rights, I should've been in class, but I'd didn't have my notebook for World Studies. The doors to all the rooms were already locked, and the only people in the halls were the monitors. I showed one of them my hall pass, then headed to my locker around the corner.*

As I turned down C-wing, something caught my eye at my locker. Someone was more like it. A tall, familiar guy I hadn't been expecting to see. Travis.

Arms folded, he leaned back against the metal, flashing an effortless smirk when he spotted me. "Looking for this?" He pulled my green notebook out from behind his back, waving it.

My stomach twisted with what I was seeing, yet I kept my pace steady and walked the rest of the way toward him, stopping just a few feet back. I held my hand out, proud that my voice stayed even. "Give it to me."

"Aww, doll." He laughed. "Don't be like that."

His stupid name, like always, had the self-conscious part of me wanting to straighten my bangs. Still, I was better without him. The best I'd been in a very long time.

"What do you want, Travis?"

"You." He lifted his brows. "Isn't that obvious?"

"Not happening." I wiggled my outstretched fingers. "Now give me. My notebook."

He leaned away from the locker, holding it out. But when I reached for it again, he snatched it back and grabbed my arm instead, holding me against him.

"Stop it," I hissed, struggling to break free.

167

"Kiss me, and I'll give it to you." He licked his lips, eying my mouth.

"No."

He quirked a brow. "You'll be sorry if you tell me no."

I yanked myself out of his hold and hissed. "Go to hell."

The notebook was so not freaking worth it at this point, so I huffed and turned to leave down the hall, back to class, only for him to say, "Bucket list number seventy."

I laid a palm over my belly. On the balls of my feet, I slowly turned back around, eyes narrowing.

Oh god. No.

"Where'd you get that?" And when had Rose added that stupid number seventy back?

"Does it matter?" He tipped his head to one side. "I've never been a bucket list item before though, let alone been part of one." He winked. "And neither has—"

"Shut up." My eyes widened. Not taking the time to second-guess my actions, I leapt forward to try and grab the list from his fingers, but he dropped the notebook and held the single piece of paper above his head now. He'd ripped it out.

"Give it to me." I clawed at his shirt, his neck, panic my driving force.

Rose was going to freaking kill me. My parents would kill me. The school would kill us. The softball coach would kick us off the team. That list was a book of evidence for all the bad stuff we'd done in life.

"You're gonna have to jump a little higher if you really want it."

"Please, Travis." I started to cry, desperate, willing to do anything for it.

"Kiss me, and it's alllll yours." He smiled wider at my tears —getting off on my pain, no doubt. Never had I hated someone more than I did right then.

"Fine. Just give it to me."

He shook his head. "Kiss me first."

168

Bile built in the back of my throat, and the tears fell faster down my face. I wanted to throw up. I also wanted to run—but not before committing murder first. In the end, I did none of those and shut my eyes; held my breath and leaned in closer, pecking his lips. Before I could pull away, he wrapped an arm tight around my waist and yanked me closer, shoving his tongue inside my mouth.

On instinct, I bit down.

"You bitch!" he hollered, releasing the paper.

Ignoring his roar, the opening of a door, and a teacher's voice, I bent over and grabbed the bucket list and notebook both, feeling my heart slow when I had them in my hands.

I turned to run but stopped short at the sight of Travis's frowning dad, who was now coming out of his classroom.

"Travis. What did you do?" He looked at me, concern in his gaze. "Are you all right, Becca? Did my son hurt you?"

My bottom lip trembled, but I knew I needed to stay calm so I could leave without any further issues. "I'm fine." *I sniffed.* "Just allergies."

Leaf scowled at his son from over my shoulder. "Get to class, Travis."

"But she bit—"

"Go!" *Leaf pointed his finger down the hall, gaze softening when he refocused on me.*

"I'm sorry," *I told the guy.* "I just...I needed my notebook, and—"

"It's okay." *He came out into the hallway even farther, leaving his classroom door propped open. He put his hand on my forearm, squeezing a little.* "Did my son hurt you?" *he asked, keeping his voice low.* "If he did, you can tell me."

I shook my head. Travis didn't hurt me physically, but I was irreparably damaged from being with him at all. Still, I said nothing.

Leaf searched my face for something. He didn't look mad.

169

Instead, he seemed, well, confused. "My son is hurting. You broke his heart."

I stiffened.

He pursed his lips and looked to where Travis had gone. "He struggles to understand real-world relationships. Women in general. I think it's because his mom was never in the picture."

And he was telling me this because...?

"I need to get to class," I blurted, uncomfortable.

"Right, yes." He patted my arm—the arm he never let go of. Suddenly, all I could think about was him and Sienna that night of the dance. The two of them so close, and Rose's comments about being "hot for teach". Who really was this man?

"I'll write you a new pass. Hang tight."

Leaf guided me back to his room and did just that. But instead of sending me on my way, he walked out of the room with me and stood there, searching my face like before.

"Look, my son...he means well. And I do believe that he still cares deeply about you too."

"I don't understand what you're trying to say." I took a step back, then another. His vibes, his words...I didn't like them.

"No. I'm sure you don't." Then he turned and went back into his class, leaving me dumbfounded. Not to mention a little disturbed.

10

August
Present Day

AN UNTRUTH. A falsehood. A fib. A fabrication. Those are just a few synonyms for the word *lie*. But the one that seemed to fit the situation when it came to my dead best friend this past week, along with her idiotic brother?

Deception.

It feels wrong to hate your best friend when she's no longer there to defend herself. It also feels wrong to hate the boy who just confessed his love to you too. Real friends don't lie or keep secrets though. And boys who say they love you are supposed to be honest.

That's why this all hurts so much.

I didn't tell my parents about Rose and what I found out. There's no point. Their judgment of her would have been warped like mine and putting them through this with me didn't seem fair.

One thing's for certain now. Something else has

begun to fuel my motivation instead of grief: anger. Instead of leaving this all behind me like I should, I'm now ready to face this entire mystery head on. Not only will I be looking for someone who may—or may not—have been a part of Rose's death but I now need to hunt for a man who might have gotten Rose pregnant—the same someone who could've very well slipped her drugs too.

I needed to talk to Adam again, bottom line. Possibly Rose and Ben's mom too.

There was another matter I had to deal with first though. A *Ben* matter.

I'm still not sure if I believe his words...or if I *want* to. The timing for a love declaration is crappy, that's all I know. Regardless, out of everything I learned the night before, that was the *one* thing to truly keep me awake all night.

Well, that and his fifty million texts begging me to understand and forgive him.

Either way, he's leaving to go back to school in a couple of days, according to his last message. He says he wants to see me at least once more to try and explain things. *Work through this,* is what he said. After I slept on it, I realized he was right on one end: we do need to talk. I'm just not sure about what first.

"I'll be home later," I call from the front door, slipping on my flip-flops. It's Sunday afternoon, and I've barely gotten out of bed today. I want to continue wallowing, but I also don't want my parents to know something's up. They've been through too much.

"Oh? You're leaving so soon? We just got home," Mom says, approaching me. Her dark eyes are sad, the lines beneath them proof that, like me, she isn't sleeping well at night.

"You got home three hours ago," I tell her. "We've

hung out all afternoon." And believe me, I needed it. Mom and Dad's stability—their calm, most of all—are the meds I require for my ailing heart.

"I just figured we could have had dinner together." Mom frowns, brushing hair away from her eyes. "As a family."

"Sorry. I should have told you." I wince. "Sienna and I are going to dinner together."

Her eyes widen with obvious interest. "Sienna from school?"

I haven't hung out with anyone but Ben since the funeral so Mom's likely thinking I'm finally on the emotional road recovery. Too bad for her, I feel like I'm spiraling all over again. Just in a different direction.

"Yep," I say with a little too much pep.

Mom pulls a fifty from her purse hanging by the door, then presses it into my hand. "Buy yourself dessert. Then keep the change, maybe get yourself a new shirt from the mall if you go anywhere else afterward."

"Oh, um, thanks, Mom."

Five minutes later, I'm out the door and heading toward Sienna's flashy car. It's bubble-gum pink, special ordered, and I feel like I'm about ready to jump into a hot air balloon, not a vehicle. Either way, I have to play nice. Other than confronting Adam or Travis again— something I'm *not* excited about—she's my final link to Rose.

According to her Instagram, Sienna was at the bonfire the night of Rose's death. I was hoping she may have seen or noticed something when it came to my best friend. If she left with anyone or hung out with someone beside Adam and Travis, maybe.

My stomach knots as I slide into Sienna's car.

"Hey, girl. It's so good to see you. I'm suuuuper glad you called," Sienna says, bouncing a little in her seat.

"You, too." I throw her a small smile, wishing I felt the same.

"I'm honestly surprised you did though." She looks over her shoulder and starts backing out of the driveway.

I put on my seatbelt, deciding just to dive right in. "Yeah, I, um, was hoping we could talk about something."

"What's that?"

"The night of Rose's death."

She doesn't respond right away, but the purse of her lips tells me she's not too interested in my request. I'm probably going about this all wrong, but I feel like I'm running out of time for some reason.

"What do you want to know?" Sienna juts her chin out once we're on the main road, the corner of her right eye twitching. "The police already questioned me. And it's not like she *died* at the actual party or anything." She huffs.

"Are you..." I squint at her. "Are you seriously mad right now?"

"I'm *mad* that you only invited me out to talk about Rose's death. You know I was never really a fan of hers."

But she was at the funeral. She *cried* at the funeral. I don't say this though. If she's got secrets, I have to play my cards right.

"That's not true." I reach over and squeeze her arm. "I've missed hanging out with you. You're the first person I've called since the funeral."

"Really?" Her shoulders slump, and she pushes out her bottom lip into a pout she probably thinks is cute.

"Yes. Really."

She exhales, flipping her brown bob. "Well, I'm sorry for being rude. It's just that I'm over the whole ordeal, you know? Rose was never nice to me. You know she accused me of sleeping with our English teacher?"

My lips part as I play it cool. I saw her the night of the winter formal. That was not a normal student-teacher interaction. "She did?"

"Yep. And that kind of accusation really hurts, you know? Especially since I've tried so to be a friend to everyone, including her."

"Wow, I had no idea."

"It's fine." She rolls her eyes.

I hesitate, nervous on how to proceed, deciding to just go for it in the end.

"I'm sorry, I just...I really need to fill some holes. And since you were there the night of her death, I'm hoping you can help me fill them. You know, for peace of mind."

I'm an Academy Award–winning actress right then. Thankfully, she plays into my part.

"Fine." She sighs. "What exactly do you want to know?"

I take a deep breath, hold it for a second longer. "What was she like that night? Do you remember?"

She seems to think about her answer, turning on her blinker before heading down the road that leads us into Winston and away from the farm. The corn stalks grow taller, keeping us closed in as we drive, while the sun's just starting to lower in the sky.

"I was with my boyfriend mostly that night. And I never actually talked to Rose, unless I was with you." She pinches her lips together before she says, "I do know that she was with Adam for a minute. And I think she was crying. And I'm also pretty sure he was yelling at her." She shrugs. "I didn't see her after that."

I knew all this, of course, aside from the yelling part. "Do you know what Adam said to her exactly?"

"Nope."

My shoulders slump. Yet another dead end. Now, sadly, I have to spend the next few hours with a girl that does nothing but talk about her boyfriend, hair products, and which filter is best for certain hours of the day for photo shoots.

Still, the lie about Leaf and the dance...something about that doesn't settle with me. Maybe she was lying because she had a crush and didn't want anyone—especially her boyfriend—to know about it. It makes sense.

Like I knew she would, Sienna begins to chat about colleges, where she's wanting to go and how her boyfriend is joining the Marines. A minute later, she's onto where to take the best pictures in eastern Iowa, about a field of sunflowers that's not too far from Winston.

I look out the window, bored out of my damn mind. I would much rather discuss softball or baseball to this. But she's not Rose. She's Sienna.

"Becca?"

"Hmm?"

Sienna hesitates long enough that I look at her. She chews on her bottom lip for a second, then releases an audible breath. "I really am sorry for getting snappy with you. I didn't mean to be rude. It's just been a rough, few weeks, what with Alex going to boot camp."

"It's okay." I smile, meaning it this time.

AFTER DINNER, I'm not ready to go home yet. But at the same time, things with Sienna feel awkward, so I ask her to take me to Ben's house—not that I *actually* want to go there. It's inevitable that he and I meet. And I think I've calmed down enough to hear him out. I kinda want to see if I can get Ginger alone too. Maybe talk about what drugs were in Rose's system. If she'll tell me, that is. Ben, as far as I know, has yet to find out. Or he's lying again.

Ben's car is in the driveway when I get there. Ginger's truck too. The lights are all on in the house, signaling they're both here, which is rare.

After saying my goodbyes to Sienna, I make my way to the front door, palms already damp with sweat. In the past, I would've just walked right inside and made myself at home, but everything is different now.

For the first time in ten years, I lift my hand to knock.

Only...I can't do it.

It feels wrong.

So, I lean my forehead against the door instead and try to check my emotions.

This will be the first time I've been in Rose's house since she died. Naturally it's going to be hard. That doesn't stop my heart from throbbing at the thought of seeing her empty room without her in it.

I'm not prepared. I never will be.

The front door flies open, and I lurch forward, caught by the hands of Ginger. Her eyes widen, and I can smell the alcohol on her breath already.

"Becca, honey? You okay?" She squeezes my elbows and helps me stand upright. She looks nothing like Rose, except for the eyes. Her hair is dark, her skin tan. Rose and Ben's father was never in the picture, but I'm assuming they got their fair complexion and light hair from him.

"Yeah, fine." I bite my lip, take a deep breath before I say, "I'm actually looking for Ben. Is he here?"

Her gaze softens. "Yes. But he's been staying in his loft apartment above the garage since...you know."

"Yeah." My throat burns, as does my nose. I will not cry. Not yet.

Instead, I glance over my shoulder toward the tiny, rundown garage, the light in the window at the top just barely lit. It sits to the left of their home, which has definitely seen better days. Pieces of siding are missing, overgrown grass stands to my knees, and untrimmed bushes line the front of the house to my right.

Ginger hesitates, studying me. "Would you like to come in and wait? I'm on my way out and can run over and tell him you're here, if you'd like."

"Sure, that'll be great. Thanks." Still, I can't bring myself to move.

"Is there something else?" She cocks her head to one side.

Ask her, damn it. I open my mouth to do just that, but a voice sounds from behind me.

"Becca?"

I shut my eyes as footfalls close in on us.

"Hey. What're you doing here?"

I turn to face him, watching Ginger slide by me and head to her car. Her purse is on her shoulder, and she hikes it up even higher, giving Ben a cheek kiss before she leaves.

When we're alone, Ben searches my face under the porch light a moment later, his gaze hesitant, but hopeful. "You okay? Something wrong?"

I glance at his mom's car, watching it pull away. "Where's she going?"

"Don't know, don't care."

"She's been drinking."

He swallows, looks to the ground at the same time. He knows this, yet he lets her go. I'm not sure what that says about him, but at the same time, I don't blame the guy either.

I point to the door of the house. "Can we, um, talk?"

His eyes meet mine, and I hate how my body warms from the intensity there. It doesn't matter. I refuse to get distracted by his pretty-boy face when it'll only distract me.

"Yeah. Okay. Sure."

We make our way inside, then into the living room. I brace myself to look around, and my breath catches with what I see. Or, should I say, what I *don't* see.

Sparse, white walls meet my gaze, and I press a hand over my mouth to stifle my gasp. Everything Rose is gone. Her pictures, her decorations...even the succulents she loved to put on the bookshelves. It's like Ginger has completely ripped away her daughter's memory.

Above the couch there was once a family portrait of Rose, Ben, and their mom. But even that's gone now too. All that remains is a sofa, a table, a chair, and a TV.

"W-what happened?" I ask.

Ben moves in beside me. "Mom's new boyfriend's moving in." He shrugs. "Apparently, she wants to redecorate so he doesn't get *freaked out* or something by the ghost of my sister. Who knows? I didn't ask because this hasn't been my house for a long time."

I look at him, eyes narrowing. "*Leaf* is moving in?"

Ben's brows furrow. "How do you know the guy?"

"He's a teacher at the school, and.. " I gulp, looking at the floor. "He's Travis's father."

"You're messing with me."

I jerk my head back. "You didn't know?"

"I've never met the guy. Mom barely mentioned him, other than saying he's moving in." He frowns. "How'd you find out they were dating?"

"She was with him at my house last weekend after you dropped me off and left."

Ben stays quiet, thoughtful, even. Now's the perfect time to change the subject, even if the alternate makes me more uncomfortable.

"We need to talk," I say.

"Yeah, sure." He motions for me to follow him into the kitchen with the tip of his chin. "Let's do it in here though."

In the small square space, I watch from the door frame as Ben leans over into the fridge and yanks out a box of cold pizza. Wordless, he sets it on the table, avoiding my eyes. I can tell he's nervous.

"Ben?" I set my hand on his arm. "Please. Just...sit for a second?"

He yanks a chair from the table, points at it, then at me. "If I sit, then you've gotta sit too."

I do, taking the stool next to him. We reach over in unison, both grabbing for the same slice of pizza. Our elbows bump, then our eyes meet. He grins at me, which makes my face go hot, but I'm not sure exactly what he's trying to say with his eyes either.

Instead of figuring it out, I grab the slice next to that one, then bite into it at the same time he does his. The second the spicy sausage begins to battle with my taste buds, though, I can't help but moan. Ben's currently got the key to my stomach here, and I'm pretty sure he knows it too. Cold pizza is to me what diamonds are to most girls: pure, unadulterated treasures.

"Hungry?" he lifts a brow.

"Starved, actually," I say, around another bite. "I went to dinner with my friend Sienna tonight. She wanted sushi and I *hate* sushi."

He nods. "Rose hated that crap too."

"I'm aware." I laugh a little, remembering the first time she tried it, then puked it all back up into her glass of soda. "That's just one of the fifty million reasons why she was my best friend."

His face falls a little. Talking in the past tense about his sister isn't something either of us have really done yet. It feels so final.

Clearing his throat, Ben reaches over the table and grabs two bottles of water, handing me one, then keeping the other. I fiddle with the label once it's in my hand, chewing my food until I can think of what else to say.

"So, about last night..."

"Which part?" he manages.

I hesitate, then blow out a slow breath. "All of it, actually."

He hums to himself, finishing his pizza. My heart races the entire time, and when he's down to his last bite, I'm ready to scream.

I hate how he's tossing and turning my question around in his mind. It's unnerving. I look at my empty plate, wishing for a teleportation device to get myself out of here. He's the one who started this, now he's taking his dear sweet time to explain.

"Becca." Fingers graze my chin, lifting my head up, then pulling it around so I'm facing him. My breath catches when Ben's gaze bores into mine, and my stomach leaps with those slimy fish again.

"Yeah?"

"I meant what I said last night."

I wait a beat, lick my dry lips, then ask the question which I already know the answer to. "What did you say, exactly?"

He shakes his head, smiles a little, then lets his finger fall from my chin. "If I recall, I *said* that I'm in love with you."

"Oh yeah. That." I swallow hard, his confession even more powerful than last night—so much so that goose-bumps scatter across my arms. Now that I'm not so consumed with the bombshell about Rose's pregnancy, I can truly *feel* his genuineness. It terrifies me.

"I'm surprised you didn't know, honestly." He runs his fingers through his mop of hair.

I blink. Then blink again. "I-I don't understand. You're in college, and I'm..." I look down at myself, my roly-poly stomach, the thickness of my thighs. "Me." I'm normally not the body-conscious type but being around Ben has always left me feeling subpar.

"Bullshit." He turns in his chair to face me, then moves my chair around to do the same. We're knee-to-knee, but he doesn't make a move to touch me otherwise. "You're everything, Becca. Y-you're funny and smart and witty and..." His eyes nearly twinkle as he finishes, "so damn beautiful it hurts."

My heart beats faster, yet my words come slow and singular. "Really?"

"God yes. I've been crazy about you for years. Yet you were too stubborn to notice."

Words don't come. I can't find them, no matter how hard I try to drag them from my brain. How is it that I'm so suckered into his declaration now when just hours before I was sure he'd been lying last night to distract me from being mad at him for keeping secrets about Rose? Either he's really that good of a conniver or he's actually being truthful.

"Talk to me," he says. "Not knowing what you're thinking is driving me mad."

"I...I don't know what *to* say." For so many years, I've had such strong feelings for him. And if I'm being honest with myself, I'm not sure they ever went away. But do I love Ben? Or am I latching on to him because of my desperation to have his sister in my life somehow?

Seconds later he moves in closer, pressing a hand to my cheek. "I'm sorry for not telling you about Rose."

I shut my eyes at the weight of his words, while my

skin prickles from his thumb rubbing across my chin. It's a sweet spot that he seems to know too well.

"Please believe me that I was only trying to keep your heart safe."

I blink my eyes open at that. *"I'm* in charge of my heart, Ben. Not you."

He nods, moving even closer. I part my knees to let one of his in between, and my body melts the second I feel him there.

"Do you believe me though?" he whispers, sliding his hand into the back of my hair. Our foreheads touch, and my mind blanks out, while my breaths quicken.

"I don't know." I'm confused, not sure what he wants me to say either because this isn't what I was expecting. Fifteen-year-old me is totally fist pumping over the revelation that her crush is actually into her; almost-eighteen-year-old me isn't so easily swayed now.

Even though I want to believe him, a part of me still waits for him to move, to laugh and say he's joking because that's what we do, him and I. We joke. We banter. We flirt in our own weird way, and that's it. We don't feel real feelings for each other. And we definitely don't fall in love.

But Ben does none of those things.

And neither do I.

Instead, he leans even closer and does the very last thing I ever expected him to do.

He kisses me.

"I SERIOUSLY DON'T THINK this is necessary," Rose sighed and laid back on my bed, yawning as she folded her hands behind her neck.

"Of course, it's necessary." I spread our bucket list flat on the bed, lovingly rubbing the crumpled surface. "I don't think you realize what might happen if anyone ever got their hands on this." It was bad enough Travis had. But the thought of my parents, a teacher, or even our coach finding it was too reckless for me.

Rose yawned again, then shrugged, which spurred my next question. I felt more like her mom more than her best friend. "Did you make a doctor's appointment yet?" I asked.

"My mom did, surprisingly."

"When do you go?"

"Friday morning."

"Good." I studied her a minute longer, watching as she struggled to stay awake. It was seven o'clock on a Tuesday night, yet she looked like she hadn't slept for weeks. "I bet you have mono."

"Maybe. I did have strep not long ago—don't they, like, go together?"

"No clue."

She opened one eye to look at me, her lips curling in that mischievous, adorable way that only Rose could pull off. "I've got an idea."

"What's that?" I asked.

"Let's write one last list down, something simple, then burn it? You know, for old times' sake?"

I hesitated, looking at the numbers—the memories; the simple tasks; the regretful ones, most of all. "Do you?"

"Kind of?" She pushed herself up, more awake now it seemed. "I still hate the fact that half of these aren't checked off."

I nodded, looking some of them over. The ones that made me smile. Ones we'd undoubtedly do together.

#21. Bungee jump.

#33. Fish in the Gulf of Mexico.

#47. Get a tattoo.

#54. Ride a subway train.

At the same time, I ran my finger over the things that I didn't want to be added back on. Things I'd say hell no to if she even thought about re-writing them down. I was all for letting my friend go wild, but if it meant jail time, I'd put my damn foot down.

#42. Streak in college.

#55. Steal something huge.

#75. Sleep with the forbidden.

"How about this: we start a new list but keep it PG, that way if it gets in the wrong hands, we won't be going to prison."

"You're no fun." She stuck her tongue out, but I knew the second I pulled out two fresh sheets of paper and a couple of pens, she was relenting because she didn't hesitate to start writing stuff down.

This time, I'd be pickier. Do little things that might not have meant a lot to others but would to me. I tapped the pen against my lips.

"How many should we start with?" Rose wrote furiously, gaze never leaving her paper.

"Four? Five? Simple and easy."

"Yeah, okay. I can do that."

Since there were only two things left on the old list that I was truly passionate about, I decided to write them down first, then add two new ones. This time when I signed my name at the bottom, I felt no shame.

#1. Go to Paris

#2. Adopt a puppy.

#3. Dance in the rain.

#4. Kiss someone I'm actually in love with.

"Done," Rose said just seconds before me.

A minute later, we swapped papers so we could see what the other wrote. When I looked down at Rose's list, my smile grew wide, to the point where my cheeks hurt. Her list was so...so normal.

#1. Get married.

#2. Have a baby.

#3. Become a teacher.

#4. Make sure Ben is always happy.

"You're serious about all these?" I looked up at her, warmth in my chest. "You're not messing with me?"

"Well, I'm not, not-serious, if you know what I mean." Her cheeks pinkened with her admission.

Having real goals embarrassed her, apparently. But her maturity made me so freaking proud.

"If you tell anyone, I swear to God, Becca, I'll punch you in the boob."

"Shut up." I shoved her shoulder. "You know I wouldn't dream of risking your badass reputation by sharing with the world how amazing you can be."

We looked at each other, stoic faces...until we busted up laughing. Nothing about what I said was even that funny, but it felt good to be goofy, like our cares and worries, any bad and good that might've lingered in us, washed away with the sound of our giggles. In a way, this felt like a new beginning: Rose and me ready to tackle our senior year in four months, only to maybe, just maybe, tackle our new bucket list after graduation.

"You ready?" she asked, pointing at the old list. The one

that seemed so meaningless now, even though the memories would never really go away.

"Absolutely." I pulled out matches from my pocket, then reached over to my nightstand for the bowl of water sitting there.

"You do the honors," I said, holding up the list.

She grinned and took the matches from me, striking one, then lighting our old list on fire.

Together, wearing super-stupid grins, we watched it burn until it was too hot to touch. I dropped it into the bowl of water, barely able to make out the words of our past as they disappeared before our eyes.

11

August
Present Day

I'M NOT sure what drives me to do it, but soon I'm crawling onto Ben's lap, straddling him. His fingers drive into the mess of pink hair on my head, digging into my scalp. My insides are on fire, sizzling in my stomach. Between my legs, too, in a way that I've never felt before.

It's terrifying.

It's exhilarating.

It's electric.

It's everything I've been missing.

#4. Kiss someone you're in love with.

I squeeze my eyes shut tighter at the thought of my number four, refusing to believe what might have always been true.

I'm in love with Ben. Always have been. Probably always will be in some way.

With that thought spurring me on, I let myself go,

despite the uncertainties. Regrets aren't right when everything feels as it should be. And this? This feels more real than anything I've ever experienced.

Ben's hands glide under my shirt, graze my skin like I'm his treasure. He spans them across my ribs, hesitates, before pushing them around to my back. Fingers on my spine, he deepens the kiss, squeezing me closer. His touch is searing, makes my head spin too. I'm on fire, Ben's the match, and the space between us obliterated and ready to spur on the flames.

Only then does he slip his tongue between my lips, and that's enough to make me die. He's an expert, gentle yet firm, and the moan in my throat rises before I can stop it.

Lust, greed, and the need for a boy-turned-man who's supposed to be a liar but is now my best kiss ever makes me crazy as I grab the back of his head, tangle my fingers deeper into his hair. Ben smiles against my lips, but I'm too frantic for sweet when he tries to take it slower. I need more, otherwise I might never feel like this again.

"God. I've wanted to do this for so long," Ben manages between breaths. The anguish in his voice is enough to make me pause. When I try to pull back to look into his eyes, he won't let me go. Instead, he tangles one hand into my hair, angling my head just right, while he uses his other hand to squeeze my hip. It's like he's afraid I'm going to disappear.

I deepen the kiss, and our teeth clink together. It's messy and rushed, but it also doesn't matter because this is Ben and me. *Finally*, I think to myself.

Desperation has me grasping at the back of his shirt and tugging. "Skin," I say, needing to feel it against me.

He shudders but obliges, barely breaking apart from me to do so, only to return the favor and slide my shirt up too. It's magical, this feeling of flesh on flesh, and I wonder how it's possible that I've never felt this good before. It's like I've woken up from a long sleep. Like I'm living for the first time.

My heart races.

My belly twists.

He reaches beneath me, his hands under my butt, and soon he's picking me up, carrying me somewhere that's not the hard stool. I wrap my legs around his waist, head falling back enough that his lips are on my neck. He carries me into his living room, then finds my mouth again, his warm breath tasting like cheese, and as awful as it sounds, it's not.

I'm pretty sure I'll never look at pizza the same way again.

Our bodies stay latched, our kisses never cease. We're getting the hang of it now, slow, careful, nipping and sucking... I could kiss this guy for hours and never get tired.

With ease, he lowers me onto my back against his couch, taking his time to look me over when he finally lifts his head. His stare lingers on certain parts of my body, and when he does, his chest rises and falls almost quicker than my own. I don't know what he's thinking, but I want to. Except I'm afraid he'll stop this if I do. In the end, I let my emotions go and lead with my body, hoping he understands.

I pull him down on top of me, and our lips touch again. This time, the kiss is softer, sweeter, and I like it just as much. It really does feel as though he's been waiting for this moment his entire life, just like he said. My heart beats even faster, practically going into over-drive. I don't know what to do now that I have him against me, but I do know I don't want to stop. Not ever.

The room around us is quiet, other than the sound of

our lips touching, the blood rushing through my ears. I moan a little more when he does this thing with his hips against mine, rubbing and arching and grinding and...

God, it feels so good.

I grab at the back of his bare shoulder, needing him to do it again, only this time it's Ben's grumbles that fill the room. I thrive on the idea that he's loving this just as much as I am.

Our kisses deepen—battle, even. Taking, giving, needing things I didn't understand before but silently adore and desire. Ben feels so right, so protective, even. It's as though he's actually mine and I'm his, and this whole thing between us is meant to be. Like Rose died so the two of us could find each other and...

"No." I gasp at the thought and push him back by the shoulders. "We can't do this."

I roll off the couch from beneath him and land on my knees, my back to his front. There must be something wrong with me. It's not normal to think thoughts like this.

God, you two just need to screw already and be done with it.

I shudder at the memory of Rose's voice, not bothering to wipe the tears when they fall. This...can't happen. Ben and I are too emotionally raw, and there're too many what-ifs at stakes. Most of all, I refuse to think that losing Rose wasn't an accident or a tragedy but some sort of life purpose instead.

"Becca?" Ben sits down on the floor behind me, his hand on my shoulder. "Are you okay? Did I do something wrong?"

I squeeze my eyes shut, torn. That's the thing. Ben did everything so right. He's good. He's nothing like I ever assumed. But if he knew what I thought just now...

"You lied to me," I blurt, no real plan as I do.

191

"I'm not sure what you mean." He shifts to face me, but I can't look at him.

I push his hand away when he tries to take mine and stand. I'm a freak. An abnormality.

"Y-you didn't tell me about Rose being pregnant."

"You're kidding." He scoffs. "I...I thought we were past that."

"Nooo. Not past it. Just because I kissed you doesn't mean I forgive you." I move to the kitchen, grab my shirt, and tug it back on.

"Forgive me?" He laughs from the floor. "Jesus, Becca. I told you I was going to tell you in my own time."

"Yeah, well, I'm a grudge holder. Sue me." I need to push him away. Need to figure out what I'm doing. What I want. And most of all, I need to be of sound mind, not grieving.

He's silent then. To the point where I wonder if he's still here. Because I'm a masochist, I turn to see he's, in fact, still in the same place. His head is bowed, hands on his face. His shoulders are shaking, and...

I blink.

Oh God. He's crying.

Heart in my throat, I rush back over, sitting beside him again.

"Hey," I whisper. "It's okay." I touch his knee, holding it there. "Don't cry. I'm sorry. We'll figure this out together, I promise."

When his hands fall away, he looks at me...but his eyes are dry. And he's—

"Are you seriously *smiling*?" I yank my hand off his knee.

"If I don't smile," he growls through gritted teeth, "then I'm gonna yell. And I don't want to yell at you because I *love* you."

I flinch but don't look away. "You're the one who's yell—"

"Just stop." He stands, shakes his head as he does, then walks over to the front window that looks out over his driveway, elbows on the window ledge. "Maybe you should go. I can't deal with this right now."

I shoot to my feet, anger licking its way up and into my throat. "You can't deal with *what* exactly?"

"Your whiplash." He faces me, his eyes wet for real this time. "You push me away. You pull me back in. You kiss me, then you pretend I'm a villain."

"You don't get to be mad at me for being confused. Especially since I thought you hated me." I huff, nowhere near done. "Then you lie to me about Rose being pregnant yet expect for me to forget about it and, what, just *be* with you?"

"You didn't act like it was such a chore when you climbed on my lap." He folds his arms, words slicing through me like a knife.

"Screw you, Ben." I turn to leave, but he grabs me by the back of my shirt, his body pressed to my back.

He groans and drops his forehead to my shoulder, his words a desperate whisper that have me wringing my hands together. "I get it." he squeezes my waist with one hand. "You're scared. Hell, you've *always* been scared. Of me, of letting go of Rose. Of dealing with your grief by finding out what *really* happened to her. But I'm not the enemy, B."

"No." I shut my eyes and blow out a slow breath. "You're not the enemy. But you're acting like an ass, and I don't deserve to be treated this way."

And with that, I pull away, yank my phone out, and shoot Mom a quick text, asking her to pick me up. I'm sure she'll have a million questions for me when she gets

193

here, but this is the only option I can stomach because getting a ride home from Ben won't work.

"Becca, please. Don't go." His voice cracks as he follows me across the room. "I'm sorry. Everything is coming out wrong, and I don't mean the things I say. I just... I'm a mess."

"Yeah. You're not the only one."

I slip into my slides by the front door. I've got another twenty minutes or so before Mom gets here but staying inside this house is killing me.

Seconds later, Ben's behind me again. Only this time, he keeps his distance. "I'm sorry," he tells me. "I didn't mean to be a jerk."

"Whatever. It's fine." And a huge lie because, honestly, making out with Ben should *not* make me feel the way it just did when it comes to Rose. Which is why I'm as much in the wrong here as he is. It's just easier to place blame on him than myself. Getting attached, only for him to leave, is going to make this all so much worse.

"It's not fine." He tugs me around, lifts my face with a finger beneath my chin. "You're upset and I said things I shouldn't have." He squeezes his eyes shut. "I'm *always* screwing up with you."

I want to tell him that he's not in the wrong. How *I'm* the one who's screwing up for thinking what I did, for continuing to bring up Rose's memory—her pregnancy too—when really, I don't even have a right to know the entire truth. She was my best friend, yes. But she wasn't blood. And despite the years we spent together, I know I'm only allowed so much when it comes to the secrets she kept, even if it kills me.

"It's fine," I say, my shoulders slumping.

"You can't lie to me, you know." He traces a spot next to my left eye with his finger. "You get this cute little twitch right here when you do."

194

I open my mouth to go off on him, but something else comes to me instead—the need for a truth that he can *actually* give me. One I'm owed after almost years of wondering.

"I tried kissing you that night in your kitchen two years ago, but you turned away. Why?"

He shrugs one shoulder. "You were fifteen."

"It's not like it would've been illegal."

"I know." He searches my face, his eyes a little sad now. "That's the night I realized I liked you. A hell of a lot, actually. I thought you were cute and would've been fun to make out with especially, but I wasn't ready to be what you deserved. Not then."

"Oh."

"I'm sorry if I hurt your feelings, B. I was just trying to be good."

"It's alright," I say.

I've always had it bad for Ben McCain, even when I was fierce to deny it. For as long as I can remember, I doodled tiny hearts with his name inside of them, only to scratch them out seconds later. Everything's happening so quickly, and it's an emotional overload. What I need is to focus on one thing, and that's figuring out what *really* happened to Rose. Who the baby's father was most of all. It's weird how quickly my priorities in life change. Especially when being with Ben, forgoing everything else in our life, is exactly what I would've wanted just a month ago. Not Ben necessarily but the ability to move on once and for all from losing Rose.

His face falls. "You don't believe me, do you?"

"I do." I swallow a lump in my throat.

"But...?" he asks, a pang of fear in that one word.

I take a breath, release it slowly. "It's just that we're two different people who share a common goal, right

195

now. And that goal shouldn't necessarily include kissing."

Even as I say it, there's a pang in my chest because, *God*...the kissing is soooo good. So much so that my chest burns from the denial I need to make, despite knowing it's the right thing for us. Ben is the only good link I have left to Rose, even if he's not being honest all the time. Losing him over a failed relationship or something as simple as a make-out session between us can't happen. Not right now, at least.

"So, that's a no then. About us?"

Before I can clarify—how I'm not dismissing the idea of *us* in the future—a car pulls into his driveway outside, distracting us. Ben looks over my shoulder, and his scowl deepens.

"It's probably my mom," I say.

He doesn't reply. Just cracks the door open in time for the both of us to see Ginger stepping out of her car.

"Why's she back already?" I hear Ben ask as he starts her way.

Fast words are exchanged between the pair when they meet at the bumper of her car. Then before I can make it out the door, Ben's kicking the side of his mother's truck.

I close the distance between me and them, confused.

"Oh, Becca," Ginger looks to me, sobbing now. Her eyes are swollen. I can tell, even in the dark. It's like she's been crying for hours. My bottom lip starts quivering, yet I don't even know what's wrong yet.

"What's happening? Is it my mom? Dad?"

"No." She shakes her head. "That's not it at all."

"Then what is it?" I rub a hand across my neck, praying my knees hold me steady. Ben crouches to the ground when I look his way, hands tucked behind his neck, not answering.

196

"They arrested someone in connection to Rose's death."

My dry lips part. "B-but I thought the case was closed?"

"It was until Adam Martin came forward."

I cover my mouth with both hands. "What did he say?"

"H-he admits to being the father of her child..." Ginger chokes, a hand to her throat. "And then confessed to drugging her the night of her death."

12

August
Present Day

IT's 4:45 in the morning, yet I haven't slept but for maybe an hour all night. Every bump in my mattress keeps me from getting comfortable, along with the thoughts running through my mind. I roll from my side to my back to my other side, stopping just long enough to stare out my window, my door, my floor... I'd do anything to relax long enough to fall asleep. But last night's revelations have given me enough anxiety to stay awake for days, maybe even weeks.

Everything feels too easy as far as Adam's confession goes. Yes, I *want* this to be the answer Ben and I have been searching for, only so we can finally begin to move on. But what if knowing still doesn't ease the heartache?

With a sigh, I pull my phone out and type a message to Ben, desperate to talk, but scared of where we stand now. Either way, I type up a message I won't be sending, just to try and slow my rushing thoughts.

I'm sorry.

I do want to be with you.

I'm just scared.

Send is never hit...but *Delete* isn't either.

Instead, I click off my phone and set it on the bed by my side. This isn't something to talk about via text, and it should also be the last thing I'm thinking of right now.

Adam drugged Rose.

Rose is still dead.

DARK SHADOWS REFLECT from the giant willow tree outside, dancing along my walls and drawing my gaze like night-growing flowers. I blink, slowly sitting up as they hit the roof of the porch outside. Rain echoes lightly against the glass of the window as well, tapping a rhythmic beat against the siding.

Not thinking, I reach into my drawer and pull out my new bucket list, heart racing as I trace over my finger over the darkened number three: *Dance in the rain.*

I shiver when the wind picks up, stirring the trees' limbs and branches even more. I swear it's Rose, ordering me to go outside. To do this for her.

Despite everything, this could be the start of a new beginning. And even though my best friend is gone, I refuse to let our new dreams go away with her.

Sliding my feet over the side of the bed, I click on my light, stand, and grab my slides before heading out into the hall. I tiptoe past my parents' room, even though there's no real need. Dad snores so loud it shakes the house, and Mom sleeps like the dead and snores almost just as badly.

In the kitchen, I don't bother grabbing the umbrella

by the back door. What's the point when there's a bucket list item that needs to be checked off? Unlike the last time when I went out into the rain, I'm not crying. I'm breathing. Living. Wondering what's next. I'm so oblivious to the world around me that when I step out onto the porch, then the gravel drive, I don't see the shadow...until the shadow sees me.

Until the shadow strikes my head from behind.

———

FINGERS TOUCH MY FACE, the voice above me low and fearful. Ben is here.

Why are you here?

"Becca, damn it, wake up, please."

I blink, but my eyes won't stay open. I'm too weak. So tired. The heat of the early morning sun caresses my exposed skin, while my damp clothing clings to my body. My shoes are off. My favorite slides. The ones I put on after we won State last year.

I need them.

The words stick in my throat, and I groan instead.

Gravel is stuck to my cheek, my skin; the throbbing in my head reminds me I was struck, as does the still dripping blood falling over my temples. It's so warm.

Arms wrap around me, picking me up. I manage to inhale, catch the faint smell of Ben's cologne. Why is he here? He curses, almost trips as he walks up my driveway.

Thud, thump, thud, thump.

"Mr. and Mrs. Thompson! Help!" he yells.

And that's the last thing I remember before shutting my eyes again.

———

THIS TIME WHEN I WAKE, I'm in a soft bed. Unnatural lights shine above me, and I want to lift my arm to cover my eyes but it's easier just to keep them shut than move.

I'm weak. And so tired.

There's a beep, a gushing of liquid too. Is that a heart monitor I hear? I remember that sound from when Rose broke her leg when she was eleven after sliding into home during a game.

We won! she'd said. *All because of me, of course.*

She was so freaking cocky, just like her brother.

"Becca?" Mom's cold hands touch my face, and I lean into them, automatically opening my eyes. She looks awful. Bloodshot eyes and pale cheeks...

"Hey," I manage, only then taking a second to look around. Indeed, I am in a hospital.

Dad's there next, taking my hand in his. "You scared the hell out of us, sunshine."

"Water?" I ask.

Mom orders Dad to go get a glass. Once he's gone from the room, she helps me sit up, fluffing my pillow at the same time. My head throbs, but otherwise, I'm okay.

"Where's Ben?"

Mom takes a seat in the chair next to my bed but won't let go of my hand. "The waiting room. He's been here all morning."

I frown, looking for a clock. "What time is it?"

"Almost noon."

I cringe when the throbbing moves from the middle of my head to my temples.

"Do you remember what happened?"

I squint. "Something hit me from behind. I blacked out. Then I woke up when Ben got there for a little bit, but that's all I remember." I pause, letting that all sink in. Someone attacked me. Someone—possibly—tried to *kill* me.

"What time did Ben find me?" I ask.

"Around six. Dad and I were just getting up, and Ben was coming to work one more day on the farm since he's leaving tomorrow." Mom sighs, continuing on about how scared she's been, how she doesn't understand why I was out there. She talks about how I have a concussion, agreeing with Dad when he says things could've been much worse. I think she even calls me stupid at one point, asking if I have a death wish for going outside in the middle of the night like that.

"Who could've done this to you?" She rubs at her own temples, like she can feel my pain.

"I don't know."

An image of Travis flashes through my mind. His warning from Saturday night, not that I actually saw him. Not that he has any *reason* to hurt me at all, other than the fact that his best friend is currently sitting in jail. Still, that doesn't leave me with many options, unless it was random.

"The police will be stopping by soon to take a report," Mom tells me. "I'm worried this wasn't just a one-time incident."

She isn't the only one.

"Can I go home today?" I ask.

Mom squeezes my shoulder. "Absolutely."

A soft knock sounds on the door frame. I look, and my heartbeat kicks up enough that my monitor takes notice. Ben's standing there, looking like he's seconds from passing out. His face is paler than normal, and the shadows under his blue eyes are even worse than my mom's.

Still, he smiles. A soft smile that says, *Hi. I'm so glad you're okay.*

And just like that, I know what I have to do. What I

202

need, most of all. Screw fearing the future when tomorrow isn't even promised.

Mom clicks her tongue against the roof of her mouth, and my cheeks warm when I look at her. Her lips pull down into a confused frown, and she stares between us. I wonder if she's putting two and two together. Still, she doesn't say anything.

"I'm going to go check on your dad and see what's taking him so long with that water." She stands, tips her chin in greeting at Ben, then leaves the room.

I open my mouth to speak, but a nurse comes in and takes my vitals in that exact minute. Ben's still there, moving closer, tentatively so. I feel his gaze on me when he takes a seat at the end of the bed. It's unnerving—yet comforting too. I'm glad he's here. I'm also glad he found me when he did.

Once the nurse leaves the room, and it's obvious my mom and dad are staying away, I pat the side of the bed, inviting him to move closer. I could still really use that water, but I need this more.

"How are you feeling?" His Adam's apple bobs as he swallows. I can tell he's nervous.

"Like I got hit upside the head with something," I say.

Ben shakes his head, sitting next to me now. "I hate this, B. I should've been there."

I lift my brows, though it hurts my head. "You wouldn't have known."

"No," he says. "But I slept in. Hit the alarm twice. I was supposed to be at the farm at four. Except it started to rain, and your dad said if it rained that I didn't have to come."

"Stop." I take his hand in mine, squeezing. "My *dad* wasn't even up yet, so don't blame yourself."

He sighs, looking unconvinced. I don't want to talk about this anymore though. Not when time is running out. Not when my revelation's hit. Not when I'm terrified of how to say the words, most of all.

I clear my throat. "You're really leaving tomorrow? On a Tuesday?"

He stares at our fingers. "Yeah. Coach wants us there at five first thing Wednesday."

Taking a breath, I gather the courage I need to say what can't be put off any longer. "What if I told you I don't want you to go?"

His head jerks and looks at me—like *really* looks at me. His eyes are narrowed, as though he's both confused and angry, but his lips part too in what looks like awe.

"Listen," I continue. "I, um...got freaked out last night when you kissed me." I lick my dry lips. "I mean, I've had this crush on you for so long. And you rejected me that time I did try to make a move, and you've pretty much treated me like crap since, so you can't blame me for being iffy, right?" A muscle ticks in his jaw, but I can't tell if it's regret or anger causing it. "Plus, you haven't been honest, and I currently have a huge issue with dishonest people, if you haven't noticed. And I've also convinced myself that I'm a huge bitch because I wonder if Rose was supposed to die so we could actually be together."

I wince and look away. Saying the words out loud feel even worse than they did when I first thought about them.

Slowly, Ben moves up the bed, getting closer. Once he's by my side, he nudges me over with his thigh. I scoot like he silently commands, and soon we're lying on the bed, on the same pillow, facing each other, his hand never leaving mine.

"Keep going," he tells me, lifting the fingers on his other hand to brush my bangs away from my face. I wonder if he thinks I look like a doll too.

"Um, I pretty much just told you how I felt."

"You didn't," he says with a smirk. "Keep going."

I roll my eyes, which makes him laugh—and makes me wince in pain too.

"Fine. Then let *me* start." He lowers his hand to the side of my neck. The stroke of his thumb against my pulse has me gulping. I'm emotionally balled up inside, and all I want to do is hug him and kiss him again to try and ease the pain.

With Travis, I never felt this way. If anything, it was exciting for a while, kissing him and stuff. But after a few weeks, I shut myself off whenever he touched me. With Ben, though, it's been different from the second I laid eyes on him. He makes me feel real. Important too.

"I've wanted to kiss you since that night in my kitchen when you were fifteen, B. Like I told you last night. I wanted to kiss you and touch you, and it scared the hell out of me because I'd never felt that way before about anyone."

I blink. Then I blink once more. "You did?"

"Yes." He smiles. "I thought I made that clear last night."

Tears well in my tired, swollen eyes. Denying this isn't a possibility anymore though because I've pretty much felt the same way for the last three years of my life.

"And as far as you thinking Rose is dead so we could be together? That's dumb. Because I knew we were inevitable years ago. I just didn't have the guts to do anything about it."

My breath catches. I look at his lips, but it doesn't ease the sting of my thoughts. Instead, it puts them in perspective.

Reaching forward, he brushes a lock of hair from my eye. "I lied to you. I hate that I did. But you know why." He takes a deep breath.

"I do." Even though it hurts to think about. I'm a big

girl who can handle her own, no matter what anyone else thinks.

"I promise you though, Becca. I will *never* do it again, all right?"

"How do I know you won't?"

"You don't, that's the thing."

I frown. "You're not being very reassuring."

"I'm not perfect, by any means, but I want to be perfect for you, which is why I'm telling you this now."

"That's pretty much the cheesiest line I've ever heard."

He wiggles his light-colored brows up and down. "Did it work?"

I sigh to myself. This boy... I'm not sure what to make of him anymore.

His eyes turn serious then. "I also didn't want to mess up your and Rose's friendship. So, I pretended it didn't bother me when you started dating Travis. And the fact that I couldn't come home all that much helped. But every time my sister talked about you, it hurt a little more because I realized you didn't feel that way about me."

"I'm sorry," I whisper, punched in the stomach with way too many feels—the best and worst kind.

"Don't be." He brings my hand to his lips, kissing the knuckles. "It's in the past."

Slowly, I nod. "So..."

"So, what?"

"Can we do this, then?" I swallow. "Be...an *us*?"

Ben's eyes sparkle as he traces a line down my cheek with his thumb. "Hell yeah, we can."

My entire body relaxes. Despite whatever worries I still have—about us, about his lying, about Adam—I can't ignore what feels right. Not anymore. Ben and I deserve to be happy.

"I'm still messed up, Becca," he offers, losing his smile. "Maybe even more than I've ever been, but I promise you, I'm all in when it comes to me and you."

"Me too." I touch his lips with my finger, tracing them. Ben needs to find peace. And I'm going to be the one to give it to him. He'll go back to school, and he'll live his best life. We can be together when he comes home too.

But when he's gone, I *am* going to find out the truth—whatever is left of it. He won't have to know about it either.

I'm being a hypocrite. I know. But I get it now, why Ben wanted to keep me in the dark about Rose's pregnancy. He cares for me. Loves me, even. He wants me to be emotionally free. And now I want the same thing for him. Because despite what Adam said or admitted, I know deep down there's more to the story when it comes to the night Rose died.

"I'm messed up too, just so you know," I say.

His nose brushes against mine, and he hums a little. "We can be messed up together now. That okay?"

I close my eyes and snuggle closer, my forehead against his, fingers tangling in the front of his shirt. I have a plan. And now I have a boyfriend, which is why I can honestly tell him, "That's better than okay, actually."

13

August
Present Day

FORTY-EIGHT HOURS HAVE PASSED since I got home from the hospital, and I'm bored out of my mind. Mom's in the kitchen making a bunch of noise, which also makes it impossible to concentrate on the TV. I'm guessing she's making me another peanut butter and jelly sandwich for dinner—my fourth in two days.

The woman won't leave to go to the store. She's afraid of me staying here alone, apparently. I can't blame her. My stupid attacker hasn't been tracked down yet, though the police assure us they've got *several credible leads.* Travis, though, is not one of them. Apparently, he had an alibi for that night.

More and more it looks like the attack was random, but that doesn't mean my mom's taking any chances.

"Can't you just order takeout?" I yell, turning the TV volume down.

"Nope. Delivery's too expensive."

I groan. "Please? I reaaaaally want a rice bowl from Chipotle." I set the remote on the couch beside me. "I swear I'll be okay alone if you don't want to pay the delivery fees and want to go pick it up. I'll lock the doors and windows, have nine-one-one on the ready."

Dad left this morning for a farming convention in Ames. He went late because of what happened to me. But as much as I'm glad he's able to still go, I do know things would be so much better if he were here.

She sighs heavily from the kitchen but also doesn't come right out and say no this time. If Ben were still in town, I bet *he'd* bring me food. Though his leaving, too, was kind of on me. Like my dad, he said he'd be fine with calling off his pre-season training to stay home with me. But I didn't want him to. Life has to go on for one of us, and since he's more settled than I am, this is the way it has to be.

"Fine." Mom groans, moving into the living room. She's got a towel thrown over her shoulder like she's been on a kitchen-cleaning frenzy. When she's anxious, she cleans; when she's stressed, she bakes. Right now, she's both, plus cranky—likely because she hasn't been sleeping well.

"Thank you." I grin, lying back on my pillow. The thought of that delicious steak melting on my tongue has me internally fist pumping the Chipotle gods.

"I'm locking all the doors and all the windows though."

"Wouldn't have it any other way."

Keys dangle in the air from behind her as she all but runs to the door. I stifle a laugh. For someone not wanting to leave me, she sure is rushing.

"And you are *not* to answer the door, you hear me? No matter what."

I salute her, voice sugary sweet as I say, "Will do. Love ya, Mom."

Three minutes later, I hear her backing out of the driveway.

Five minutes after that, I fall asleep.

———————

IT'S dark when I wake up. The house is quiet, other than the sound of the shower running upstairs. Mom must have gotten home and let me sleep, which means my food's probably in the fridge.

When I get up, a chill skitters through me as a light knock sounds from the front door. I look toward the steps, half expecting Mom to come running down in her robe. But the shower stays on. I know I shouldn't answer it. Mom said not to. But she's technically here now, so...

I make my way to the door, wrapping the blanket around my shoulders like a superhero cape—not that it makes me feel any braver. The TV stays on, and the canned laughter has me feeling only the tiniest bit better. Taking a deep breath, I flick on the outside light, gasping when I see Travis standing there.

He lifts his head, meeting my gaze through the glass with hardened eyes. I shouldn't open the door, I know this, but I do anyway, mostly because I'm curious to see why he's here.

"What do you want?" I ask, leaving the screen door shut and locked between us.

"I need to talk to you."

I tap my chin, pretending to think about it as I look him over. His hair is even greasier than normal, and there are black oil stains all over his T-shirt. In other words, Travis looks like Travis. It's kind of disgusting how I used to think he was so hot.

"How about no and instead you go *screw yourself*."

Travis curls his lips, lifting his hands to frame the door. Seconds later, he presses his face against the mesh of the screen. "Don't talk to me that way, *doll*." His sour breath fills the air in front of me, and I step back on instinct, attempting to breathe through my mouth.

"You need to leave, Travis."

He cocks his head to one side, and a rush of adrenaline slides through my veins the longer he studies me. Everything he did to me, said to me, every comment he ever made or wanted to make, even, fuels my hatred for him.

He pushes away from the door, runs both hands through his hair. I'm guessing he's high on something. Travis is *always* high.

"You shouldn't have gone digging, Becca. I warned you. Now you've stirred things. Really, *really* bad things."

I cross my arms. "Excuse me?"

"If you'd have just let it all go like I told you, then everything would've been fine. But *no*, you're a snooty, nosey little bitch just like she was."

"What are you talking about?" My skin grows cold.

Shaking his head, he starts pacing along my porch, stopping in front of me again, his gaze shooting over me in several sweeps. "You've really let yourself go this summer."

"And you're a bastard. Now, tell me what you came here for, or I'll call the police."

Travis growls, shoving his face against the mesh of the screen door again. Up close like this and under the porch light, I see just how glassy and dilated his eyes are. He's definitely on something. And when Travis is high, it's like truth serum.

"He isn't the bad one."

"Who?" I ask

211

"Adam!"

A shiver runs through me, but I need to ask... "If he's not the bad one, then why in the hell did he confess?"

Travis shakes his head and steps away, down the porch, now on the gravel where he picks up a handful and throws it at me.

"Hey!" I yell, reaching into my pocket for my phone.

He leans his head back and stairs at the sky, spinning a few times. He's so blitzed out of his mind. I know I should call the police, but I need more answers. And if I have to get them from Travis, the one person I hate the most in this world, then so be it.

"I loved you, ya know." He scoffs, rubbing a hand over his face. His words stab my belly but do nothing for my heart. "I still do for some jacked-up reason. Then when you stopped sleeping with me, it ruined everything. It ruined *me*."

"You need help, Travis. Because that wasn't love. What you're feeling, now or then. That was a sick need to have something to sate your ego." I take a step back, ready to close the door, but he rushes me, pounds on the frame, rattling it.

I screech, falling back on my butt.

"I'm sorry." He shakes his head, bowing it. His words are choked, but there's no pang of sympathy in my chest for him. "I screwed up, hurting you and cheating on you the way I did."

My stomach sinks into my toes when I stand. "Y-you cheated on me?" It's a question of curiosity, that's it. Because it doesn't matter either way if he did. Not anymore. Not like it would have months ago.

"Yeah, but it wasn't good. Not like it was you."

Yeah. That's hilarious—seeing as how we only slept together that once. I don't say this, of course. Not when

212

I'm terrified of stirring the beast inside of him anymore than I already have.

"Let me make it up to you." He comes even closer, his face shoved farther into the screen, making only one eye pop wide. He looks crazed. "I'll even tell you the truth."

"What truth?" Sweat beads between my shoulder blades while an incessant hammering pounds my skull. If Mom comes down, there's no telling what might happen. Still, I don't close the front door. Not even when I hear her calling my name from somewhere upstairs.

"About the night Rose died."

Another chill slides down my spine. He's talking in circles, making no sense. "What happened, Travis?"

Seconds later, he begins to cry, blubber really. "Now Adam's in jail, and it's only because he loved her and would've done anything to help her. She was a manipulative bitch. And she deserved what she got."

My throat burns as I growl out, "Leave. And *never* come back, you hear me?"

"Why don't you ask that new boyfriend of yours what happened the night Rose died," he shouts.

"Ben wasn't around. He—"

"You don't gotta be around to know the truth." He wipes at his wet face and laughs. It's manic. Crazed. "Ain't anyone ever told you that?"

My heart races so fast it makes me dizzy. I grab the table by the door to stay upright. Travis must see the panic in my face because his smile grows wide as he steps backward down the steps.

"It'll all make sense soon, doll. Trust me."

And as much as I don't want to believe him, I do.

14

August
Present Day

ADAM POSTS BAIL the following morning. It's all over social media. I'm not sure how his family got that kind of money. He lives in a tiny house with his dad, mom, and little brother about a mile outside of town, so it's not like they're rolling in cash. Either way, I'm glad he's out, especially after last night's confrontation with Travis. Adam lied. And it was time to confront him.

The problem is, I don't know how to go about leaving my house without Mom freaking out.

I wind up calling Sienna, offering to pay her this time to pretend we're hanging out. I hold no qualms in using her like this, mostly because I'm desperate. After our dinner disaster, I was sure she'd tell me to go to hell. But she immediately says yes, surprising me.

"And you've got the mace I put in your purse, right?" Mom fusses over me as I open the front door to leave,

214

fingering the end of my ponytail and yanking up the strap of my tank top.

"Yes, Mother."

"Don't mock me. I just worry. I wish you weren't going, but I know we can't keep living like this."

My attacker hasn't been caught yet, but I agree with her a hundred percent. That doesn't mean fear isn't keeping me awake at night. Thankfully, I'd gotten rid of Travis before she came downstairs, otherwise she'd be locking me in my room.

"Sorry." I hug her close, inhaling the scent of her perfume. It's the first time we've hugged since the funeral.

When I pull back, I notice tears on her cheeks. The view has guilt spiraling in my belly even more. There's so much I want to tell her. But if I do, she'll never let me do what needs to be done.

"It's just dinner, Mom. And I'll be with Sienna."

"I know." She waves her hand, then wipes her face. "Just call and check in when you get there."

"Okay." It's the least I can do.

———

SIENNA ISN'T TOO chatty when I get into her car. Her eyes are red though, like she's been crying. I ask if she's okay, and the second we pull out my driveway the flood-gates open about her boyfriend.

"I'm just going to miss Alex so much, you know?"

For once, I can relate. Already, I miss Ben. But he and I are not where she and her boyfriend are relationship wise, so I don't want to drop comparisons because it might seem insensitive.

The only thing I can say is, "I'm sorry."

Despite my apology, Sienna keeps going—blubbering

by the time we get on the main road toward town. I can almost hear Rose in my ear, like she's there whispering to me. *Sienna's a narcissist whose whole life revolves around two things: making sure her boyfriend gets a blow job in the bathroom every day before fourth hour, and getting straight As.*

"...and what do you want to go to Adam's house for anyway?"

I clear my throat. "To check on him."

That's not a total lie. More so, I need to find out what he's hiding and why.

My phone buzzes from my pocket. I pull it out, already knowing who it is before I look at the screen. Ben's been texting and calling non-stop since last night, yet I can't bring myself to answer him. Not with the fresh hell that is Travis's accusation. Just when I think I can trust him, something else leaves me doubting things again.

Why don't you ask that new boyfriend of yours what happened the night Rose died?

I hit Ignore and pocket my phone.

"He's weird," Sienna continues. "But he was, like, in love with Rose, right?"

It's the first time Sienna's has asked me about anything related to my best friend's death. I don't realize how much I want to talk to someone who's not associated with this whole thing until now.

"Those are the rumors, yeah," I tell her.

"I never liked Adam, but he's, like, I dunno, too much of a stoner to kill anyone, don't you think?"

"I don't know." And last night, Travis only confirmed my doubts "But I need to know why he admitted to it if he didn't do it."

"Shouldn't that be a police thing?" She scrunches her nose.

"The police don't know the whole backstory." And I wasn't about to go to them until I gathered more info.

"I don't know how you ever dated Travis."

I purse my lips and look out the window. "I'm not proud."

"Yeah, I mean, he's *nothing* like his dad, other than how they look."

"I guess."

It's silent for another minute. Uncomfortable because I don't know what to say. Sienna and I are not all that close, but at the same time, she's the only other friend I have.

"Thanks, by the way," I say.

"For what?"

"For taking me." I pull out the twenty shoved inside my shorts pocket and set it inside her cup holder.

"Keep it." She sighs when we stop at a stop sign. "It's not like I have anything better to do."

Fifteen minutes later, we pull up to Adam's house. I've only been here once before, and that was with Travis when we were picking Adam up to go to the alcove.

"Should I have brought a hazmat suit for this?" Sienna shudders but also unbuckles her seatbelt.

I look over at the tiny home. It's a sad, decrepit mess of overgrown weeds mixed with Mickey Mouse décor spilled all over the front lawn. A deflated baby pool that's half full sits on the front porch with a metal chair half in and half out of it.

The front screen door hangs on its hinges, looking like it's seconds from falling off. There are three air conditioning units under the windows, instead of in them, all lined up along the front of the house in the space where flowers or bushes would normally grow.

"You don't have to go in," I tell Sienna, opening my door.

"And be responsible for your death if he's actually a killer?" She huffs, following me out. "Please. I'm trying to get into Princeton. I don't need an accomplice to murder on my record."

I'm the first one to make it up the stairs, the one to knock too. It takes less than a minute for a man to greet us. He's tall, brown haired, and has Adam's face but older. His stomach protrudes over his belt, and he's holding a beer.

"Not interested," he says.

"Wait." I stick my foot into the door before he closes it. "Is Adam here?"

My stomach pitches at the snarly look on his face. Sienna must see it too because she presses even closer to my back. "You two friends of his or something?"

"Yes. I'm—I mean, I *was* Rose McCain's best friend, but Adam and I are friends too."

His eyes narrow. "You shouldn't be here." Then he tries to shut the door again, only this time, I push my shoulder through it.

"Please," I plead. "I'm not angry at Adam for what happened. I just want to talk to him."

"That dead bitch nearly ruined his life."

I dig my nails into my palms. Sienna grips my forearm so tight I wince.

"Did you know that *Rose* is also the reason that son of yours even passed junior year, sir?" It's a huge lie, but every parent has a soft spot in their heart for the smart kid, don't they?

"Little good that does him now, huh?" He snort-laughs.

I cringe.

"It's bad enough the kid was friends with Travis. Now I find out he might be responsible for a girl's murder.

218

Shit ain't right, lemme tell ya." He rubs a hand down his face. "We raised him better than that."

My brows furrow. Adam's dad didn't like Travis?

"I dated Travis," I blurt out, a last-ditch effort to get the man on my side. "He isn't a good person. I can agree with that wholeheartedly."

His upper lip curls in disgust, but he opens the door a little wider. "Glad we got something in common at least."

Releasing a quick breath, I glance back at Sienna, whose face is pale, while her eyes look seconds from popping from their sockets.

Go to the car, I mouth.

No, she mouths back.

"Sit. I'll get him," Adam's father says, pointing to the plaid couch once we're inside their living room. The springs are poking through the cushions, so I'm not one hundred percent it's safe, but I nod and take a seat on the arm.

Sienna stays standing and clings to me for dear life. "Are you sure this is a good idea?"

"Yeah." Though I am definitely not as sure as I had been.

Two minutes later, when Sienna's cut the circulation off to my arm, Adam moves into the room. "Becca?"

I look up, meeting his eyes—eyes which look as though they've sunk into his head overnight.

"Hey," I manage. "Can we, um, talk?"

He hesitates, looks over his shoulder, then says back to me, "Sure. But outside."

The door squeaks behind Sienna once we're outside and she jumps, almost toppling me over. I turn and take both of her hands in mine, whispering with annoyance, "Go. I'll meet you in the car."

She nods this time. Whatever fears she must've had

219

about my supposed safety disappear when she takes off down the drive. Some good she is.

Once it's just me and Adam, I look at him again. He smells like peanut butter and dirt. It's such an innocent smell, so childlike. His arms are folded now, and he's leaned against the side of his house, eyes to the crumbling ceiling of their small porch. With an impending court date and a possible thirty-year sentence hanging over his head, I'm surprised he seems so calm.

I don't beat around the bush, needing answers, stat. "Tell me why you gave her the drugs. Especially since you knew she was pregnant with *your* baby."

He shoots me a glare. "You shut your damn mouth, bitch."

Ignoring the bite in his words, I keep going, getting in his face. "You don't get to do this, Adam. She wasn't yours."

"And she sure as hell wasn't yours either." He scoffs.

I hold his glare, despite the pang in my chest. Rose and I knew each other for almost a decade. I had more years of friendship with her than he ever had. But saying so won't win me any brownie points.

"Please. I just..." I step back, take a breath that hurts my chest. This is too much. Too painful. But I have to keep going. "I need answers. I need to know what happened."

He narrows his eyes, bites the inside of his cheek. Just when I don't think he'll say anything else, he surprises me, words soft and filled with the kind of pain only someone in love can feel. "I gave her the weed that night. Nothing else."

"OKAY. THEN DID YOU..." I trail off, hesitating. "Did you get her pregnant?"

220

He squeezes his eyes shut and bows his head. "No."

I swallow hard, wishing it was that simple after all. It's the not knowing part that hurts so much.

"What happened that night? Can you tell me what you remember?"

He pushes away from me, moving to sit on the steps. "She came to the party, crying," he murmurs. "I asked her what was wrong, and she told me she was pregnant." He rubs the back of his head. "She said she was afraid and didn't know what to do. I just...I wanted to help her however I could, you know? That's why I gave her the joint. I thought it'd help calm her down. But when I came back from taking a piss, she was gone."

Because giving a pregnant girl weed is the answer to everything, I want to say but don't. It's important to pick and choose my battles.

"What was she scared of? Being pregnant?"

"No." He shakes his head, laughs a little. "She was scared of what her *boyfriend's* reaction would be when he found out she'd gotten pregnant by another dude."

I jerk my head back. "Wait. She was still seeing her mystery boyfriend, but he wasn't the one who got her pregnant?"

What kind of messed up BS was my best friend into?

"Yep."

My heart thunders in my ears. "Do you know who the father was, then?"

No hesitation, Adam says again, "Yep."

I press a shaking hand to my lips, then stand on the step beside him. "Can you tell me who he is?"

"Are you gonna go to the police if I do?" He looks at me, eyebrows lifted.

"No," I blurt, probably too fast to be believed. I'm at Adam's mercy here, is the thing. He could tell me false-

221

hoods, twists words to try and get me on his side or get me in trouble, even. But I'm not good under pressure.

"Liar." He stands, towering over me. His personality jumps to white-hot anger in a flash, and spit flies out of his mouth and over my nose as he talks. "Always the goody-two-shoes friend. Stuck up, smart little bitch. I don't get why she ever picked you."

I ignore the insults, understanding what's really going on. Adam doesn't want me to know the truth. He's still trying to cover up for someone. I know this, but don't know who. Or why.

"I swear, Adam. I won't tell anyone. Not Ben, my parents, not the police either." And I mean it. I just want to know.. For peace of mind.

He lowers his voice to a whisper, almost like he's worried someone might hear. "You really wanna know why I went to the police and admitted to being the dad and giving her the drugs?"

"Yes." I hold my breath.

He curls his upper lip. "Because the guy Rose was seeing threatened my family. Said if I didn't take the fall, he'd hurt my little brother. Or my mom one night after work. He'd make it look like an accident, but it wouldn't be."

"Oh God." I reach out to touch his arm. "Adam, I'm so sorry."

"Your sorry don't mean shit to me."

"I know, but—"

"Leave it, Becca." He growls, shoving my hand away. "Trust me. You don't wanna know anything else."

"I can handle myself." Way more than he probably thinks.

"Yeah. Don't think you can. You don't know what the dude's capable of."

Rose told me very little about her secret *boyfriend*,

even after I confronted her. If the asshole is this terrible, no wonder she never wanted to introduce us.

"Did he hurt her? That night by the river?" I hold breath, wanting the answer so badly I can taste it. Knowing at the same time what might happen if I do. I'd never stop trying to figure things out, no matter the threat.

"No." Adam lifts his chin. "She killed herself. Jumped off the tire swing and wound up getting stuck in the dam."

"But that's not what—"

"Enough." He rushes me, sets both hands on my shoulders. His grip is tight, fingernails digging through my shirt. He won't hurt me, but my heart goes faster all the same. "I told you to just leave this alone. So did Travis."

"Why would Travis want to warn me away?"

Adam drops his hands and stares at the boards beneath his feet as he digs the toe of his sneaker between the crevices of the wood. I touch my throat, trying to keep my voice steady.

His lack of answer makes my stomach twist.

"Adam. What does Travis have to do with this?"

He opens his mouth, then snaps it shut when a kid runs outside. "Adam!" the boy cries, his joy so big and real. I watch as he wraps his short little arms around Adam's legs.

"Hey, bud. You're supposed to be watching a movie." Adam picks him up and sets him on his hip. I study the little boy's profile. Brown hair, sunken-in cheekbones... He's the spitting image of his older brother. Only, there's an innocence to him that's been untouched by the world.

"I got bored without you." The kid sets his head on Adam's shoulder. The image warms my chest. Adam really is a good guy, just like Rose said. It sucks that he's been put into an impossible position. One I want to help with...if only I knew how.

"I'll be right back in. Promise. Just give me a sec."

"When's Mommy going to come home?" The boy yawns.

"Soon, buddy."

"Daddy's snoring again."

Adam sets him down on his feet, dismissing him with the rustle of his hair. "Go back into your room. I'm almost done."

The boy looks at me, all sparkling eyes and curious gaze. Then just as quick as he came out, he's gone again. I look at Adam again, half expecting him to tell me to leave. But he doesn't this time. Instead, he takes a heavy breath and begins to speak, like his brother's presence re-energized him.

"Rose was blackmailed into having sex with the guy who got her pregnant, Becca."

"What?" I jerk my head back. "Who?"

He bows his head. Then says the one thing I never expected to hear.

"Travis."

I DON'T SPEAK when Sienna pulls away from Adam's house. I'm pretty sure I don't breathe either. My head hurts. My stomach too. And everything inside of me spins in circles of confusion; of disgust; worst of all, of betrayal.

My best friend was sleeping with Travis.

Travis blackmailed her into doing so.

Travis was also the father of Rose's baby.

I didn't ask any details of Travis when I found out. Didn't push to know anything more about who Rose's mystery boyfriend was. Not when it might put Adam's life in even bigger jeopardy.

"Becca?" Sienna touches my hand when we pull into Rose's driveway. *Ben's* driveway. I need to talk to Ginger. I need to tell her the truth—better yet, I need to hear her version of it before I break the news that her new boyfriend's son was blackmailing her daughter.

"Are you okay?" Sienna asks.

"Honestly?" I hesitate and stare back at the McCain house. "No. I don't think I am." With that, I shove open the car door, throw a quick goodbye over my shoulder, and head toward the house.

When Ginger doesn't answer right away, I grab the spare key that's always in the light fixture and let myself in. For now, I'll do some detective work, maybe see if I can find something in Rose's room. If Ginger hasn't packed it away like she did everything else, of course.

If it wasn't for Ben questioning things—Ben, who thinks everything is likely all cleared up, who's back at college and living his best life while I continue to deal with this fresh hell—then I'd still be blissfully unaware. Or maybe *stupidly unaware* should be the right words.

I make my way up the stairs and head down the hall before I can stop myself. Rose's room is the last on the right. I haven't been inside for almost two months. Slowly, I push the door open, blinking in surprise at what I see. Nothing's been touched. It's like a shrine. Her bed's unmade, blankets on the floor, dirty clothes piled high in the corner. Water bottles half empty on her desk and there's even a bag of unopened chips.

I blow out a shuddering breath, imagining her there, and grief takes me by the throat and squeezes. Makes my knees weak at the same time.

Regardless, I have to keep going.

Her softball glove hangs on a coat rack, and pictures

of us are scattered throughout the room in frames. I can't look at them, not when they feel like nothing but lies. The ones not on the wall, I push face down. That was another time. Two different people.

My hands shake when I yank open her desk drawer, her dresser drawers too. I search through books, journals, anything I can find to clue me in as to why she was being blackmailed. I'm also on the hunt for pictures or letters, something to show who this mystery boyfriend of hers was.

An angry sob rises into my throat when I start to toss clothes from her closet, followed by shoes and boxes of old books she'd never read, all dusty and dirty like my soul. Sweat gathers along my temples from exertion, the emotional and physical kind. I'm so tired of all the lies that after ten minutes of searching, I fall to the floor of her room and start to cry into my knees. I've got no more answers than I did before.

My hands itch with the need to grab her softball bat from under her desk and smash things with it. I want to destroy the world and everything in it. But rage isn't me, and I'm determined to stick to my roots...even if said roots have me standing, grabbing the blanket on the foot of Rose's bed, and wrapping it around my shoulders.

With a heavy sigh, I lie on her bed, staring up at the white ceiling. If I shut my eyes, I can almost smell her lotion. Weak in the heart, not sound in the mind, I drop my head to the side and look closely at the one framed picture I forgot to push down on Rose's nightstand. The two of us are side by side, arms wrapped around the other's shoulders as we stand outside the front door of our old junior high. We were in eighth grade, I think. A simple time. So easy.

Rose looks back at me through the glass, a smile on her face that I barely remember now.

"Why did you do it?" I ask, not sure which part I want to know the answer to more.

I need to talk to Ben. To find out what other secrets he's keeping about the night Rose died. I also need to tell him about the threats on Adam, that Travis is—was—the real father of Rose's baby.

I lie on my best friend's pillow for a long time, thinking; and crying; and wondering, most of all. Then when it all gets to be too much, when I can't take the pain in my chest any longer, I shut my eyes and, somehow, manage to fall asleep.

15

August
Present Day

THE BUZZING of my cell phone wakes me. I pick it up, blanching at the time: 9:45. I've been sleeping for almost two hours. The phone buzzes again. The number's unrecognizable. With the fourteen other missed calls, I'm starting to wonder if Mom's gone to the police or formed a search party.

I answer, wincing before I can speak. "Hello?"

"Becca? Jesus Christ. Where are you? I've been calling you all day, and now you've got your mom all freaked because you haven't been answering her calls all night."

It's Ben.

I immediately start looking for my slides on the floor. "Sorry. I, uh, I fell asleep."

"You're home?" he asks.

"No, no..." I pull in a slow breath, release it. "I'm at Sienna's house. We've been hanging out, watching

228

movies." The last thing I want is for him to know that I'm currently a mess inside his sister's old room.

"Sienna's house," he deadpans, obviously not believing me.

"Yep."

"I thought you didn't like her."

"That was Rose who didn't."

"Huh." He clicks his tongue. "I'll swing by and grab you," he tells me. "I'm twenty minutes outside of town."

"Why are you coming home?" I rub the sleep from my eyes.

"Why do you think?" he asks.

"I don't know. It's why I asked you." I don't look back when I leave Rose's room, too terrified that if I do, I wouldn't want to leave.

Ben sighs. "You're still so clueless, aren't you?"

I furrow my brows, not understanding why he's so mad, but also too tired to ask. "Look, I need to go. I'll call you later?" I hang up the phone, but Ben calls right back. This time I hit Ignore and stuff my phone into my pocket.

That's the exact moment I hear noise coming from downstairs.

Someone's here.

I tiptoe to the stairs. The sound of laughter and three distinct voices grow bigger the closer I get. They pull me in, capture my attention, even though I don't want them to. I peek over the banister. Leaf is here. Ginger too. And Travis...he's also there, leaning back on the couch, checking his phone. My chest squeezes, anger my driving force. The fact that I was just in the same bed that he and my best friend may have been having sex in has my skin crawling, makes me want to go bleach myself. With every breath, the rage in me boils hotter, leading me to do what I know I shouldn't.

Screw Travis.

And screw Rose too.

My footsteps are purposely loud and heavy when I walk down the stairs. By the time I reach the living room, both Leaf and Ginger are standing in front of the couch staring back at me, while Travis looks me up and down, a lazy smirk on his mouth that I want to rip off with my fingernails.

"Becca?" Ginger speaks first, brows furrowed. "What are you doing here?"

I don't look at her. I can't. I've only got enough wrath inside of me for one person right now, and he's looking back at me with green eyes that no longer haunt me in a good way.

"Why did you do it?" I whisper, though it comes out more as a growl.

"Hey to you too, doll."

Ginger steps in front of me, blocking my view. "What's this all about?" She frowns, and Leaf soon stands beside her, a hand lingering over her shoulder. But Ginger's blockade doesn't work on Travis and instead, he moves next to his father.

"You had sex with Rose," I hiss.

Ginger gasps.

Travis's smirk fades into something cynical. That doesn't stop me though. Nothing will.

"Was the first time in a car when you were high and drunk like it was with me?" I walk to him, shove his chest with both hands. "Did you pass out while you were still *inside of her too?*"

"What is she talking about?" Ginger intervenes, her shaking fingers now wrapped around my wrist.

"Hey, let's just all calm down." Leaf takes Ginger's free hand and tries to pull her away.

I turn to the man my best friend once admired—a

teacher who is so obviously oblivious to the dark side that makes up his son. "Travis is a complete and utter douchebag."

Leaf glares at me. "Just hold on a minute. You can't come in here, insulting my son like—"

"*Your son* was the father of Rose's kid." I turn to Ginger and jerk a thumb at Travis.

Ginger takes a step back, a hand on her mouth. She looks at Leaf, whose face has gone pale. She then narrows her eyes at Travis, who's yet to move a muscle since my declaration.

"You son of a bitch!" Ginger screams before I can blink, reaching for the front of Travis's shirt. She shoves him, then shoves him again, pulling a hand back, like she's going to slap him.

Leaf grabs her arm before she can get a shot in, twisting it behind her back. Ginger wrestles and yells and roars until she bends at the knees, giving up...sobbing.

"Bitch," Travis growls at me. He moves closer, gets in my face. The smell of weed has my stomach twisting. Or maybe that's fear instead. "She really did get what she deserved."

He leaves then, strutting down the hall and out the door like there's nothing on earth that could stop him. My stomach heaves at the view, while shivers dance their way down my spine. I want to kill him. I want him to die.

I look up, blink, angry tears falling down my cheeks as the roar of voices fill my ears once more. Ginger argues with Leaf, a finger pressed to his chest as she screams at the top of her lungs. Leaf stays quiet, his head bowed, hands at his sides, clenched into fists. He's ashamed—I see it in the purse of his lips, the slump of his shoulders too.

It seems like his parenting skills are just as bad as Ginger's.

Maybe the two of them were meant to be.

With that thought, I turn and head toward the front door, taking my first real breath in minutes when I reach the sidewalk outside. I'm halfway down the street before my teeth begin to chatter. I'm not cold. I'm alone. And the last time I was alone outside was when I was attacked. If I can just get to the gas station down the road, then I'll be okay. I know I will.

I have to be.

When my phone rings again, I bring it to my ear, already knowing who it is. "Hey, Mom."

"Becca, where are you? Are you okay? I've been trying to call you for hours."

A sob releases from my throat, but instead of anger, all I can feel is grief. Betrayal that stings like a thousand wasps have burrowed inside my chest.

"Becca, honey, where are you? What happened? I'm coming to get you."

"I'm at…"

A car pulls up beside me a second later. I turn, terrified it's Travis…only to feel a slight rush of relief when I see it's his dad instead. He's wearing Coke-bottle glasses tonight. I've never seen him wear them before. Not that I pay much attention. His dark hair is styled in some weird pompadour way. I'm also pretty sure his long-sleeved shirt is pink.

He slows his car, pulling close, before rolling down his window. "Hey, Becca. Hop in. I'll give you a ride home."

I freeze in place, debating. Maybe I can talk to him, pinpoint details about Travis's whereabouts that night…his son's relationship with Rose and whether or not Leaf was aware of it.

232

"Who's that?" Mom asks. "Becca, what's going on? Who are you with?"

"It's fine, Mom," I reassure. "I-I've got a ride. Promise I'll be home soon."

I end the call and start toward Leaf's car.

16

August
Present Day

"I'm sorry about what happened back there." Those are the first words that come out of Leaf's mouth after I shut his car door. It's neat and tidy but smells exactly like the aftershave Travis used to wear. "I'm very upset with my son for what he's done, and I promise I'll make this right for you *and* Ginger both."

"It's not your fault." I cross my arms over my stomach, crouching down in the leather seats to try and ease the cramping in my belly. Rose might have been okay with hanging out with the guy for study sessions, but he's Travis's father, not my teacher.

"Not technically my fault, you're right." He chuckles. "But Travis is my responsibility."

We're quiet for a while. The silence has me squirming, unable to sit still. Leaf maneuvers his way throughout the dark streets of Winston, whistling like

234

this is the most natural thing when it's not. Things feel awkward, and five minutes into the drive, I'm already regretting my decision of getting in the car.

I pull out my phone, checking for texts from Mom or even Dad. Ben too. But, like always on this road, there are zero bars of service.

After a while, Leaf speaks up. "How have you been feeling? You know, since..."

I look out the window. "As good as I can be."

"Hmm. Understandable. I'm so sorry for your loss, Becca. Rosie was a very good student. Loved by all."

I frown at his nickname for her. *Rosie.*

A few more minutes of dead silence passes between us. He's stopped humming completely and now taps both thumbs on the wheel. With each moment, tension fills the air, makes my skin crawl too. I'm not sure if it's me, him, or us together. But something doesn't feel right.

"Were you two very close?" he asks.

"Yes, very." I narrow my eyes when we pass the turn leading to my house. "Oh, um. That was my road. I live on Thompson Farm."

"I'm aware." He glances at me, smile tight. "You dated my son, remember? Therefore, I know everything there is to know about you."

Goose bumps form on my arms and the hair on the back of my neck stands on end. "I want to go home, please."

"In due time, doll."

My heart skips. "It's actually just Becca."

"Ah yes. Travis said you were sensitive about that name. Forgive me."

I shake my head, breaths suddenly uneven. I glance down at my phone. There's one bar. I open the screen, send Ben my location, an SOS text, then tuck it away. Leaf doesn't notice, thankfully.

235

"W-where are we going?" My voice shakes with the question. "My mom's expecting me. She's—"

"I figured you had questions."

"Questions?"

He makes a clucking sound with his tongue, like a clock. Over and over and over... I chance a look at him. His upper lip's curled. Even in the dark, I see the shadow of hate on his profile.

"Please. Take me home," I repeat, seconds from grabbing the door handle and jumping out...until a loud, drawn-out *buzz* falls from his lips.

"Time's up." He laughs—cackles, really. "You don't want to play. I get it. I make you nervous. But you would've liked this game. Rosie did."

"No, please. I just wanna go home."

"*Not yet.* I told you this already."

"But—"

"Shut up, you little bitch, and listen to me."

I screech when he slaps the wheel with an open palm. Fear paralyzes me to the point where even looking at my cell phone when it buzzes against my thigh has me terrified of an inevitable death.

"Your information is wrong." He heaves a giant sigh, fingers squeezing around the wheel.

I don't nod, I don't blink. I don't dare try and speak.

"And I'm here to set the record straight. About everything once and for all."

A whimper escapes from between my lips when he slams his foot against the accelerator. "Don't cry, please," he coos, glancing at me. "I loved Rose. God, did I love that beautiful, beautiful girl. No need to cry tears, lovely girl."

I suck in a sharp breath.

No. No, God, no.

"And she loved me just as much, you know." He hits

236

the accelerator again, harder this time, pushing eighty in a forty within seconds. I grip the door handle, breathing labored, heart racing...

#75. Sleep with the forbidden.

Oh my God, Rose. You did it.

"You can stop playing dumb. I know you found out. That little shit Adam..." He grits his teeth. "Guy just couldn't keep his mouth shut. Always hated that kid." He slams on the brakes, swinging a sharp right off the main road, tires screeching. We pull into a private lot I'm not familiar with. A broken fence sits to the left, while the rest is surrounded by waist high weeds.

"Adam only told me about Travis." I look around, desperate for an escape. But he blazes down a bumpy side road, through the grasses and weeds. Turning my body away from his, I manage to get my location to Ben again, only for Leaf to grab my phone at the last minute, then throw it out his rolled-down window.

"None of that, doll. You're safe with me."

Please, Ben. Please find me.

He laughs mockingly. "Now, I'm gonna tell you what you want to know, then I'm gonna make sure you keep your damn mouth shut about it. Just like I did with Adam." He tsks.

I curl against the door, pull my knees up, and wrap my arms around my calves. Sweat forms along my temples, my back too. "I-I don't care," I cry. "Whatever happened is on Rose, not me. You don't need to say anything else."

"I do, if only so you can see what *you* did wrong."

"M-me?"

"Always you," he growls. "*Everything* was always about. You."

I cover my trembling lips.

"Rose was lonely and lost until she found me," Leaf

237

continues, slowing until we're near a dead end with a sign ahead that says *Road Closed*. Around us stands more waist-high weeds and an empty field beyond the sign. There are no main lights from streets—not a single house, farm, or building for miles.

Please, Ben. Please find me.

"All the people she loved ignored her. You, her brother, even Ginger." He balls his hands into fists on his lap. "But not that little shit Adam. He wouldn't stop. He wouldn't leave her be. She was mine. Since the moment I saw her in class last year. I knew we were destined for each other."

"I-I didn't know. Please, take me home. I—"

He backhands me, forcing my head back against the window. I groan when red-hot pain ricochets across my cheek.

He puts the car in Park, turns to me, a knee pulled to his chest so casually that it looks like he's in his teacher mode. "Nobody understood what she needed except for me. But she never listened, that girl. Always getting in trouble. Always so reckless."

Even through my tears, I have to ask... "D-did Travis know?"

"About me and her?"

"Yes." My questions may taunt him more, but I'm in too deep to stop them. "Is that why he b-blackmailed her?"

Leaf hesitates, opening and shutting his mouth, before setting his chin on his knee. "She loved *me*, not him. Said she was saving herself for love. Said that I was the only one to ever be inside of her."

There are a lot of things I knew about Rose. The main one being she lost her virginity at fourteen to a guy who was sixteen. After that, she swore off boys. But if I admit this to him, there's no telling what my words will do to his already demented mind. So, I do what I know might save me from another slap to the face...or worse: I nod.

Satisfied with my answer it seems, he begins again. "Rose started coming by my class after school last year for help—her and that boy, Adam. After a while, I told the boy not to come. Said he didn't need the help. That's how I got her alone. How we got to know each other too." His smile is lecherous, his eyes distant when he glances over my shoulder. My stomach twists even more, and the tears come faster, blurring my vision.

Still, I don't move. I'm not sure what'll happen if I do.

"Every Tuesday we had sessions," he continues. "She'd come in, wearing her tight little dresses, tempting me with her body..." He hisses and squeezes his eyes shut, like he's experiencing something for the first time in his mind.

It's disgusting, and I want to puke.

"I told her no at first. That I couldn't cross lines like that. Already, I'd been approached by other young girls. I could've had my pick of the litter." He chuckles. "But sweet, sweet Rosie. She made me feel so very much."

My breath catches at his confession. Other young girls... One of them was likely Sienna. I remember Rose commenting about their closeness the night of the formal. *She's hot for teach*, my best friend had said. I didn't know it at the time, but I do now. Sienna wasn't the only one who'd been looking to get her teacher in bed.

I shudder at the thought, hating how I'd miss the signs. If I hadn't been so wrapped up in Travis, then this could've been avoided. I could've stopped it. Put her on the right path or told someone. Gotten Leaf fired.

I still can. If I'm able to get out of here.

"Her name was *Rose*," I hiss. "And you had no right to touch her."

239

Ignoring me, he whistles low. "God, she was a beauty. So much going for her. Rosie and I were meant to be." He drops his head back against the seat and sighs.

As he continues to speak, I lower one arm from around my leg and slowly reach for the door handle. If he stays distracted, I might be able to slide out of the car and run.

"I knew I wouldn't get her out of my system," he says, chuckling. "So, we slept together one night. Just once. During a study session."

I clench my hands into fists, wanting nothing more than to punch him in his smug face, then resurrect my best friend from the grave just so I can shake some sense into her. Even still, I can't change the past.

"Rosie was so desperate for me. Almost as much as I was her." He drops his foot back to the floor. "We belonged together."

The need to scream burrows deeper into my throat. There's no way he's going to tell me all of this, then let me go alive. I'm not stupid. That means I need to make my escape, now, before it's too late.

"Go to hell, you sick asshole." I yank the door hand, pulling, ready to bolt.

But it's locked.

Horror builds inside me. I yank and tug, yank and tug.

No, no, no, no!

"Yeah, doll. Don't think that's gonna happen," he murmurs, reaching across the console, grabbing my hair, then shoving my forehead against the door.

Oh God. Oh God, oh God, oh God.

He shoves me into the glass again.

Thump. Thump. Thump.

Blood spills in between my eyes and down my nose.

I can't see.

The night blurs.

I want to puke, but I can't breathe to do so.

Seconds later, he crawls over the center console, shifts me onto my back. His hands are around my neck, squeezing before I can scream. Spit flies from his lip as he stares down at me, empty evil eyes so calm you wouldn't know he was seconds from helping me find my maker.

"She was a tease." He squeezes harder, nails digging into my neck. "All of you young girls are. She told me she was eighteen and legal, but she lied to me." I gasp, choking for air that doesn't come. Stars form in my eyes. "Rosie's intentions with me were supposed to be pure. Yet she was pregnant with my own son's kid when it should've been mine!"

I claw at his hands, his wrists, his cheek, but he grabs my hair, yanks and yanks, until a chunk is pulled from my scalp. I scream, but there's no sound. The adrenaline fades.

"Stop fighting." Leaf hovers, eyes flaring, teeth exposed, gnashing. "I knew I should've taken care of you that night. Stupid, stupid girl, going out in rain. You were warned to stay quiet, yet you didn't listen. I should've killed you, but my boy begged me not to."

The inside of the car grows darker, my vision blurring. I learned somewhere that a person can survive four full minutes without oxygen, which means I'm one minute away, maybe less, from dying.

"I'll lose everything if you tell, which is why this needs to end. Now."

Faces flash behind my eyes. Mom, Dad.

Ben.

I refuse to die. Refuse to let this be the way I go, most of all. With those thoughts, those people, fueling me, I lift my weak leg once more and jam my knee between his thighs. It does exactly what I need it to.

Leaf grunts, then groans, falls back into his seat with wide eyes.

Gasping for air, no hesitation, I turn, unlock the door, and leap out, landing on my hands and knees in the dirt. Body shaking, I push to my feet and take off into the tall weedy field, stumbling once but righting myself before I can fall again.

"You're just as stupid as she was, thinking you can get away from me."

I slap my hand over my mouth to keep myself from crying out, then in the thick of the tall weeds, twenty or so feet from his car, my knees give out and I fall between two trees, the waist-high weeds.

I'm stuck here.

On my stomach, I peer through the field, sweat falling down my temples and eyes, mingling with my tears and the blood. There's a slight breeze in the air, pushing the top of the weeds from side to side. The moon does little to light the area around me, thankfully. It's the only reprieve I have.

Feet scuffle through the weeds somewhere ahead. I feel him there, close, even though I don't see him with my eyes.

"Travis found us in the living room, you know." The laugh following his words is bitter and bitter. "All we were doing was kissing, and he walked in. My own *son*..."

The words *bribery* and *blackmail* find solace in my messy thoughts, everything coming together in a way I never expected.

"He told us he was going to tell everyone. Including you. Rosie...she started to cry. Saying you couldn't know. You wouldn't understand. That you'd *tell everyone.*"

My breath shudders with every exhale. I shut my eyes, barely holding on to consciousness.

"She said she knew of a way to keep him quiet. To distract my son. I told her it wasn't necessary, that he was my child and should respect my wishes."

My stomach twists at his words.

"But she kept talking about this number on a bucket list of yours." Leaf laughs again. "Does number seventy sound about right, *doll*?"

I stiffen even more.

No.

Rose wouldn't have shown him our list. That was private, for our eyes only.

How could you, Rose?

"She didn't want you to get hurt," Leaf says, tsking. "She really did love you. She talked about you all the time and told me she couldn't wait to tell you about us."

I squeeze my eyes shut and bury my face into the dirt. Something bites at my arms, the back of my neck, my exposed thighs. I hate bugs. I hate the mud. I hate everything.

"Her plan to use you as Travis's distraction was so perfect for a while."

"I'm not going to say it's fine because it isn't. But I am going to help you achieve your goal anyway because I love you."

Rose didn't want to help me achieve my number seventy for the sake of our list. She wanted to use me as a distraction so she and Leaf could continue to have their affair.

All those times when she told me to get back together with Travis, to give him a chance... It was to benefit herself, not me.

How could you?

"That list was rather adventurous, I'd say. So much

243

so, I kept a copy in my safe at home. I particularly like your seventy-one."

His feet crunch in the dry grass ahead. He's only a few feet away. I grip the dirt, willing to use anything as a weapon.

God, please don't let him find me. Please, please.

"Liam's father and I are actually close friends. We do drinks together on Fridays. He's my accountant." Leaf sighs. "He wasn't happy that someone practically destroyed his son's vehicle in the parking lot outside of the football stadium last fall." He clicks his tongue against the roof of his mouth.

I bury my forehead deeper into the wet ground in attempt to mask my sobs.

"Things took an unfortunate turn for the worse after you stopped sleeping with my son though," he growls. "And now the truth comes out. *Rosie* wound up having sex with him just to keep my son satisfied and quiet." He growls. "Stupid girl, thought she could trick me and say that kid was mine. I believed her too. But lo and behold, I went to the doctor and found out the truth: I'm no longer able to have kids, you see."

I want to stand, to run at this man. To hit him square in the face with my fist, most of all. But I can't get up. I'm too weak. My head hurts. I'm dizzy. I want is to go home to Mom and Dad. Sleep. Cry. Sleep some more.

"I'll always miss her. I will. But you see, Rosie did this on her own accord. She's the one who pursued my love, not the other way around. Her lying broke my trust, which is why I did what was necessary, and I went to her mother. Told Ginger the truth. That I was worried about Rosie because she'd been inappropriate with me."

That lying, ugly asshole.

"Turns out, Ginger wasn't the terrible mother her daughter had made her out to be. Sure, she struggles

244

with drinking, but she's a wonderful woman. She's even promised to go to rehab for me. The two of us have fallen in love, and I'm afraid I can't let you ruin that for us, Becca."

A door slams in the distance.

A voice echoing beyond. "Becca?"

It's Ben. He followed my SOS. He followed my phone location.

"Becca? Are you here?"

I open my mouth to scream—tell him to run, that he's not safe. But to my surprise, Leaf curses under his breath, and soon I hear the brush of his feet rustling through the field in the opposite direction.

I release a huge sigh, my entire body trembling with relief this time, not fear. The man obviously isn't armed because if he was, he wouldn't run away.

Tires screech in the distance. Leaf is gone.

Leaf. Is. Gone.

"Becca? Jesus, where are you? Answer me, damn it. Answer me!"

Knees shaking, I claw at the mud, struggling to stand. Still, I'm on my feet in seconds, swaying one way, then the other as my dizzying head makes it hard to stay upright. The last of my adrenaline rushes through me just enough that I move forward a few feet...only to crash into Ben's waiting arms.

When I don't speak or answer his questions, he sighs, picks me up, and cradles me against his chest. "It's okay. I've got you. You're safe now."

The feel of his lips against my temple is like a calm in the storm, and my body instantly relaxes, reveling in the safety of his arms, the sound of his heart against my ear, most of all.

17

September
Present Day

"IT'S BEEN two days since you've touched anything but water. You have to eat something." Dad hovers over me on the couch, a perpetual scowl on his face. He's home early from his conference, but I don't even feel bad. I'm glad he's here, safe with us, especially since Travis and Leaf are still on the run.

"I told you guys, I'm not hungry." *Wheel of Fortune* plays on the TV. I never considered myself a game-show watcher up until recently. They help to numb my mind and thoughts.

The fear brews constantly inside me now. Every knock on the door, creak of the floorboards at night, or tick of the siding from outside has me curled in a constant ball.

Dad puts a tray of junk food on the end table. I look

246

over, mouth not even watering at what I see. Takis, Starbursts, and my favorite energy drink won't even pull me out of this funk I'm in. It's like I'm losing Rose all over again. Only this time, showers are happening. And instead of sadness, I feel both disgust and terror.

Leaf ruined Rose's life. Leaf was a sick, sick man. And now he has the ability to ruin mine...if not end it first. Still, I can't tell anyone the truth out of fear that something really bad will happen to them—to me—if I do. So, when the police asked for a name and description, I blurted out the first one I could think of. Travis.

Travis, who is, like his father, now MIA.

I'm not sure if my accusation will make things worse or better. Either way, I need to make a plan. Maybe go to Adam and get him on my side. Then we could talk to the police together, a united front. The thing is, I don't want to do it until I know for sure where the father-son team is.

"Still no word from the police," Mom tells us, standing in the kitchen entryway, cell phone squeezed between her hands.

"He couldn't have gone far," Dad says. "I wouldn't worry."

"Well, at least we know this time, right?" Mom pats my arm.

"Uh-huh." I swallow again, the throbbing not as bad as it'd been the night before. The lie though...it's bitter. Coats my throat in shame instead of pain and makes me want to vomit.

"That boy is filth," Mom continues. "I knew that the second I laid eyes on him." She bends over, kissing the top of my head. Her truth does little to ease my guilt, mostly because I know she's right. It's too late for regrets now.

After Ben found me in the field, I'd clung to him until the tears dried, his hand in mine the entire way to the hospital. I'm pretty sure he called my parents, told them to meet us there, but everything about that night is blurry, to the point where I've blocked a lot of it out.

I wrote the lie about Travis on a piece of paper, unable to speak because of my swelling throat. Since then, even with my voice coming back some, the bruise on my cheek now an ugly shade of green and yellow too, I've refused to open up more than I have to. Not even to Ben, who still has zero clue that Travis was the father of Rose's baby.

"They'll call when they find him, won't they?" Mom asks Dad.

"I'm sure. And Ginger told me if she saw Leaf, she'd—"

"Can you guys just stop?" I growl, instantly regretting it. I cough from the pain, a once burning sensation that's more of a throbbing ache now.

Mom and Dad blink back at me, eyes wide, sad, and confused.

I breathe in through my nose, then finish on a whisper, "I'm sorry, but I just want to forget things. Please."

Dad nods slowly.

Mom, though, isn't as forgiving. "I get that this is upsetting, Rebecca, but you have to know that we won't be letting Travis get away with this. He kidnapped you, he assaulted you and nearly choked you to death."

"Fine. Whatever." I get to my feet and head up the stairs. "Just leave me out of it."

"Get back here, young lady," Mom calls out. "We're not done talking about this."

I don't listen. Instead, I go to my room and do what I've gotten so good at.

I cry.

———

AN HOUR LATER, when both my eyes are nearly swollen shut, the doorbell rings. I grip my sheets, panicked, and my heart leaps into my throat. Even though I'm pretty sure I know who it is, I can't help my reaction.

Footsteps thump on the stairs. Voices echo. I swear I hear my mom say *good luck*, which has me rolling my eyes. A minute later, there's a knock on my door.

"Come in," I mumble.

Ben pushes it open but doesn't come directly inside. Instead, he studies me from the doorway, a line forming between his light brows.

"Hey," I manage, taking the time to look him over. He's wearing a white T-shirt that clings to his body. It's paired it with cargo jean shorts that should totally be a fashion flop but instead makes me grin for the first time in two days.

I know I'm supposed to be upset with him, but I can't stop the feelings in my chest. They explode with warmth, to the point where I have to sit up just to try and get some air into my lungs.

"You okay?" His legs are crossed at the ankles, a shoulder pressed to the door frame.

I nod.

"Can I...?" He points at my bed.

I nod again.

Ben quietly shuts the door and locks it behind him, then strolls toward me like he's been in my room million times before. His smile is curled up on one side, and that dimple pokes, making him look supermodel worthy and boyish at the same time.

"I'm here to get you de-funked," he says, sitting beside. "Apparently, your mom and dad are tired of seeing that long face." He grazes a finger down my cheek, then sets his hand back on his lap.

"Of course, you are." I roll my eyes.

If my mom and dad knew what we'd done in his kitchen and living room the other day, then I'm pretty sure they'd think twice about letting him come over to de-funk me. But I'm not gonna question it when I'm needing answers only Ben can give.

"Sooooo..." Without asking, he grabs my hand and presses his lips to my knuckles. "You miss me?"

Despite my reservations, I sigh and lay my head on his shoulder. He laces our fingers together. I let him because it feels nice. Soothing. As frustrated as I am with his evasive non-answers, I can't help but feel like being mad is pointless now that I nearly died by the hands of a psychopath.

"I'm sorry, what'd you just say?" I croak and grin. "I was just trying to imagine what it might be like to live with all that ego inside of you."

"Are you insulting me?" He fakes a gasp, and I can't help but laugh. It feels really good to do something other than cry.

"I'm just describing you. No harm in that, right?"

He pinches my side, which makes me laugh even more, and soon he's leaning over my body, urging me onto my bed, straddling my hips...

And now I'm totally *not* laughing.

"You're shaking," I whisper, reaching up to touch his cheek, forgetting all the bad things for a moment.

He nuzzles my palm like a puppy, and something in my stomach kicks at the look I see in his eyes. "I'm just glad you're okay." His Adam's apple bobs when he swallows. "If something would've happened to you..."

I flinch at the thought, the memory of Leaf's hands wrapped around my neck again. I reach up, rub my throat with my free hand for the thousandth time in forty-eight hours. It's only then that I let the bad back in, which also means asking Ben questions that can't be avoided any longer.

"Travis said something to me about you." There's no point in clarifying the *when* in that moment. My ex and his crazy dad kind of run together time wise anymore.

"What?" he scowls, upper lip curled.

I take a deep breath, urging him onto his side to face me. "He said...I should ask you what happened the night Rose died."

It's barely there, but I notice it—Ben's flinch. He rolls over onto his back and covers his face with both hands, probably to try and hide it. But I'm not stupid.

"Ben," I whisper, "what are you not telling me?"

He sets his hands on the mattress beside him but doesn't look at me. "He was just trying to get in your head, B."

I scoff. "Well, he kinda has."

He rolls to his side again, facing me. "It's not a big deal."

"If it's not a big deal, then why won't you just tell me?" I turn, facing him too. "You promised me no more secrets, remember?"

He groans. "Apparently, my Mom got a home visit from her teacher the day she died."

"Leaf?" My stomach twists. I hold my breath, waiting.

"Yeah." He draws in a breath, slow to release it. "Rose called and told me, talking through her ass about the guy lying and tricking her. I dunno. I was just getting ready to leave school and—"

"It was Travis's dad, Leaf." I rush out, wondering if I

251

can tell Ben the truth. Worried, at the same time, that his knowing might put him in danger.

"What are you talking about?" He frowns.

Danger or not, I can't keep this a secret. Not from Ben. He deserves to know. And I refuse to be a hypocrite when I've been so angry at both him and Rose for all of the secrets they've kept from me. Maybe with him being aware of the truth, he and I can go to the police together. Me, him, *and* Adam...

So, I tell him what all I know, knowing deep down that it's going to be oaky. That if loves me like he says he does, then we'll get through this. *Together*.

I start with the bucket list, jumping to Rose and Leaf's relationship. How Travis was the father of her baby, and how he blackmailed them both, leaving out my role in that whole ordeal. I even tell him how Adam's involved, that my faith in his innocence makes sense.

Throughout my confession, Ben's face pales considerably. Still, he nods here, hisses with rage there... By the time I'm finished, he doesn't speak. And out of everything, that scares me the most because I don't know if he's mad at me or Rose more.

The longer I wait for his reaction, the more my eyes burn, the more my throat swells for reasons beyond a bruised windpipe. When his quiet becomes too much, I start to cry, the shoulder-shaking kind.

"Shit, Becca. Come here." Surprising me, Ben wraps his arms around my waist and pulls me against his chest. "Don't cry. Please. It's okay. We'll figure this all out. I just...damn, I hate that you had to go through this alone. We're supposed to be a team, remember?" He tucks a loose strand of hair behind my ear, holding his palm to my bruised cheek.

I cry harder at his words, his gentle touch, pressing my forehead into his neck. After that, he doesn't tell me to stop anymore. Just urges me in between his legs while leaning us both back against my headboard.

There in his lap, I let it all go. My feelings, the pain of the last two months, up until now, this moment. The entire time, Ben kisses my temple, my forehead, murmuring sweet words. The perfect boyfriend.

"I'll never let him touch you again. You're safe with me."

I want to believe, but he doesn't know that for sure.

When my tears finally dry and my hiccupping breath evens out, it's Ben who speaks first again, but it has nothing to do with Travis, Leaf, or his sister's death.

"I remember that night." He sets his chin on my shoulder. I hear him smile, the twitch of his lips against my ear.

"Which one?" I ask through a yawn.

He moves a little, and I open my eyes just enough to see him pull the picture of Rose and me off the dresser beside my bed closer.

"That was our freshman year," I tell him. A simple time with simple lives... We had no idea what was to come, and I'm kind of glad we didn't.

"That was during the conference title game. I was a junior."

"Yeah." Rose was wearing overalls and a crop top. I was decked out in everything black, down to my hair— prior to my pink days. Both Rose and I had Ben's number painted on our cheeks in school colors. I can't remember who took the shot, but I do remember not wanting to be there. That was exactly two weeks after the night I tried kissing Ben in his kitchen.

"You sat in the lowest bleachers," he continues, "the ones closet to the field."

"You remember that?" I blink, getting lost in the memory he's describing. When I shut my eyes, I can still

253

feel the autumn wind on my face, smell the popcorn from the concession stand and the homemade cinnamon donuts they used to sell out of a small trailer close to the entrance. The last thing I'd wanted was to be there, like I said. But Rose, as always, had begged me to come to support her big brother.

So, I did.

I would've done anything for her then.

And now I would do anything for Ben.

"I remember those combat boots the most." Ben laughs. "The bright-blue laces made them look like they were clown shoes."

I laugh a little. "It's the only spirit I could muster besides the face paint."

"They were cute." He kisses my bare shoulder where my Tee has slid down. "Hell, everything you did back then drove me wild."

I lean back to put my chin on his chest. "Yeah?"

"Yep. I was mad crazy about you."

I know this. But teasing him comes naturally. *Was* crazy about me?"

"Yes." He turns his head and searches my face, blue eyes serious and pulling me in as much as his words. "Because what I feel for you now, Becca, is something a hell of a lot different."

"Yeah?" I hold my breath. Everything inside of me feels like it's suddenly on fire, blazing from a need I've never felt. My chest tingles, my stomach flutters... God, how is it possible that I can go from one emotion to another in such a short span?

Not that I'm complaining.

"Hell yeah, B." He lies back against the headboard again. "Every time I look at you, it's like someone's opening my chest up and tearing my damn heart out." He pats said chest with his fist as he finishes. "And I can't get enough of the pain."

Warmth fills my chest, which then slides deep into my belly seconds after. I'm not used to these sweet words from guys. With Travis, he'd been into me because he wanted something—my virginity. With Ben, though, things feel different, like we're meant for something greater.

I sit up and take a deep breath, then turn to face him. "You mean that?"

At first, he doesn't answer. Just reaches forward, grasps my chin with his thumb and forefinger, searching my face. I can't take the devotion in his gaze. Not without feeling guilty. I shouldn't be this happy. It's not fair to Rose's memory, and it all feels too good to be true.

"I do." With his free hand, he tugs me closer by my shirt, urging me against him. "So damn much."

Not thinking with my head, I crawl onto his lap, letting my legs wrap around his waist. It feels right. Real. It feels like I'm floating on a bubble of happiness, fearful that someone's close by with a needle to pop it at any second.

I'm tired of hurting though. Guilt, fear be damned. There's no denying this thing between us now. Not when it's always been there, festering.

"I..." I swallow, hard. "I feel that way about you too."

He looks at my mouth, his own lips twitching. "Like, maybe, you might love me?"

I bite my bottom lip, grinning. "What do you think?"

He laughs a little. I do too.

But the teasing and flirting? It doesn't portray how I really feel right now. What I want, most of all. There's this restless energy between us. It's scratching the surface of my skin. A desire to explore and kiss, feel and touch... I need more. I *need* Ben. I need him to erase what

255

Travis did to me that night in December. And I need him to give me what I've never truly felt before.

I lean closer, press my hands against his chest. His breath catches at my bold move, yet he manages to one-up me, wrapping both arms around my waist, fingers sliding beneath the hem of my Tee.

"Becca," he whispers, our foreheads grazing. "Tell me what you're thinking."

I shut my eyes, lick my lips too. "I don't want to mess this up."

He urges me back, just enough to where he places both hands on my cheeks. "It's not possible."

"It is," I argue, our eyes locked. "I'm a mess."

"It's. Not. Possible."

A second later, he closes the distance between us, his lips grazing mine not once but twice, until he parts them with his tongue, which slides over mine.

The kiss is perfect. It's *everything*. A kiss that should end all kisses.

I shiver, and goosebumps dance the tango across my arms. His fingers leave my face, diving into my hair, and we're suddenly chest to chest. Our breaths grow heavier, matching. He drops one hand to my waist and yanks me even closer, like he can't get enough. I can't either.

With Ben, I'm a live wire, sparking in the road, ready to strike the first chance I get. Yet he doesn't push for more than our kisses. I'm pretty sure he never will without permission.

Minutes later, when my lips are swollen, I dip my head back, allowing him to trail kisses down my chin, my neck, to the dip of my throat, then back up again. I moan. He groans. And soon his hands are sliding up beneath my shirt, my belly, stopping just under my bra. Frustration has me arching into him. I want him to touch me everywhere he can. So much. But instead of taking what he wants, Ben pulls his mouth away from my neck and settles his forehead against mine again.

"B," he says, shutting his eyes. "I want to touch you."

It's then that I feel myself truly falling for him.

"Okay." I smile. "Do it."

He settles me onto the bed, urging me onto my back. That's when I feel his fingers on the inside of my thighs, tracing lazy lines up and down my skin below my jean shorts. It's torturous. It's wonderful. It's everything I didn't think I could experience with a boy.

Dizzy from the contact, I bite down on my bottom lip, close my eyes, and savor everything as he crawls over me a moment later, settles himself on me, presses his hands on either side of my head. Like before, our eyes meet and hold, only there's fire in his gaze this time. A longing that I feel deep within my own bones.

"Kiss me," I tell him.

"Forever," he whispers back.

Seconds later our mouths meet again, more frantic this time. Impatient, yes, but never too much. Reaching up, I slide my fingers through the back of his thick hair, gripping it tight. He's the only thing keeping me afloat in this world I've been drowning in for so long.

My touch seems to spur him, and soon he's sliding a palm up and under my shirt, his heated skin like fire, burning me alive. I kiss him harder because I love the sensation, only to start shaking when I feel his hand over my bra. He's gentle and soft with his palm, but his mouth is hard and unrelenting, like he fears I'll disappear if he stops.

I'm worshiped at an altar by Ben, like he's been summoned by God himself.

"Starting tonight..." He pulls away, panting.

"Starting tonight, what?" I manage through another gasp.

257

"I'm yours. For as long as you want me." One side of his mouth curves into a smile. "That okay with you?"

Wordless, I pull him close again, speaking against his mouth. The entire moment suddenly feels like a dream I never want to wake up from. Maybe it is.

"Yes," I whisper. "As long as it's okay if I'm yours too."

18

September
Present Day

IT'S the wind shaking the chimes outside that wakes me. The TV is still playing infomercials, telling me I need this chopper-thing that I'm pretty sure my mom's sharpest knife could out-cut in seconds.

When I glance to my left, I notice my dad's asleep beside me on the couch, still in a sitting position with his chin to his chest. Guilt shoots through me because I know I'm the reason why he's not in his bed.

My nightmares.

My inability to sleep alone in a room without having all the lights on.

Hence why he and I fell asleep watching old movies at two in the morning.

After Ben left last night, my mind wouldn't shut off. It should have been good things running through my brain, like how Ben kissed and touched me. But it wasn't.

Instead, without him there to distract me, I was more on edge than normal. Terrified, really. About him leaving. About the possibility of him knowing too much. Of Leaf finding him, most of all. Even after Ben called to reassure me that he was home and safe later, I couldn't shake the feeling that life wasn't giving me a second chance but instead was giving me one last hurrah.

I need to go to Adam's house. *Today*. Get him on board with the plan to go to the police and end this once and for all. Ben agreed to go with us, and I'm praying that our three-person crew will be able to stand together, united, as we tell them everything we know.

I sigh and look out the window, catching sight of the suncatcher hanging there. It's the one I made when I was in fifth grade—a pig wearing a bonnet. Mom refuses to take it down, saying it's got a certain country charm to it, despite the fact that we only have horses, chickens, and corn on this farm. Not pigs.

It's what's next to the bonneted pig that has me standing and walking toward the window. Hanging beside it is the suncatcher that Rose made too. A sunflower. At the end of the day, when we were told to take them home, Rose wrapped hers up in a piece of newspaper and came home with me, saying she wanted my mom to have it, not Ginger.

Still to this day, I think about the look on my mom's face when Rose handed it to her. Admiration and love had lit up her eyes just as much as it had when I'd given her mine. Now I can't help but wonder what Mom would think if she knew the truth about us... about our bucket list. About what Rose had been like before she died.

"Becca? Everything okay?" Dad yawns.

I turn to face him. "Can't sleep. The windchimes are keeping me up."

He stands and stretches, arms high above his head, his face scruffy with a two-day beard. "Wanna give me a hand outside this morning?"

I know my dad misses the days when I'd wake early to help him with farm chores. And I kind of miss it too. More so miss the time I used to spend alone with him. I've always, most definitely, been a daddy's girl.

"Give me five minutes to get changed?" I ask.

"All right." He rubs a hand over his jaw. "Meet you in the kitchen."

I take the steps two at a time up to my room. In my closet, I grab my tennis shoes, hopeful for what might happen once this day ends. Maybe I can get back into an older routine, right some of my wrongs by helping out my mom and dad like I used to, by doing better in school and volunteering at places. Granted, that won't help me much in the long run if Travis or Leaf don't get in trouble. If the police can even *find* them either.

"Shut it down, Becca," I tell myself, sliding a scrunchie around my ponytail.

Downstairs, Dad's in the kitchen, two thermoses on the counter in front of him. Carefully he pours coffee into each. I hate to tell him that I never did actually drink the coffee he poured for me way back when, mostly because I don't want to hurt his feelings.

"You ready?" He smiles, handing me one.

I take it and pretend to drink. "Yep. Let's do this."

I follow him out the front door, feeling a little lighter. Things with Ben are *really* good now at least. Besides my family, our new relationship is pretty much the one positive thing I've got going.

"What's on your mind this morning, sunshine?" Dad bumps my shoulder with his, then pushes through the gate behind the house where the chicken coops and feed are.

I set my thermos down, then grab a handful of feed with my scoop. "Just stuff. Nothing, really."

I toss the feed into the pen, and the chickens scurry to snap it up. I used to love watching them eat when I was a little girl.

Dad sneaks into the pen, grabbing the newly laid eggs. Once my job is finished, I sit on a haystack, watching him work instead of the chickens. For as long as I can remember, Dad's always been my comforter. The one who'd come running after my nightmares—the defender against monsters in my closet or beneath my bed.

"Does it have anything to do with a certain boy?" Dad winks at me from over his shoulder.

"There's no *boy*." I stare at my shoes and frown. Other than Travis, I've never dated anyone, let alone brought him around my parents.

"Oh, I'm sorry. I forgot. Ben *is* two years older than you, so he's technically a man."

I roll my eyes. Of course, he knows.

"Mom won't like it."

"I know she won't."

He walks over and puts a hand on my shoulder. When I glance up at him, the first thing I notice is how sad his smile is. It's the type of smile that says he's worried about me but won't come right out and say it. There's something else there too.

"What?" I ask.

He sighs. "Mom and I just want you to be happy. You know that, right?"

"I'm trying."

"Well, if Ben makes you happy, then—"

The sound of the horses neighing from the barn cuts him off. We look at each other, frowning, then race

262

toward the giant red barn doors. God, I hope it's not a coyote again.

Dad sets down the collected eggs on a table outside the door, brushes his hands over his pants. "I wonder what's got them all worked up?"

I shrug, following him. He takes one side of the door and I the other, yanking it hard to get it open quicker. Already, sweat drips down my neck and into the back of my tank top by the time I'm done. Freaking Iowa humidity.

Before we can even step inside, the smell of urine and feces hits my face. I gag and turn away, while Dad asks the obvious.

"What the hell's that smell?"

He moves in front of me, into the barn, clicking on the light, only to stop in place, then yell, "What the..."

I blink, trying to look around him, but he shoves me out before I can see a thing. "Go inside. Call nine-one-one. Then stay inside with your mother until the police arrive, you hear me? Do *not* come into this barn."

"But—"

"Go!" It's his angry growl that urges me back this time. Dad never yells.

Every bad thing I can imagine runs through my head. Instead of looking inside the barn like I want to, I run toward the house, dialing nine-one-one on my phone before making my way up to my parents' room.

My stomach is in my toes by the time I reach her. Mom's face is buried in her pillow, her snores heavy. Instead of waking her up right away, I hit Send on my phone and wait for the operator to pick up. I sit on the edge of the mattress, knee bouncing. Once someone answers, I can't control the shaking in my voice as I try to explain what's going on— even though I don't know what's happening.

263

In all the chaos of the call, Mom wakes, clinging to my arm as she listens to my panic-filled conversation with the operator. Her eyes widen when she hears me mention my dad in the barn and sending an ambulance. Seconds later, she's up and off the bed, throwing on her buttercup-yellow robe that makes it look like the sun is leaving a trail behind her when she walks.

"Mom, wait," I yell.

She doesn't listen.

With my phone still pressed to my ear, I follow her, trying to call out to her again while holding the operator on the line. We're not supposed to go outside, but like me, my mom is stubborn.

The slam of the front door signals she's already gone, leaving me caught in between listening to my father's orders or wanting to play hero to my mom. Holding my breath, I make a decision that will forever haunt me as I step onto the porch, sneakers crunching through the grass when I take off after her seconds later. I'm tired of the operator's pointless questions and hang up on her, praying I managed to spit out enough information to sate her *and* get an emergency crew out here at the same time.

I reach my mom's back just before she steps through the barn doors. Yanking at the back of her robe. "Mom, stop. Dad said not to go in."

"Well, your father is an idiot if he thinks I'm going to leave him alone to deal with whatever is going on."

The second she enters and begins to scream, though, I instantly wish she would've listened. Then maybe I would have done the same.

The first thing I see when I step inside is Mom's back. Dad holds her to his chest, but his eyes flash up, meeting mine. "Becca, no, honey, don't look..."

I do though, spotting a hulking shadow hanging from

the rafters of the barn. His jeans are coated in urine. His eyes are bulged out, and his face...it's blue. But it's what's on the front of his skinny, shirtless body that makes me want to puke.

Red, bloody letters scratched across Adam's chest that say: *You're next.*

19

September
Present Day

IT WAS AROUND four o'clock in the morning, according to
the police report, when Adam was murdered and hung
out for display in our barn. When the police questioned
us, I opened my mouth, more than ready to tell them the
truth, only to remember the warning.

A warning clearly meant for me.

In the end, that's why I said what I did. *I don't know.*

Mom let me have it, talking over my head and
insisting that it had to be my crazy ex-boyfriend who'd
done this. She told the police about the attack in the car,
and since there'd been a report filed, they ran with the
idea, immediately putting out a secondary warrant for
Travis's arrest.

I didn't correct my mom. I should have but couldn't.
Travis is not his father. Yes, he's a jerk. Yes, he hurt me.
But he'd never murder his best friend.

What I needed to do was talk to Ben again. See what steps we should take now that Adam's dead and won't be able to back me up on everything related to Leaf. Nobody will believe just me. I'm nothing in the scheme of things, especially compared to a well-known, favored teacher in the community. If I went on about Rose and Leaf's affair, they'd likely think I was a stupid kid just looking for attention. What I need is some solid physical evidence.

I just don't know where to get it.

To top it all off, Ben isn't answering my phone calls or my texts. Not since I called him sobbing twenty minutes after we found Adam's dead body...forty-eight hours ago. He told me he'd be there as soon as he could. But five minutes later he sent me a text, saying an emergency had come up with his mom and that he wouldn't be able to come over after all. I'd tried and tried to call him again since then, but he's avoiding me, sending me weird replies via text, then admitting just an hour ago that he had to go back to school for training early.

A different kind of fear has been raging through me since. Part of me is worried that he's regretting what happened between us. And if that's the case, then I'm seriously going to give up on boys completely. Go to a nunnery after graduation, living out the remainder of my days as a born-again virgin, instead of a girl who'd had sex with one boy and messed around with another.

Even still with those thoughts, I can't help but call him again. And for the fourth time already today—and it's only six a.m.—his voice mail picks up.

I end the call, not bothering to leave a message this time, tossing the phone onto my bed before falling, ungracefully, back onto my pillow.

Emotions play ping-pong inside my brain, from anger to sadness, back and forth until I can't think anymore. I've needed Ben these last two days. Not just to tell him what really happened and how the image of Adam's tennis shoelaces, untied, haunt me every time I shut my eyes. Or how the vision of his blue-gray face and his wide, bulging eyes are going to be the stuff of my permanent nightmares from here on out. I just...I've *needed* him as a friend, at least.

A knock taps against my door frame. Letting my head fall to the side, I find Dad there.

"Hey, sunshine," he says, walking toward my bed. He crouches down in front of me, presses a hand to my cheek. "You okay?"

I nod. It's all I can do anymore.

He searches my face, circles as dark as mine beneath his eyes. Instead of speaking words—words that likely won't help—he kisses my forehead. "Go back to sleep," he whispers.

Even after he leaves the room, I can't shut my eyes.

A few minutes later, his tractor comes to life outside, proof that things must go on. But inside my room, the quiet is too much. Too suffocating. And going back to sleep? That's not gonna happen.

Slowly, I get to my feet and stumble toward the kitchen. I have a plan. Now to get my mom on board. "Hey, Mom?"

She spins to face me, a cup of coffee in hand. "You're up early."

There's no time for small talk, so I get right to the point. "Can we take a trip to Iowa City today?"

She frowns. "What for?"

I hesitate, forgetting that she doesn't know about Ben and me yet. It's easier to lie than explain, again, mostly because it's too early—in the day *and* the relationship.

If we even actually *have* a relationship now.

My stomach sinks at the thought, and I cross my

arms over the top to try and stop the ache. "Ben, um, forgot his wallet, and he's already back at school. His, um, license and ID are in there, and...he'll need them."

Mom lifts her brows in disbelief.

"He called and asked me to bring them. It's only a forty-minute drive," I tell her. "It'll be good to get out of the house, right?"

Her lips purse. I'm positive she's going to say no. Until she doesn't.

"Fine. We'll make a day trip of it, how about that? Do some shopping at Coral Ridge Mall, then be back in time for the visitation at five."

Shopping is the *last* thing I want to do at the moment. Same with the visitation. But if it means I get to confront Ben, then count me in.

OUR TRIP IS POINTLESS. When we get to the stadium where the team practices and plays, I'm totally set to go in and confront him, even if it means embarrassing myself, but there aren't any cars in the lot. Nothing. Which means Ben's either lying about training...or it's already over.

"We can try and find the place he's staying at until dorms open," Mom suggests when we pull away, oblivious to my frustration. "Obviously he asked you to come, so maybe you can just call him?"

"No." I stare out the window, heart climbing into my throat when I speak. "There's no point. I'll see him whenever. His loss, right?"

Mom shrugs, then starts driving us in the direction of the mall. We eat lunch in the food court, and Mom talks while I pretend that every lurking figure doesn't freak me out. At one point, she asks me if I'm okay, probably figuring it's just nerves for tonight's visitation. What I don't tell her, though, is how I'm worried that, at any given second, life as I know it could end.

_____

DÉJÀ VU ISN'T something I'm fond of, but the second my parents and I walk into the funeral home the night, I'm struck with that very feeling.

"...in Jesus's name we pray. Amen." The preacher bows his head, pretending not to notice as the three of us shuffle in late and sit in the last row.

Sniffles sound around the room. There's a low wail coming from the front row that draws me in. My heart aches at the sound. I peer over the woman's shoulder in front of me, catching sight of a lady hugging Adam's father—I'm assuming it's his mom. I don't bother looking for the little brother. That'll just hurt even more.

By the time the small service is over, I'm shaking so hard Mom has to wrap an arm around my shoulder to keep me upright. Dad asked me at least three times if I'm ready to leave, during the service, but somehow, I managed to stick it out. I'm sure they probably think I'm remembering Rose's funeral. But that's not the case.

What if Travis shows up? Worse yet, Leaf?

What if my parents are burying me next? Or I'm burying them?

Bile builds in my throat at the thought, and I'm thankful for Mom's next words. "It's time to go." She stands first and takes my hand in hers, smiling so softly it makes my chest warm. Dad hovers on the other side of me, his hand never far from my arm or the small of my back. I'm like a frail, old women, ready to crack into pieces between them.

They're both going to hate me when they find out

I've been keeping so many secrets. Everything is such a mess.

Mom squeezes my fingers and leads us out the door, her nearly silent *let's get out of here* accompanied by Dad's *it's gonna be okay* are the only two things that keep me from bawling.

"Chipotle for dinner?" Mom offers once we're on the front steps.

I haven't eaten much over the past few days, but the mention of my favorite food causes my underworked stomach to grumble, surprisingly. "Sure."

Mom and Dad speak about the funeral tomorrow, both of them deciding it's best if we don't go. I'm not going to argue—any time out in public is one more chance that Leaf can find me. Or us.

I shiver at the thought of my parents being targets, glancing around the dark parking lot. The farther away we move from the funeral home, the more my heartache lessens. But my nerves soon skyrocket instead.

It's dark out here. Too dark.

As I wait for Dad to unlock the car door, something pulls my attention back toward the building. Goose-bumps gather on my arms and my teeth chatter—but not from being cold. There's a shadow leaned back against the brick wall, tall, menacing, and thin. When I catch a sliver of his face under the roof's overhanging lights, my eyes widen.

It's Travis.

He's dressed in black slacks and a white T-shirt, the butt of a cigarette in his mouth now just barely burning. But I'd recognize him anywhere. He looks terrible. Worse than I've ever seen him. I'm pretty certain he's shaved his head too. I wonder if he knows he's a very wanted guy.

I should ignore him. Leave with my parents and

pretend he's not there. But I can't. I'm so close to answers that I'm willing to risk death to find them.

Twisting my hands together, I bend over and look into the car at my parents. "Hey, I need to pee, and I don't think I can hold it."

"Fine." Mom undoes her buckle. "I'll walk you back in."

"No, I'm okay. It's, like, twenty feet."

She looks at my dad, who shrugs, then looks back at me with a heavy sigh. "If you're not back in five minutes, we're going to—"

"Send a search party, yada, yada, yada. I get it."

Her lips flatten into a straight line. "Don't mock me, Rebecca."

Though my heart is racing like there's a flock of wild animals inside, I can't help but smile. Mom's...*Mom*. She's funny and protective and pretty much my one motivator in life, besides my dad—though I think he'd prefer to coddle me rather than push me sometimes.

"I'll hurry," I tell them. "Promise."

A few fallen leaves dance across the cement ahead while I make my way toward the side of the building. It's a musical echo of scrapes and whooshes that should be comforting but isn't. Not when every foot closer I get to my ex feels like I'm putting one foot inside my grave.

"I'm surprised you showed," I say, pretending to be brave, hiding the shake of my hands by folding my arms.

He inhales a final drag from his cigarette before speaking. "Say what you want, doll. But Adam was my best friend."

"Did you kill him?" I ask.

His jaw clenches, and he looks around me toward a group of people walking by. "No."

"If you didn't do it, then why are you hiding?"

"Because *your* dumb ass claimed I did."

I wince, taking a small step back. He's too close. It's too dark. And, again, his father could be lurking. I'm stupid for being here, yet...

He rubs the back of his neck, cracks it from side to side. "I need to talk to you about something, Becca."

Must be something big if he's using my real name. "Talk then." I lift my chin. "You have three minutes, asshole."

He jerks his head back. "*You're* pissed at *me*? That's rich."

"Yes, I'm *pissed*. For one, your *father* tried to choke me out," I hiss, counting on my fingers. "Your *father* who was also having an affair with a seventeen-year-old."

Though, from the sounds of it, Rose had technically been sixteen when their entire relationship started.

"You also cheated on me with my best friend, black-mailing her into having sex with you when I wouldn't." I tap on another finger. "And you also got her *pregnant*."

"Yeah." He laughs and rubs a hand over his chin. He's too calm and relaxed for a guy wanted for murder and assault. "Sorry about that. Got a little too eager one night, if you know what I mean." He shrugs. "Rose didn't stop me though. I think she might've even liked it."

A lump fills my throat, but I manage to swallow it. He's just trying to get a rise out of me. It's what Travis does.

"Just spit out whatever else you have to say, all right?" I glance over my shoulder, making sure my parents are still parked.

"Okay, okay." He holds up one hand, then drops his cigarette, squashing it with the toe of his boot. "I have something of yours."

I frown. "What?"

"A letter. From Rose."

I blink. "Excuse me?"

273

He pulls another cigarette out and lights it, the butt cracking under his lighter. "You heard me."

"Why do *you* have it?"

"I found it in some of my dad's shit last night. I needed money since his ass took off, and it was there in his office drawer."

I touch my lips. Why would his dad have a letter from Rose to me? And why would Travis openly offer it up?

"Anyway, I didn't think you'd show tonight, otherwise I would've brought it."

"How do I know you're not lying?"

He shrugs. "You don't. But I can tell you, all those answers you're wanting about my old man? They're in that letter. Wouldn't be right of me to turn him in, but I'm pissed enough to let you do it."

This all feels too good to be true.

He moves closer, his chest brushing mine. I take an immediate step back, somehow trapped against the brick wall of the building now. Travis hovers over me, his mouth lowered to my ear. To anyone passing by, we look like lovers, when really, all I want to do is drive my knee between his thighs.

He lifts his hands, presses both along either side of my head against the wall. Then he dips his head, lowering his mouth to my neck this time.

Travis inhales, groaning a little. "Forgot how good you smelled."

"Don't touch me." I shove him back by the chest.

He laughs.

Ignoring his taunts, I take a step to my left toward the lot. "Where and when can I get this stupid letter?" God, this is crazy. But I don't really have another choice either.

He smirks, likely knowing he's got me where he

274

wants. "Eight a.m. tomorrow. At the alcove, but closer to the dam."

My stomach pitches. I blink.

I can't go there. I *can't*. That's where Rose's body washed up on shore.

Still, if I don't go...

I know what I have to do. Even if it's the last thing I want. Even if it kills me, literally. I'm not ready to die, but if that's what it takes to get Leaf behind bars, so be it.

Lifting my chin, I look Travis dead in the eyes and say, "I'll be there."

20

September
Present Day

DAD's at the feed store in town picking up supplies, so he's one less person I have to get past the following morning.

Mom isn't so relenting.

I hold my hands together beneath my chin, batting my eyes, puffing out my bottom lip. She's sitting on the couch, folding laundry, a frazzled mess, likely because she was up all night with me again. I can't help the nightmares. I can't help how badly I scream too.

"Pretty please? It's just a bike ride, and I have that mace you gave me *and* my cell." What I don't tell her, though, is that in the pocket of my cargo army pants, I've stowed away my dad's handgun. The one he uses to scare coyotes away if they get to close. They store it in a lockbox in their bedroom closet, the key's hiding spot in Mom's top dresser drawer.

"*One* hour. Tops. As long as you text me every ten minutes to check in."

"Cross my heart."

Eyes narrowing, Mom holds her arms out demanding a hug. I hesitate, praying she doesn't feel the bulge in my pants pockets. Thankfully, she doesn't.

Five minutes later, I'm out the door, determined *not* to die today. Last night I'd been ready to. This morning's another story.

Hence the weaponry.

Not that I actually know how to use the stupid gun.

Even for early September, the humidity is brutal as I take the roads leading to the river. The dam is closer than the alcove, a mile and a half from the farm actually. But it still feels like I'm riding for days, not minutes. By the time I make it to the clearing, my tank top is soaked and sticking to my skin, likely a heat and nerve combination thing.

Travis's car is parked off the side of the road. I see a few people close by, sitting atop the brick wall, fishing. Rose used to sashay along the edge, ballerina style, like she'd do at the dam. The view has my stomach rolling, but the people help to ease the fear of being alone with Travis. Still, it doesn't stop me from wanting to circle back around and go home. Forget *everything*.

But then I think about Rose's letter. What might be in it, most of all.

I know this is probably the worst idea I've ever had, but I'm desperate, seeing as how today is my self-imposed-D-Day when it comes to going to the police. With or without Ben, I have to do this. I've waited too long.

I jump off my bike and prop it against a tree, using the back of my arm to wipe the sweat from my forehead. Swallowing a lump in my throat, I look around for

Travis, but the rush of the river in my ears is distracting. Unnerving too. My heart thuds against my chest as I walk toward the brick wall. I don't look at what's beyond the fishermen though—the small waterfall making up the dam. If I did, I'd fall to my knees, cry to the point where I might never be able to get up.

I didn't want to come here.

Not again.

I didn't want to see the rows and rows of dandelions on the ground beneath my feet, the ones Rose used to pick and tuck into our hair. The ones she used to tie together and make pretend crowns with too.

My chest tightens at the memory. I turn, unable to breathe, ready to run and—

"You came." Travis leaps out from behind a tall bush.

My hand flies to my chest. "Shit, you can't do that to me."

He smirks, his gaze lazy as he looks up and down my body. I take him in too, but more so in disgust. He looks like he hasn't slept in days—lips chapped and bloody at the corners, black bruises under his eyes. The shirt he wore last night now hangs off his body like it's four times too big, while his dress pants have been traded in for basketball shorts. Hairless like he is now, the guy looks like something out of an alien warship who's been probed one too many times.

"I forgot what a chicken you could be sometimes." He laughs.

I hold out a hand. "Where is it?"

"Always in a hurry." He tsks. "Don't I get a kiss first?"

He steps closer, and I yank the mace out of my pocket, figuring the gun might be overkill just yet. "Don't come any closer."

Travis let's out a slow sigh, studying the silver container. Oddly enough, he doesn't comment. Just pulls a white envelope from the front of his shirt pocket. Tentatively, I reach for it, eyes narrowing when he holds it above his head.

"I want something in return for this."

"W-what's that?" I ask, dropping my arm with the mace to my side.

He lowers his hand, the letter too. I reach out to take it with my free fingers, my knees threatening to buckle. I touch the paper. This is the last link I have left of Rose, yet I'm terrified to know what it says.

"Hold on now." He tugs it back, teasing me. "Something's going down for me within the next day or so, and I'm gonna need help with it. *Your* help, actually."

"Is it..." I swallow hard. "Illegal?" Worse yet, does it involve his father? I realize I'm seconds from selling my soul to the devil, but I've come too far to back down.

"It's *necessary*. Let's just go with that."

"Fine." I regret the word the second it's out.

"All right." He smiles wide. "No matter what time I call you, you're to come to me. Got it?"

"Whatever. Just give it to me." Jumping forward, I swipe the paper from his hands, taking two steps back only to rip the envelope open.

Travis sighs and leans back against the tree, waiting with his ankles crossed. A lighter flickers to life and soon the scent of a cigarette fills the air. Still, nothing distracts me from what I see.

It really is Rose's writing. *Her* words. And at the top of the letter, it reads: *Dear Becca.*

My shoulders shake as I study the blue cursive ink, and tears drip quickly down my cheeks.

If you're reading this, then you know the truth. And since I'm too much of a bitch to tell you in person, I have to write out my apology this way. You know how I am.

I take a deep breath, then look ahead toward the

brick wall, the river, too, capturing my attention. I cry harder but continue to read.

I achieved #75, aka sleep with the forbidden, but I'm not proud of it. It was reckless and stupid, and I know you probably will hate me for it, but you also need to know the truth. I slept with Leaf, my English teacher. The thing is, he's not who I thought he was. He's manipulative, let's just say. And when he doesn't get what he wants? Watch out. I really thought he loved me though. He told me so.

Leaf promised me things I thought I needed but then betrayed me in the end. I'm so sorry. Especially since I told him about the list we burned. He only knows about #72 though because he's the one who saw us in the parking lot that night. Otherwise, he doesn't know about any of the other stuff. I'd never tell him. I swear. Your friendship is way more important to me than anything else, and I wouldn't risk it. You have to know that.

I shake my head. Rose told Leaf about the list, admitted to doing what we did to Liam's truck that night of the football game, but otherwise the man knows nothing else. Which means he really is lying.

Either way, I'm done with him, especially since he came over today and ratted me out to my mom. The jerk called me inappropriate, said I needed mental help! Can you believe that?

"I can," I whisper, running my fingers over her words.

Mom freaking believed him too, is the thing. Threatened military school, then took me to the doc because, well...Leaf told her something else I haven't told you yet. Something I'm so ashamed of that I'm pretty sure I'll never be able to face you again. (Hence another reason for this letter.)

I'm just gonna come right out and tell you this.

I'm pregnant. And the baby is Travis's.

I wince, seeing those words written there. Words that

shouldn't feel like a knife in my back, especially since I know the entire story now. But still, there's a pang in my chest that won't go away as I read on. Because the truth hurts, even though I've been demanding it from the beginning.

So, this is where the letter gets hard to write. Big time. And it started with that jerk face ex of yours walking in on me and his dad.

I read the words, cringing here, wincing there. Everything she admits is the same truth Leaf told me, including the blackmail. There are spots on the paper where the blue ink is smeared, and I can't help but wonder if Rose was crying when she wrote this all down.

I forgive you, girl, I whisper in my mind.

She goes into more details than Leaf did about things. How much she wished she could take it back too. I believe every written word of it because Rose may have kept secrets but only by omission. Never because she didn't want to tell me. I realize that now.

Anyway, my mom agreed with me about not having the baby, so she got me this pill to take from a guy she knows that would supposedly abort the baby. A dealer, I guess. It's supposed to be super controversial and not even on the market yet. I dunno. I wanted to get Plan B, but she was worried someone in town would see me. I'm like, who flipping cares. Whatever. I plan to take it tonight. Adam's gonna get me high first, thinking it might help with the pain if there is any. The thing is, I want to tell you. I want you to be there with me when I take it too. But when I tried calling and asked if you'd hang out, you said you didn't want to, so I took it as a sign that I have to do this on my own. My stupid mistake shouldn't involve you anyways.

My biggest mistake ever was not going out that night. "I'm so sorry, Rose."

I called Ben just a little bit ago and told him about being pregnant. He doesn't know about Leaf's and my relationship, and obviously Mom doesn't either. Neither of them should be stressed out any more than I've already made them, you know? I really thought Ben would be pissed, but he wasn't. He's such a good brother. Told me he'd take care of things with Mom. He won't let her send me to military school, thankfully.

So, the drugs in her system were nothing more than weed and this mystery abortion pill which she wasn't supposed to take. Which means she didn't OD. And she didn't jump into the dam on purpose either, just like Ben said. She was reckless. But she wasn't suicidal.

I continue to read, my chest lightening a little knowing all this. Maybe the interaction of the pill and the weed is what actually killed her, and she fell into the water.

I just want you to know that I'm so freaking sorry, Becca. Please don't hate me for keeping secrets and lying, for sleeping with that awful ex of yours too. I swear I'll make it up to you, somehow, every day of my life if I have to. But please, PLEASE don't hate me. Be mad at me. Throw things at me. But don't hate me. You mean the world to me. Always will. You're my sister.

Forever.

Always.

Rose

I lower the paper and look at Travis again. As still as death itself, he sits with his legs pulled to his chest on the ground now, his chin resting on his knees as he stares up at me. "So, now that you know the truth, do you feel better?" he asks.

"Go to hell." Disgusted, I stuff the paper inside my pocket and take off toward my bike.

Travis is partially to blame for this, and I want him to

die a miserable, awful death. But his dad needs to be punished for messing with his students, and without this stupid letter, I wouldn't be able to do what I'm about to do.

"How long were you and Rose friends?" he asks, feet shuffling as he rushes after me.

I pick up speed. "Almost eight years."

"Damn." He whistles. "That was one hell of a bucket list."

I don't respond because I don't want to hear his stupid voice more than I have to.

Once I reach my bike, I grab it and push it toward the road leading away from the river and through the thick weeds. Rustling feet continue behind me, picking up speed. Because I'm not in the best of shape right now, Travis catches me easily. He grips my upper left arm, nails digging into the skin.

"Let me go." I wince, struggling to pull away. My phone buzzes from my pocket. And I know right away it's Mom. I forgot her *every ten minutes text or call* rule.

Just add that to my list of failures.

Travis lowers his head, presses his lips to my ear. "You owe me. Don't forget."

I don't speak. I can't. Now that I've read the letter, now that I know the truth, I need to get to the police. Screw Travis and his father's stupid threats. Screw *everyone*.

"The deal's off," I hiss, reaching into my other pocket for the gun this time. It shakes in my hand, but I'm not afraid to use it. Not anymore.

His grip on my arm tightens, while his eyes narrow at the weapon for a long second. Then, like I'm not holding his life in my hand, he grins, reaching up with his free hand, and tucks a loose strand of hair behind my ear.

I shudder. My stomach swirls with the sudden need

to hurl, but I can't show fear. Instead, I squeeze the handle even tighter, position my finger over the trigger as I aim it at his face. Thankfully, the fisherman can't see any of this.

"Move. Now," I hiss.

He doesn't try to stop me. Instead, he shakes his head and steps back. "You'll pay for that one, doll."

I should be scared.

But I'm not.

———

DOWNTOWN WINSTON IS quiet this early in the morning. I feel like people are hiding out behind curtains, waiting and watching, readying to pounce. With one goal in mind alone, I make it to the front of the police station...distracted when I spot a woman across the street, leaving the salon.

It's Ginger.

Ginger, who is supposed to be in rehab an hour away, according to Ben's latest text. My stomach hardens at the view, and I forget my destination as a new one comes into play.

Ben lied to me. Again.

"Ginger!" I holler, drop my bike, and rush through the grassy town square center to greet her.

"Becca?" Her eyes widen. "What's wrong?"

"Why are you not in rehab?" I pant, settling my hands onto my knees.

She jerks her head back. "Rehab?"

"Ben told me you went to rehab. It's why..." I wince, not wanting to bring up Adam. The visitation...the hanging.

"No, honey. I'm obviously not in rehab, though I have been going to a few AA meetings."

284

I squint at her, then take a step back. I don't understand...

"When did you last see Ben?" I ask.

"Before he left for school three days ago. Why?"

A sick feeling builds in my stomach. Ben's fine. He's been texting me. Leaf doesn't have him. Leaf *didn't* hurt him.

"Becca, what's going on?" she asks, her voice lowering.

"Sorry," I mumble halfheartedly. "It's just...there's something you need to see."

Taking a deep breath, I pull the letter from out of my pocket and hold it in front of Ginger.

"What is it?" Her gaze flits between me and the paper, eyebrows furrowing.

"Read it."

"Where did you find this?" she murmurs, reads it over, her eyes widening with each word she comes across.

"Does it matter? It's the truth. Everything in it that letter, from *your* daughter, is the only truth you'll ever need. Leaf lied, *he* slept with Rose." My breathing accelerates, squeezing my lungs as I finish with, "Leaf is also the one who attacked me when I left your house the other night. Not Travis."

"Becca," she whispers, drawing out my name. "Why are you doing this? There's no need to cover up for Rose now that she's gone."

"Are you kidding me?" I scoff. "Leaf needs to pay for what he did to her."

Ginger shakes her head, then does the last thing I expect: she tucks the letter into her purse and zips it shut. "Sweetie, there are things you're unaware of when it comes to Rose and Leaf's...*situation*."

285

"No. That's mine. Give it back." I reach for her purse, yanking it.

"Stop it." She hisses. "Right now, young lady."

My mind races, dizziness washing over me. My phone buzzes, louder and louder. Still, I don't take my eyes off Ginger. She looks empty. Tired. It's like she's...she's *done*. Not just with life but with her daughter too.

I growl, disgusted and angry on behalf of my best friend. "That letter is mine."

"Not anymore, I'm afraid." She grunts and pulls her cell phone from her pocket, tapping the screen.

"Leaf is demented!" I scream. "He had a sick obsession with *your* daughter, yet you're going to take his side?"

"Yes. I am. Because Leaf is a good man who loves me." She lifts her chin. Both defensive and oblivious. "Rose was sick, Becca. She was mentally unstable and jumped over that dam because she was unwell."

I shake my head. "That's not true. She was dealing with a lot of bad crap, but—"

"It is true." She stuffs her phone into her pocket, looks at me again. "And that letter..." Ginger pats the side of her purse. "It's proof of that. I'm just sorry you didn't know."

"You're wrong!" I reach out, grabbing her purse-strap handle, tugging, tugging some more.

"Let go!" she screams. "Right now, Becca. I texted your dad, and he's coming to get you. You're not well either; I can see that now."

"That's my letter!" I yank and yank and yank. "You stole it!"

Ginger steps back, hands on her hips. "And what exactly do you plan on doing with it, hmm?"

"I'm going to take it to the police."

286

She lifts her brows, laughs a little. "And ruin Leaf's life while you're at it? I'm sorry, I can't let you do that."

"He ruined your daughter's life!" I scream, loud enough to draw eyes my way. Several people stand around us now, watching on, including a police officer, several women from the salon too.

I know I look crazed. But how is it that I'm the only person who believes the truth?

"Just give the letter to me, okay?" I lower my voice, trying for calm, reaching for her strap again.

"Officer!" Ginger calls out. "Please, I need help."

My lips part. Shock renders me speechless. She's really doing this.

"What's the problem here?" the officer asks, eying me as she takes her place beside Ginger.

When I look up, the first thing I see is the cop's hand on her gun, the second? The mistrust in her eyes. The officer doesn't know me, but the situation is not in my favor. Which means if I try to tell the truth, she won't believe me.

I've lost my proof. Still, I have to try.

"She stole something from me." I point to Ginger's purse.

Ginger turns on the tears like a trained actress. "She found a letter my daughter wrote. Rose McCain?" She faces the officer head on, and what I'm sure are practiced tears fall down her red cheeks. It's an award-worthy performance, honestly. Didn't know she had it in her.

The officer looks between us, her lips flat until finally she relents... ust not in my favor. "Go home." She says to me. "This is your only warning, young lady."

She surveys me. It's then that I remember the gun I'm carrying in my pocket.

Crap. I'm screwed. So much, in so many ways.

A minute later, a car horn honks. I look toward my

bike, seeing Dad's truck. He gets out, door slamming, looking as though he's ready for the apocalypse—all badass and touched by anger in a way I'm not used to.

The thing is, it's not Ginger or the officer he's glaring at.

It's me.

288

21

September
Present Day

MY FACE IS blotchy and tear stained by the time I make it home. I've never heard my dad yell so much in my life. Mom's on the front porch, a hand to her mouth as she watches me get out. She looks one part relieved I'm alive, the other part ready to murder me herself.

Surprisingly, the only thing she says as I walk past her and onto the porch, then into the house is, "You're grounded."

Without them knowing, I put the gun back into its case and place the key inside Mom's drawer again, glad to be done with it. When I get to my room, all I can hear is their arguing in the kitchen below. They fight about what to do with me. Therapy, a doctor, or possibly sending me to live with my mom's sister in Maine.

To drown them out, I shove my ear buds into my ear and click on Spotify, pulling up my playlist. During the third song, when I feel like my life is over completely, I manage to fall asleep, awakened later in the afternoon by the buzzing of my phone somewhere under the covers. The ear buds fall out, disorienting me, and my eyes burn from crying so hard that I struggle to open them so I can see who's calling.

Though when I do look, I wish I wouldn't have.

"What do you want?" I bite.

"Hey, doll," Travis murmurs. "I'm gonna need your help tonight, not tomorrow. Plans have changed."

My body goes rigid. "No. I told you, deal's off."

"You're gonna *wanna* help me, is the thing. I mean, if you ever wanna see lover boy again."

That's when I hear it.

A muffled voice, low, panicked...familiar.

Ben. "Becca, no. Don't come."

My eyes widen and panic steals the breath from my lungs.

Oh God. Oh God, no.

"Travis, please," I cry out. "Don't hurt—"

"Gonna need you to come down to the river alcove, alone. No cops, no friends, no mommy or daddy. One hour, that's all you get. If you do what I ask, then I won't make it look like an accident this time."

The phone clicks. Something in my head does too.

I won't make it look like an accident this time.

"No," I whimper. "No, no, no." I scramble to my feet, look left, then right. Thunder rumbles outside, distracting me. A storm has come, literally and metaphorically. I jump in place, a hand on my mouth while I pace back and forth in my room.

Before I can think about what I'm doing, I dial a number. It rings and rings...until finally, on the fourth one, she picks up.

"Hello?"

"Sienna. I need your help, please."

———

FIFTY-SEVEN MINUTES LATER, after sneaking out my window, then running through the muddy fields to meet up with Sienna's car at the end of the farm, we're pulling up to the road next to the river.

Mom and Dad are going to kill me. But I need to save Ben first.

The rain pours in heavy sheets, the thunder louder than earlier. Sienna think's I'm having a crappy day, that I needed a moment with the Big Guy in the form of visiting the alcove. What she doesn't know is that I'm leading her toward my possible demise. Hers too, if I'm not careful

"Ugh, you could have picked any other day to have a come-to-Jesus moment," she groans and pulls up next to a car. It's Travis's.

I slap a twenty into her cupholder and mumble, "I'll get my own way home."

If I even make it home.

I shut the door, managing to do so without crying, then rush around the front bumper, stomach in my toes. It's bad enough I asked Sienna to drive me here. Getting her involved any deeper isn't fair. Still, it's not like I could've asked my parents.

"Helllllloooo?" she calls after me. "You left your—"

I run to her window, slap a hand over her mouth, looking left, right, then back behind me. If Travis heard her, she's screwed as much as I am.

"Quiet. Just turn around and leave. Now. It's too dangerous for you to be here."

Her eyes widen, and it's only when she nods that I

pull my hand away. "Becca?" she whimpers. "What's going on?"

"Please," I say, shirt soaked, hair stuck to my cheeks, my knees. I'm shaking, my knees, my hands... "Just go, Sienna."

Unfamiliar voices sound over the rush of the river, the rain and thunder and wind. They're loud enough I recognize at least one of them.

"Is that...Travis?" Sienna points to something behind me through the trees.

"Leave, Sienna. Right now."

"But—"

"I said go!"

Sienna's bottom lip trembles. It's the last thing I see before she rolls up her window. Without waiting for her to pull away, I turn and begin to run. There's no time for second guesses. No time for comforting her either.

My feet sink deep into the mud, and my overgrown bangs drip across the bridge of my nose and eyes. I make my way closer toward the tree line, pushing the hair from my face, chest tight, eyes surprisingly dry for once, even knowing what's waiting for me.

Dropping to my knees with a deep breath, I peer through a small gap between the trees, spying two figures hovering over a third body...a body that's on the ground, unmoving.

I'm close enough to see the blood dripping over the unrecognizable, swollen face, and the rope hanging from his neck, ripped and frayed at the end too. Close enough to see, that Ben stands hovering over the figure. Something the color of oak in his hands, hanging lifeless against his thigh.

"Ben!" I scream, then push through the tall grass, rush down the small hill until I'm ten feet away, then five...

It's only then that I recognize the beaten and strangled body, unmoving on the ground.

Or what's left of it.

Ben's cheeks are whiter than I remember them being. He's wearing a T-shirt and shorts...both of them ripped and unwashed. There's a Hawkeyes baseball cap tucked low over his head, but the brim is broken, the top button torn off and hanging.

It's the same outfit he was wearing the night he left my house.

But it's what in his hands that forces a cry up my throat.

A bat, covered in blood, with the initials *RMC* on the handle.

Rose's old softball bat.

"Ben," I whisper, hands in the air, approaching him. "Put it down, okay? Please."

He doesn't move. Doesn't look at me either. All he does is stare at Leaf's dead body.

"There you are." Travis chuckles, stepping between us. "Didn't think you'd show, doll."

Ignoring Travis, I keep my gaze locked only on Ben. Ben, who's covered in bruises, half of his face almost unrecognizable as he slowly stands and turns to face me.

Our eyes lock from over Travis shoulder.

"Ben," I whisper, lips trembling. "W-what happened?"

"He hurt her." He chokes on the words but continues. "He had to pay. He had to pay for what he did to my sister, to you."

If Ben did this to Leaf, his life will be over. No football, no future, no nothing . . .

A wicked smile forms on Travis's face as he jerks my chin away from Ben. "You owed me, remember?" he yells over the crackle of thunder. "Lucky for you, lover boy did the job instead. Works well, seeing as how he'll be going down for it. Not you. Not me either."

"No." I try to walk around Travis, but he sets his hands on my shoulders, blocking me.

"*Yes*," Travis mocks. "And he had one hell of a good time doing it, didn't you, buddy?"

I cover my mouth with both hands, knees growing weak.

"You wanted him dead, didn't you?" Travis yells at me when I don't speak. "You wanted my dad to pay for what he did to Rose, right? You wanted him to suffer like she did? Because he pushed her in, Becca. *He* pushed her over that dam, not me. Yes, it was my idea, but the old man here is who did it in the end. She's dead because of him."

"No," I cry out.

"I told him not to just seconds beforehand. She was crying, calling *your* name too. Nobody else's. Just. You."

I fall to my knees, shut my eyes.

"I knew how upset you'd be about losing her. I told my dad so. But he shoved her in anyway. Told her she had to pay for being a slut. Getting pregnant with my kid." He laughs.

I try to stand, sobbing as I do, only to fall back onto my butt, the wind and rain too much.

"He was gonna blame me." Travis hovers over me, green eyes crazed. "His own son. I mean, who the hell does that?"

Travis's words are like fire running through my ears, burning me alive. I squeeze my eyes shut and rock with my arms around my knees to try and put out the flames.

I'm so sorry, Rose. I'm so, so sorry.

"In the end, it's all your fault, doll. Everything would've been fine if you hadn't broken up with me." He keeps going. And going and going and going... "I didn't want her. I hated her. Hell, Becca, I was drunk when I first had sex with her. She told me that if I slept with her, you'd get jealous and you'd come back to me, but you never did. Bitch lied."

"Stop it." I cover my ears with my elbows, soaked in mud, frozen from the cold rain. "Stop it, Travis, please."

"That twisted slut. She just wanted to keep me quiet so I didn't nark on her and my old man. So, I kept screwing her. A lot. She even let me call her Becca when I did." He laughs. "Then Adam found out. Stupid, clueless Adam. He threatened to tell on my dad. My dad told him he'd kill him—his kid brother too—if he did. Adam tried taking the blame, but Dad wasn't about to let it go. It was too risky."

I knew it.

"He was my best friend, and my dad *killed him*. Can you believe that shit?"

Travis falls to his knees beside his father, jumping from one emotion to the next. Fingers in his hair, he pulls. "Adam...was m-my best friend."

Then he does the last thing I expect, he openly sobs.

I feel nothing—see nothing—except for Ben. He's looking at his hands now, eyes widening as he moves his gaze up his forearms.

"Oh God. What did I do?" he mumbles.

Next to Leaf's unmoving body sits the bat covered in fresh blood. My stomach curls and twists, and bile threatens to climb up my throat. I don't know what Ben's thinking, but I can only imagine the pain he's in, especially since he, too, now knows the truth.

I take his hand in mine. Squeeze it just once. "It's okay. We'll figure this out." The words feel dry, untrue because they are in fact not true. Ben can't get out of this. Not when the evidence is so real.

"Leaf hurt her, Becca," Ben whispers. "I had to..."

"I know he did." I touch his cheek.

"He pushed her over the dam. He *killed* her."

All I can do is nod, cry, nod again.

When I slide my thumb over his bruised cheek, he winces.

"What happened to you?" I ask.

He shakes his head. "Travis...he stole my phone. Knocked me out on my way home from your house." Ben lunges forward, taking me against his chest, clinging to me as tightly as I do him. "God, Becca. I'm so sorry I wasn't there for you. He pretended to be me on the phone, texting that whole time. *Fuck*, I was right there. He said if I didn't do this, he'd hurt you."

I grip the back of his shirt and squeeze my eyes shut. "How did you get away?"

"I didn't. Travis just...he snapped. Tied me up, beat me. Then came down this morning and started saying something about you and him getting together again." His body shakes against mine. "Then he untied me. Told me we're gonna kill Leaf. He told me what happened to my sister, and you..." He chokes on a sob. "I-I didn't want to kill him, Becca. I didn't. But...I just, I lost my damn mind. Helped Travis get the guy in the car." He scrubs both hands over his face. "I started changing my mind after that, but then he called you and..." He sobs harder, shoulders shaking. "Oh God, what did I do?"

"Shhh, it's okay." I grip his shoulders, pressing my mouth and against his neck, tasting salt, rain, and regret. "Everything's going to be..."

Slow clapping starts. I stiffen at the sound, while Ben growls, the noise of it vibrates against my temple.

"What a damn good performance." Travis stops clapping. "I almost believed you. Sure seems like Becca does."

"Fuck you, Travis." Ben turns slowly, his arm now around my waist.

Travis picks up Rose's bat by the handle and studies the bloody end. "*You* did this," he barks. "You're a murderer who *killed my father*. Not some *hero*."

I wipe at my wet cheeks, look up and face him again, blanching at what I see. Travis is smiling, soaked and muddy, maybe even worse than we are. His eyes are red and bulging. In his hands, he still holds the bat, tapping it once, twice, three times against the toe of his shoe.

"Put it down," Ben tells him, sounding stronger.

"You killed my dad." Travis cocks his head to one side, face pinched. His tapping stops. It's like he's seeing the scene in a brand-new light—because he starts to yell. Scream, really. "You *killed* him!"

Seconds later he lifts the bat and jumps over his father's body, coming at us. I scream and hold my hands over my head, only to be shoved back. My body throbs in pain when I hit something on the ground. I curl into a ball waiting for the pain and...

Then I hear it.

Thunk.

A cry.

Thunk-thunk.

A groan.

Thud.

Then...silence.

22

September
Present Day

I CAN'T MOVE. Everything hurts. Still, I have to look.
When I move my arm to do so, I immediately wish I
hadn't.

"No, no, no, no..." On hands and knees, I crawl
toward Ben, eyes blurring from tears.

Blood drips from his temple. His eyes closed...chest
no longer rising and falling with breaths. I know before
even reaching his side that he's gone.

"No, Ben, no!" Fingers shaking, I touch his face. I
scream. I kiss his head, hold it on my lap. He's so cold. So
wet. I need to warm him up.

Oh God, no, Ben.

"Shut up, ya dumb bitch." Travis stands over me,
grabs my hair and yanks me away. "Shut up, or I'll dump
you in the fucking river after I beat you to death too."

298

A sob breaks through my lips, so loud it burns my throat. He shoves me down and into the mud, then starts pacing back and forth with the bat by his side.

"So stupid," he mumbles, smacking his forehead.

Over and over and over. Smack. Smack. Smack.

Through my sobs, I hear the rev of an engine. Travis must too because he stops moving. Drops the bat too. I turn toward the noise, already knowing who it is.

Sienna. She didn't leave.

"Who the hell is that?" Travis growls.

Her lights flicker through the rain, bouncing with the divots in the ground. She drives closer, faster, never stopping, never slowing. Her headlights flash. Maybe she's trying to tell me to move. I won't. I *can't*. If Ben's dead, then I might as well be too.

Travis jumps backward, over Leaf's lifeless body. Wordlessly, he continues moving until he's next to the river's edge, his hands in his hair again. His eyes are wide and frantic, almost comical.

Just five feet away, I feel the heat of Sienna's engine. Then as quickly as she races toward us, she slams on her brakes. The car stays running when she jumps out, probably because she thinks I'm going to escape with her. Still, I won't leave Ben.

"Becca, oh my God!" She runs my way, crying, the sloppy, sobby kind of tears. "I called the police. They're coming. I saw him hurt Ben, and... Oh my god. Is that..." She points to Leaf, panic in her eyes. "Is he...?"

I nod.

Her face pales, and she loses it completely—falls to her knees and sobs beside his dead body like he was the great love of her seventeen-year-old life. As horrible as it sounds, I'm thankful the man is dead. He won't hurt or prey on the innocent anymore.

A gun clicks before I can try to pry her up. I turn, finding Travis along the edge of the river with the barrel of a handgun pointed against his temple. He blinks at me. I blink back.

Then he smiles and pulls the trigger.

23

THERE'S an old song my father used to sing when I was a little girl. Something about life, not taking it for granted, loving and losing things when you least expect. I haven't been able to get it out of my head since that day at the alcove.

Just two days ago when my life forever changed.

Two days since Travis killed himself.

One day since the police came to their own conclusions: that a son beat his father to death, then killed himself because of it.

Ten hours since the police found his lifeless body washed up on a shore near the dam.

Dad sits on the couch next to me, a bowl of Mom's homemade chicken soup in hand. "Eat. Mom's worried you're going to starve to death."

This is becoming a pattern, I've noticed. Me, not

301

eating. Mom and Dad, pushing me to do so, no matter what kind of mood I'm in. Food doesn't fix the pain, but I'm pretty sure they don't know what else to do for me.

He sets the bowl, along with a slice of fresh bread, on the TV tray in front of me.

"Thanks," I tell him, my body numb.

I know both he and Mom feel guilty, even after countless bouts of reassurances on my end that I'm not *completely* traumatized. They won't let me out of their sight either. Not that I mind. Having them close gives me the strength I need to close my eyes and sleep at night. I'm guessing it'll be like that for a while.

They couldn't have known that Ginger's boyfriend was Rose's psychopathic lover and Travis, his son, was a chip off the old block. They couldn't have known because I didn't tell them. I didn't tell anyone, other than the one person who's currently fighting for his life in the hospital.

Ben.

Ben, who is alive but in a medically induced coma to try and reduce the swelling on his brain that Travis caused when he hit him in his head with the bat.

"Have you heard anything?" I hold my breath. This is the fourth time I've asked in two hours. I can't help it.

"No, sweetie," Dad says. "I'm so sorry."

Throat tight, I lean back against the cushion and stare mindlessly at the TV.

"He'll come out of this okay. He's a tough kid."

"You don't know that. He's in coma and his brain is swollen. He's like...Jell-O."

"Becca," Mom scolds from the kitchen—it's déjà vu in the worst sense imaginable, only this time, I'm not the one fighting to live.

"It's the truth," I mumble, eyes burning yet again with tears.

302

"Rose wouldn't want you to think like that."

The sad part is, I know she's right. And even though Rose made crappy, destructive decisions, she'd want me to be strong. For her, for Ben, for myself most of all.

"Ginger wants to talk to you." Dad sets his hand along my arm.

I blow out a breath. "I don't think I'm ready."

The last time I saw her, she was still Team Leaf, believing her psycho boyfriend had done nothing wrong. I'll never get over that.

"She's broken, Becca," Dad whispers.

Mom huffs, stealing a bite of my bread as she approaches. "You don't actually feel sorry for that woman, do you?"

"Of course, I do," Dad argues. "If I lost you two, I'm pretty sure I'd lose who I am as a man."

Mom says *aww*, while I groan, and soon they're leaning over my lap to kiss.

"Stoooop." I shove them apart. "You two are gross." But I'm not gonna lie. I actually love how affectionate they are, even after all these years of marriage.

Dad laughs, Mom winks, and for a second, it almost feels like everything is going to be okay again. Until the sinking sensation in my chest returns. I press a hand over the spot, rubbing it a little, knowing it won't ever go away.

"Are you okay?" Mom leans in, pressing the back of her hand to my forehead. She's been doing that a lot lately. Like she thinks my witnessing hell is going to cause me to break out with pneumonia or something.

"Just tired."

She hums a little. She and my dad share one of their looks, but I'm too exhausted to try and figure out whatever it is they're thinking.

"Let's get you in bed, then." Mom motions for Dad,

who then helps me stand like I'm an invalid. Physically, I'm bruised a little, but it's my heart that hurts the most. Curling up in bed sounds way more promising than continuing to lie on the couch, honestly. At least there I'll have a pillow to soak up my tears. A pillow which may or may not still smell like Ben.

When I make it to the top step, Mom's cell phone rings. She slides it from her pocket with a finger in the air and moves into her and Dad's bedroom.

"Okay, feet up." Dad urges me onto the edge of the mattress in my room, helping to swing my legs out on the bed. I smile my thanks, suddenly too tired to even keep my eyes open. Until Mom enters the room.

"Ben's awake," she tells us.

Adrenaline has me sitting back up, clinging to the sheets with fists. "I have to see him."

"Not tonight." Dad frowns. "You're exhausted. We'll go first thing—"

"I'm *going*. Now." My chest burns with both fear and excitement. Fear of not knowing what's going to happen when I see him. Excitement over that same thing. This is what I've been waiting for, the only thing getting me through the past two days.

There again, I'm paranoid that Ben will admit the truth only the two of us know about. That *he's* the one who beat Leaf to death, not Travis.

"I am *going* to see him," I argue, my thoughts jumbling when stand. "Whether I have to call a cab to get me there or you guys take me instead doesn't make a damn difference to me."

Silence permeates the room, followed by a set of dueling sighs.

Mom, surprisingly, is the first to break. "I'll get her shoes."

Dad breaks in with, "I guess I'll start the car."

I smile. It's the first time I've done so in days.

Fifteen minutes later, we're on our way to the hospital, my stomach so tight with nerves I feel like I could vomit. Thirty minutes after, we're pulling into the hospital parking lot.

"Can you walk?" Mom glances back at me from over her shoulder.

"Yes. My legs are fine." My sanity? Not so much.

"Attitude," she warns, then glances at my dad, who's smirking. I should tame the inner diva, but my nerves are too far gone for me to do much of anything.

With my parents flocking me on both sides, we make it through the doors, then reach the elevator. I hit the corresponding floor, assaulted with the starchy smell of the hospital, cleaning products, and something I can't figure out—maybe the scent of death.

I hold my breath, waiting for the elevator doors to open. One floor, two, then three, until we jerk to the stop on the fourth. My heart kicks into overdrive, and I grab at Mom's hand beside me for strength. She probably thinks I'm nervous about seeing Ben, which I am. But for something else entirely.

Please, Ben. Don't tell them what you did.

We walk down the hall, too slow for my taste. If I rush, I might look guilty, and looking guilty is the last thing we need. What I need to do is compose myself. Get it together. Deny, deny, deny most of all.

It's seven p.m. Visiting hours are over at nine. We're fine as far as the time goes, but that doesn't mean Ben won't be questioned by the police like I was.

Travis beat his father to death. That's what I'd told the police. *Then he beat Ben after that, before shooting himself in the head.* With Sienna backing me up, how could they had no choice but to believe me. Sienna, who also admitted to having an actual relationship with Leaf a

305

few months prior to Rose, after I told her what had happened.

Please don't tell. Please, Ben. Don't. Tell.

Dad sighs loudly, drawing my attention away from the floor. Sitting against the wall next to Ben's hospital is Ginger—the last person I want to see. Her legs are outstretched, crossed at the ankles. She's staring at the wall across from her, a blank expression on her haggard face.

My upper lip lifts with hatred and disgust. She's a living, breathing, and untouched reminder of failure.

I told the police about the letter Rose wrote and how Ginger had taken it from me. I'm not sure if they ever got it from her. I'm guessing she burned it so she wouldn't get questioned about giving her teenage daughter drugs.

Dad walks down the hall first, crouching before Ginger. I fold my arms, rubbing them. Mom doesn't move from beside me, but she tenses.

"You sure you want to do this right now?" Mom turns to me, frowning.

"Yes." *Please, don't tell, Ben. Please. Please.*

"All right." Mom touches my elbow, squeezing lightly. "Let's go."

With my bottom lip now pulled between my teeth, I follow Mom as we move toward my father. The entire time, I'm trying hard to pretend Ginger isn't there. But her grief fills the space so much so that I can't not look either.

The second our eyes lock, she stands and closes in on me, almost like she wants to hug me. But I'm pissed off and want nothing to do with her.

"Do you believe me now?" I ask her.

She flinches. "I'm so sorry, Becca. I—"

"No. You do not get to apologize. It's too late."

306

Once I've said my piece, I place my hand on the door-knob, ready to go in and see Ben. Tell him that I love him, that nothing else matters now that Leaf and Travis are both dead. As long as we never tell a soul what really happened, things we'll be okay.

But Ginger stops me, whispering, "Becca, wait. Ben's awake. But..."

Alarm bells immediately ding in my head. "But what?"

I hold my breath, face going cold when I look at her from over my shoulder.

The cops are inside. He's cuffed to a bed. Life in prison, for the both of us...

Ginger winces, rubs a hand over her face too.

"Tell me," I plead.

Her bottom lip trembles. "H-he's not the same."

I laugh with spite. Relief rushes through me at the same time. "Yeah, that's the thing, Ginger. None of us are anymore." With that, I open Ben's hospital room door and step inside.

When I spot him, I can't help but gasp. He's sitting up, alert, watching TV. Head covered in bandages; face so pale he looks as though he's never seen the sun... Still, he's alive.

My knees shake when I walk to his bed. His beautiful blues are glazed over for another second, before he blinks, seemingly coming to life when he looks my way. He smiles, but it's lacking something. Still, it's enough for me to forget everything I've been fearing for the past two days, even if it's only for a moment.

I jog the remainder of the way to his bedside and immediately go in for a kiss. Lips to lips, heartbeat to heartbeat, it's like I've died and been reborn all over again, knowing he's here, with me.

Before I can deepen the kiss, though, Ben stiffens.

He doesn't try to kiss me back either.

Instead, he pushes me away just enough so he can laugh, then whisper, "Uh, what're you doing, Thompson?"

I touch my lips and pull back, staring back at him. Seconds later, I try something else, thinking he just needs a moment to focus, then thread my shaking fingers through his.

"Being with you." I swallow hard. "I love you, Ben."

His eyebrows dip together while he searches my face. He also doesn't say it back.

"Are you okay?" I ask, chest squeezing.

"Uh, yeah." He stares at our fingers. "I'm fine. Just got knocked unconscious at practice, I think." He squints out the window to his left. "I'm not sure why the hell they brought me all the way back home for a concussion though."

"Um..." I glance over my shoulder when I hear the door open. Mom stands there, a trembling hand over her mouth. She looks like she's seconds from crying.

Confusion pulls my brows together when I refocus on Ben. I don't care what Mom may or may not know about us. It doesn't matter if she hates the idea. Ben is my destiny.

"You didn't do this at practice." I take my hand from his and run it across his bandaged temple. The image of the blood still haunts my mind, but I swallow the tears that want to come.

"Yeah, I did." He hisses then, pressing a hand to his temple. "I'm assuming Rose is too busy to come see me? Not that I mind seeing you, especially if you've decided we should make out."

My stomach drops.

"W-what are you talking about?"

Ben's smirk grows wider, even as he closes both eyes

308

and leans back against his pillow. "I'd explain it to you on a level you'd understand, but I don't have any crayons with me."

The blood drains from my face.

I'm frozen, too confused to move or speak.

Inside of me, a swarm of unsettled bees buzz around my heart and chest, my stomach too. I study him, his confused expression. And when I pull my hands away and take two steps back, the room seems to come crashing down on me.

Oh my God.

He's not the same, Ginger warned me. She told me, but I didn't listen.

"Doesn't matter, I suppose," Ben continues, yawning too, "especially if one little knock in the head finally made you realize how in love with me you are." His eyebrows hop up and down, and that dimple make a momentary appearance.

Ben doesn't remember.

I take a step back, then another, fingertips pressed to my shaking lips. Mom approaches my side, settling an arm around my shoulders. I want to curl into her chest and cry, but she won't let me. Not in front of Ben.

"I think we need to go. Let Ben rest, okay? Maybe we'll come back and visit tomorrow," she says.

I stare at him as she says this, thinking it's a dream. He's leaned back against the pillow, and he's watching the TV again, laughing now. A deeper sob builds in my throat. It's only when Mom gets me back out into the hall do I finally let it go.

Tears for Ben.

Tears for what we've lost.

Tears for something that might never be again.

"It's amnesia," I hear Ginger whisper to my dad just a

few feet away. At her words, Mom hugs me tighter, like she fears I might fall.

I think I might.

Seconds later, Dad's there too, his arms around both Mom and me. We hold onto one another, none of us speaking. No sounds made either, other than my low sobs.

Mom's the first to pull away, but her hands go straight to my cheeks. "You're strong, Rebecca. You'll get through this."

Dad kisses the top of my head, nodding and taking his place at my mom's side. Their hands interlock, palm to palm. "The kid will be back on the playing field in a matter of weeks, no doubt in my mind."

For the first time in my life, I don't believe either of my parents.

"Doctors are unsure how long it will last," Ginger confesses a few seconds later. I nearly forgot she was there.

I pull myself together long enough to look at her though. "And you couldn't think to tell us this when you called?"

"I'm sorry." She sniffles. "I tried before you went in."

"Not good enough," I say.

A thought hits me. Painful. *Guttural.* To the point where I want to curl over.

"Does he know?" I whisper, like hearing the words will break me all over again.

Ginger frowns at me. "Know what?"

"About Rose," I grit my teeth. "Does he know she's dead? Does he know she was murdered and pushed into the river?" I add that last bit just to dig deeper into her wounds. She deserves to hurt for not believing the truth.

"I...I didn't even think about that." Panic fills her

features. Pain follows. For a second, I almost feel bad for her, though it doesn't last long.

I shake my head. "When are you going to tell him?"

"I-I don't know that either. I—"

"You're a chicken," I hiss. "You can't keep this from him. He thinks she's alive—his *dead sister*. He doesn't know the truth, and because of *your* mistakes, Ben has to relive that pain all over again."

"You think I don't know that, you little brat?" Ginger yells, her eyes narrowing into slits.

"Hey." Mom jumps in between us. "Don't you talk to my daughter that way."

Dad's there too, a hand on Mom's shoulder. "You go in there right now, Ginger," he orders. "Tell that boy, or I will."

She shakes her head, takes a step backward down the hall. "I-I'm sorry. Truly. I don't want to lose my temper, but I'm on edge here. Everything is messed up, and I...I didn't even think about having to tell him about Rose."

Of course, she didn't. Because, like always, Rose is still nothing but an afterthought, even in death.

"Rose may have had drugs in her system that you gave her the night she died, but it was your boyfriend who pushed her over the dam," I snarl.

Now that both Travis and Leaf are dead, true justice will never be served. And even though Ben got his desire for vengeance, it's not the kind that he would've wanted. He was kidnapped. Coerced. Broken to the point of no return.

Maybe it's a blessing he doesn't remember what happened.

But if he ever does remember, I'm going to be there to remind him that he did what he had to do.

More tears fall down Ginger's face, but I feel nothing. I am, and always will be, #TeamRose.

"Now's the time we walk away, Becca," Mom whispers in my ear from behind.

The thing is, it's not time. I have work to do. Work that Ginger is apparently too scared to tackle like always.

"No." I take a deep breath, chin high. "*I'll* tell Ben. He deserves to hear it from someone who actually gives a damn."

Mom turns me around and searches my face, hands gripping my upper arms. "You don't have to do this," she says. "But I'm not going to stop you if this is what you want."

I shut my eyes and lean closer, press my forehead to hers. "It needs to be from me, Mom."

She sighs, then kisses my cheek, whispering, "I know. I just wish it didn't have to be."

I fight against the urge to run, to tell her I'm no better than anyone here. I have secrets of my own, ones that will likely haunt me for the rest of my life. I know what really happened two days ago by the river...and nobody else likely ever will if Ben doesn't get his full memory back. This isn't the legacy Rose would want in her death. Not a single one of us did what we set out to do in order to clear her name. We tried. Ben more than any of us. And now we have demons to deal with because of it.

In the end, we all could have prevented my best friend's death, had we been more mindful and aware— less selfish. And me telling Ben the truth now, is my first step toward repentance.

I pull in a deep breath and move past my parents, barely sparing Ginger a glance. Then with my hand on the knob of Ben's hospital room door, I acknowledge what lies ahead, terrified but ready.

This is my fate now. Something I won't give up on. A fate I both need and want, even knowing the road ahead will always be bumpy.

For Rose, I'll move on—love her brother like she always wanted me to. And when the time comes where he's ready to face her death again, I'll be the person right there by his side, holding his hand, grieving with him all over again.

Rose's death has always felt like the end for me. Starting tonight, I'll discover how to find peace again somewhere in the middle, even though peace and murder would never hold hands had they been alive and real like me.

EPILOGUE

Ten months later

A HUMID BREEZE whips my hair in front of my face like the willow trees dancing above. The grass beneath my knees is damp from the rain, seeping through the denim of my jeans and chilling my skin.

Reaching forward, I trace the words etched onto my best friend's headstone, a small smile on my lips knowing she's at peace, even if it means I will likely never be.

ROSE MCCAIN
BELOVED DAUGHTER, SISTER, AND FRIEND
MAY 13, 2001–JULY 8TH, 2018

TWELVE MONTHS AGO, I lost her. I lost myself too. But with the help of Rose's spirit, which still lives inside me, I've managed to make it through the last year, one moment and one deep breath at a time.

Rose is in the wind, hugging me. Her smile is the sun, bright and radiant with every passing, cloudless day. The scent of her favorite lotion is in the flowers surrounding her grave by my feet. Even in death, she's unrelenting when it comes to hanging on, and I don't mind it one bit. Without her spirit, I'd be nothing.

A warm hand settles on my shoulder from behind. I smile at the heavy sensation, already knowing who it is without looking.

"Sorry I'm late." Ben sits in the grass behind me, straddling his legs around my hips. Leaning forward, he nuzzles his nose against my neck, and I can't help but sigh at the feel of him there.

He's my peace in a never-ending storm. My life vest in deep, unrelenting waters.

"Everything okay?" I lean back against his chest, tipping my chin to look at him.

"Yeah. Mom was just having a bad morning. Needed my help functioning, pretty much." He settles his chin on my shoulder.

I want to say *When doesn't she?* but Ben doesn't feel animosity toward his mom like I always will. So instead of speaking, I press my lips to his chin, holding them there for a selfish moment.

"You're her sanity," I tell him.

"Yeah, well, it's time she gets her shit together without me."

I nod in agreement but, again, choose not to speak ill will. Ginger's life this past year has been spent in and out of rehab, her own demons getting the best of her most days. Come next month, she's supposed to be checking into a facility that keeps her until she's beyond her twelve steps, all thanks to my parents. Hopefully, for Ben's sake, it'll be enough this time.

I reach for one of his hands. Bringing it to my mouth, I kiss his open palm, no words on my end needed. Telling Ben everything that had happened to Rose, to us wasn't an easy feat. In fact, he and I didn't speak for two months after that night in the hospital. He told me to leave, that he didn't want me around until he could "figure shit out". And though it hurt to walk away, I did just that, knowing I'd never be able to tell him what truly happened. Not without losing him completely. So, I live with his secret. Bear the weight of a pain he'll likely never remember. It's not good for my soul, but my heart still beats, unlike his sister's.

Every Monday when we were apart, I called to check up on him. And every single Monday, he ignored my phone calls. Six weeks after getting out of the hospital, he was actually well enough to go back to school. His recovery was swift and something the doctors hadn't foreseen. But I thank God every day for it.

For a while there I was pretty broken myself, even though I accepted his choices and understood why he made them. Ben had to figure things out on his own, without me this time, and because of that, I did the same, with the help of my parents, therapists, meds, and even Sienna, who moved to another school close by after her parents discovered she'd hooked up with Leaf. She and I talked often about that night by the river, and though she's handled it better than I have, probably because she only believes what she saw, it's comforting to have someone else to share pieces of that tragedy with.

I still wake up every night with nightmares. Mostly ones of Ben with the bat in his hands, hovered over

316

Leaf's dead body. The dreams of Rose still haunt me too; her face and voice grow more distant with each one.

Though I'll never know for sure what went down before I got to Ben that day, I can't help but wonder if I could've helped prevent it somehow. They're regrets I share, just like the ones I have with Rose.

I live each day with a knot in my gut that never seems to go away.

During my and Ben's time apart, I told my parents everything having to do with Rose and my bucket list. Everything we did together and apart; everything wrong and everything right. I spared some of the details, especially where Travis was concerned, but they got the gist of it all, I think. Mom was the hardest on me. Angry, not just because of that list but because I'd kept so much. Even if Ben and I had been together then, I wouldn't have been able to see him. I was grounded for pretty much the first six weeks of senior year. Though I didn't mind. Home is where I'll always want to be.

But the day I got ungrounded, just weeks before Homecoming, I got a phone call. One that would change my life for as long as I allowed it to be changed. It was Ben.

He was ready to talk to me.

That was, unofficially, the happiest day of my life.

Not to mention a story for another day.

That summer Ben and I spent together after Rose's death is still absent from his mind, and I know it bugs him. He doesn't know about what he did either, though I'm glad he's been spared the pain. The guy is hurt enough as is, deserving a fresh start that I've been all too happy to give him.

"I still can't believe it's been a year," I say, changing the subject.

"Me neither."

The silence blows between us in the form of the wind. I swear I feel Rose in it, hovering above us. I worry someday that my memories of us together will fade with time.

Ben's arms tighten around me, like he knows what I'm thinking. "I wonder what she'd say if she knew about everything that happened after she died." He points at the headstone.

I lean forward to arrange the flowers I brought. "Probably call us idiots," I laugh, losing my smile a second later as I think to myself, *Or, she'd ask us why we even bothered at all.*

Out of everything, I think that's my biggest regret in life—not feeling like I was enough for her. Still, regrets never solve anything, so I continue to push forward, achieving the goals of our two bucket lists, instead of just mine.

My number one priority on that list? Make sure Ben is *always* happy.

"I miss her." He sighs. "Sometimes I still hear her voice in my head. Like she's in a room with me or something."

"I wouldn't put it past her to haunt us," I manage around a lump in my throat.

Ben chuckles, nuzzling my neck again as I lean back against him like before.

I'm moving into the University of Iowa dorms in six weeks. It's a time I once feared after Rose had died, but now am looking forward to because it means more time with Ben. It's bittersweet knowing I'm done with that chapter of my life. But knowing I have the rest ahead of me gives me a sense of peace.

Knowing I'll be forced to do this without Rose, though, will never be okay.

Until the time I leave this earth, though, I *will*

continue to live my life for my best friend. Push my doubts and fears away, too. I'll not only go to college and get a degree, but I'm determined to visit Paris; get married, even; and hopefully have a daughter of my own somewhere down the line. I can't wait to tell her all about her mother's forever best friend. How she got her name, Rose, from her too.

I'm not sure if Ben will be that guy for me. I want him to, of course. But there's no surety about anything in life. He's set to graduate in two years, while I'm just getting started. He's hoping to get a coaching position somewhere in the Midwest, close to me. He doesn't want to go pro anymore either, saying all it'll do is drag up his past again, something he doesn't want to deal with. I don't blame him.

Only time will tell what happens, of course. He's twenty; I'm nineteen, and life doesn't always work out the way we want. Rose is proof of that. Either way, we're happy where we are right now. In love too. Rose was right on one thing: Ben and I were definitely inevitable.

"Only six more weeks." He kisses the spot just in front of my ear, grinning against my cheek. "Then if she does haunt us, we can be together when it happens."

"Yep. That also means no more FaceTime dates for us though."

"Yep." He pokes my ribs, and I can't help but giggle. "I get you all day, every day, in the flesh."

"So confident." I smother a smile.

"I've waited years to have you look at me the way you do now, B. I'm not gonna waste a second of it."

He's right on that end. And the fact that we come to Rose's grave every week together since we got *officially* together at the end of last October only certifies that we're one in the same; two people who lost something, only to find something else to ease our pain along the way.

Ten minutes later, when the rain above us begins to sprinkle down, Ben asks if I'm ready to go.

I draw my knees up to my chest. "I'll never be ready to leave her."

He's quiet for a second before he pushes to his feet. Seconds later, he moves ahead of me, a hand pressed to the top of Rose's headstone.

"I won't either," he whispers.

Instead of crying like I would have a year ago, I stand and move in beside him. like that, I take his hand in mine and squeeze. I know he wants me there with him, and more often than not now, words aren't necessary between us.

"It's gonna be okay." He sniffles and stands up straighter before facing me. When his arms wrap around my waist this time, and his face falls to my shoulder, I can't help but believe him—though the devil sits on my shoulder knowingly as I nod. Some secrets hurt. Others are killer. I keep them all.

Ben pulls back, enough to cup my cheeks. His face is as red as his wet eyes, but I don't call him out on the tears.

"I love you," he tells me.

I blink, smiling, wondering, too, if Rose can see us. "I love you too."

Our foreheads touch when he bends over, as do our hands. And like that, we say our silent goodbyes to her, together, like we always do. Only this time, something clicks in my head when the rain begins to pour.

#3. Dance in the rain.

I look at Ben. He looks back at me. We smile, and before he can ask what I'm doing, I wrap my arms around his shoulder and start to sway.

"Are you dancing with me right now?" He laughs.

"Don't question it." I pull him closer, lay my head on his damp shirt. Like that, I close my eyes, letting the rain engulf us, smiling at the same time.

Once the music in my head quiets, I pull back, taking Ben's hand in mine. "Let's go."

The thing about Ben? He doesn't question my quirks. Maybe he understands. Maybe he doesn't. He's just there for me, like I am for him, no matter the situation.

With our backs to Rose's grave, we head to our cars, the giant willows stirring even faster. The sky opens wider, and the rain drenches us in a matter of seconds. I shut my eyes and smile, head back when we reach the front bumper of my mom's car.

It's Rose. I feel her again. She's telling us goodbye, telling us to accept one final truth: That Ben and me together like this? We'll *both* be okay.

Someday, at least.

ACKNOWLEDGMENTS

The Liars Beneath is a seven year story in the making. It went through 3 major rewrites and a lot of tears to get here. Of course I have a mile long list of people to thank for that, so I'll keep this short and sweet.

To my family, Chris, Kelsey, Emma, Bella. You all know I wouldn't be here without your love and patience. And though you continuously try me on a day to day basis, you have never stood in the way of my dreams—that support means everything to me. More than you will probably ever know.

To Jem, my rockstar agent. You're the one person who never stopped believing in me and this story. You came into my life when I was at my writerly lowest, and I will never forget that. Without you, TLB wouldn't be here. Thank you for being my cheerleader, my rock, and most of all, my friend.

To the Wise Wolf Team. You saw something in my book that nobody else did. Thank you for taking a chance on me. For letting me tell Becca's story, most of all.

To Sabrina. You saw the rough bits of TLB and

helped me turn it into something magical. If you wouldn't have picked me to mentor, then I one-hundred percent believe I wouldn't be where I am today.

To the entire #Writementor team. You're small, but mighty, and I won't ever forget what you've done to help me get where I am. Thank you for creating such an amazing program.

And finally, to my writerly bestie Jess. You know what you mean to me. Love you, J.

ABOUT THE AUTHOR

Heather Van Fleet is a Midwestern-born author with a love of all things spontaneous, like road trips. She enjoys TV shows that leave her questioning her morals and book boyfriends. As a graduate of Black Hawk College, Heather took her degree in early childhood development, tossed it into the garbage, and is now living the dream of writing young adult novels sprinkled with suspense and lots of kissing. She's currently living out her own version of a happily ever after with her high-school-sweetheart-turned-husband, their three hugely feminist daughters, and two fur babies with bad attitudes. When she's not being a mom or writing books, you can find her drinking way too many energy drinks or crashing out on her sofa with a romance novel of some sort.

CPSIA information can be obtained
at www.ICGtesting.com
Printed in the USA
LVHW032132080122
708053LV00015B/906

9 781953 944580